ST. MARTIN'S

MINOTAUR

MYSTERIES

SECRET SERVICE AGENT SEYBOLD'S LEFT EYE TWITCHED AS HE FACED THE PRESIDENT.

"It's the personal effects of the deceased, sir. He had the usual: wallet, checkbook, cell phone. He also had an empty medicine bottle, evidently something he took for his heart condition. The police gave all these things to Burton with the exception of one item."

"What item?" Dad and I asked simultaneously.

Seybold glanced at me as if he'd forgotten I was there.

He colored slightly, then reached into his pocket and brought out a scrap of paper. It was a torn piece of a photo. "He had this on his person. Luckily, the lead investigator realized the possible political implications and turned it over to me as a matter of national security."

Dad motioned for me to come over and I stood behind his chair, peering over his shoulder. It was a black-and-white glossy photo of a man and a woman. You could see most of her naked body and enough of his to understand which position of the Kama Sutra they were trying . . .

Seybold pulled a small, square magnifying lens from his jacket pocket and handed it to my father.

"If you'll look at the rug and this part of the table."

Dad and I stared at the photo, using the magnifying glass.

My supper started doing flip-flops in my stomach. I was pretty sure I recognized the flower pattern in the rug . . .

I looked up at my dad. "It's the Lincoln Bedroom."

DOUBLE EXPOSURE A First Daughter Mystery

SUSAN FORD WITH LAURA HAYDEN

St. Martin's Paperbacks

DOUBLE EXPOSURE

Library of Congress Catalog Card Number: 2001048751

ISBN: 0-312-98827-3

Printed in the United States of America

St. Martin's Press hardcover edition / April 2002
St. Martin's Paperbacks edition / June 2003

St. Martin's Paperbacks are published by St. Martin's Press, 175 Fifth Avenue, New York, NY 10010.

10 9 8 7 6 5 4 3 2 1

This is dedicated with love to my parents,
who gave me the opportunity to see the White House as a
   First Daughter,
and to all the First Daughters, past, present, and future,
for the experiences we have shared.

And to all the first dads from their first daughters
—the ones without the capitals and Capitols.

People keep telling me that I ought to write a book.

I've always figured that this is because of the things I've seen as I've lived my life, not because of my prose style.

Maybe they have a point. Certainly, I know that I'm lucky to be among the handful of people who can say that they grew up in the White House. I remember when my mother and I were getting our first official tour of the White House after my father had become President. As we heard about the rooms, their furnishings, and the history behind the building that had just become our home, a feeling of awe swamped me. I kept thinking about all the people who'd stood in these rooms before me, people like Andrew Jackson and Abraham Lincoln. F.D.R. gave many of his fireside talks from here. I could imagine Abigail Adams hanging her laundry to dry in the East Room, and one of Theodore Roosevelt's kids sneaking a pony up the elevator and into the room of his ailing brother, in hopes of cheering him up (the pony kicked a dent in the elevator's side—the damaged panel is still in the Smithsonian), and all the other wonderful stories about the White House and the people who have lived in it.

The first week after I moved into the White House, every time I saw a matchbook or a notepad imprinted with the words "The White House," I took it, almost as if I was afraid I'd be leaving soon. At the beginning, I found it hard to believe that this bastion of American history was going to be my home for the next several years. As time passed, it did start to become home for me.

When I told this story a couple of years ago at a function, I mentioned that after my father left office, I used up all of the matchbooks and notepads I'd taken in those early days, and that I regretted not having the mementos. Rex Scouten, the White House head usher, found out and sent me several of each, which I treasure to this day. Many of my favorite White House memories were the result of the kindness and professionalism of everyone on the staff while we were there. I can't say enough good things about those people. They made my White House years very happy and special ones.

So when I think back to my own days living there, it's easy to play the "what if" game. I guess you can say that the character of Eve Cooper is a product of my "what if" moments. Eve and I have some things in common, share some experiences that are unique to the White House. I gave Eve a younger brother, Drew, for this book. In reality, I'm the youngest Ford child, and I have three older brothers. By making Drew a kid brother, I could work some of the difficulties of being a teenager in the White House into the story without having to relive the problems through Eve.

Then again, I want you to know that this novel is a work of fiction. All the characters, though I've done my best to portray their job titles and responsibilities accurately, are fictional. Though the portrayals of official functions are based on the realities I observed while I was living at the White House, the events in the book are composites or inventions. I certainly never stumbled across a body in the Rose Garden. I suppose you can say that the reality I experienced has become merely a springboard for Eve's adventures. She's not me, nor do her exploits and escapades reflect my times in the White House. The only character in this book that is not an invention is the White House itself, which I tried to make as real as I could. That was a labor of love.

But my "what if"s could have happened. . . .

Maybe. . . .

I hope you enjoy the book.

CHAPTER ONE

After only three weeks, I wanted out.

Badly.

During the campaign, the idea of living in the White House had sounded almost exciting. Almost exotic. Almost fun.

Almost.

But then again, my mother had always warned us to be careful what we wished for; we might get it. I wish she were still alive so I could tell her, "We got it, all right, Mom. So . . . now what?"

My name is Evelyn Ann Cooper. Most people call me Eve. The press really loves that—a First Daughter named Eve. Some genius stumbled onto that little story hook back in September on a slow news day. I cringe every time I see it in print.

So now, post-inauguration, I'm stuck here, essentially living in a national monument, surrounded by museum pieces I'm afraid to touch, people I don't know, and legions of Secret Service agents whose faces would probably shatter if they dared to smile.

So far, the only person I've met who seems to be able to smile around here is Michael Cauffman, Dad's hand-selected official photographer. In fact, Michael's constant—and may I say sappy—grin is beginning to get on my nerves.

Jealousy on my part, I guess.

But he can afford to be happy; after his daily duties in the White House, he goes home at night to his apartment. He doesn't have to deal with the same problems my family has facing them. No Secret Service agents. No hovering ushers, afraid that you'll leave a Diet Coke can on a $65,000 antique table. No slinking through the hallways trying to avoid the public areas and hordes of tourists, with Secret Service agents dogging your every step.

What I want to know is—who decided it'd be nice for the President, and his family, to live in a freakin' museum?

With armed guards?

But then again, when I look out my window and glance down to see a group of visitors trooping toward the house, the reality of the situation hits me like a fist in the solar plexus.

I live in the White House.

Me.

Eve. The same Eve who came here when she was nine and wrote her "What I did on my summer vacation" paper about her once-in-a-lifetime tour of the President's house.

It's times like these that I wonder what weird set of cosmic forces decided I belonged here, rather than in the midst of the tourists taking that famous twenty-minute tour. Somehow I suspect I'd fit in better with them, all those hordes of earnest citizens visiting the White House on vacation, than I do actually living here, dealing with all the rules, the regulations, the ushers, the history, the grandeur, and, oh yeah, don't forget, the antiques. Sometimes it makes me stop in my tracks and I have a hard time catching my breath.

When the feeling hits me, I can't help but sigh.

"Quit sighing," Michael ordered, "and lean a little to your left and tilt your head down a bit."

I crossed my eyes and stuck out my tongue.

He snapped a picture. "Okay, that takes care of *The National Intruder*. But *Ladies' Home Daily* will want something a bit more traditional."

"The *Ladies' Home Daily* can kiss my rosy rump."

Michael laughed. "Don't be surprised if they offer. They're begging for the lowdown on the Cooper administration, and they might sink that far to get it." He drew an imaginary headline in the air. " 'President Prefers Oatmeal for Breakfast. Poultry and Pork Markets Suffer Unprecedented Drop.' "

"Forget the pork." I stretched cramped muscles. "*I'm* going to be the one dropping if I don't get some fresh air." I stood up and yawned.

Michael reached down by his feet for his camera bag. "Then let's go outside and grab some shots. I'm ready for a change in venue, too."

"Outside? Sure. Anywhere but"—I paused to shudder—"the Rose Garden. There's nothing worse than a cheesy picture of the First Daughter admiring the roses."

So far, every First Daughter since the invention of film has posed for a beauty shot like that, and the press always run the things forever. Heck, those carefully posed portraits even show up in their obituaries.

"I'd just as soon be different," I added. Lord knows I felt different—like I didn't quite belong here, even if my father did.

Michael packed away his Nikon. "Trust me, Eve, this picture will be different. Besides, it's February. The snowstorm yesterday buried most of the greenery. No roses in bloom. Not even an apple tree to tempt you." He laughed at his own joke. "In fact, the Democrats will be the first ones to tell you there's no Tree of Knowledge anywhere on the White House grounds. Not for the last four years and not for the next four, either."

"Very funny," I said with a muffled snort.

All right, so it *was* funny. But I wasn't going to give Michael the satisfaction of letting him know I thought so. I hadn't figured the guy out yet. Dad had latched onto him somewhere along the campaign trail. Michael appeared to be a stand-up guy, and even *I* had to admit he was a good photographer.

In any case, my father sure seemed to be fond of him. Maybe it was a matter of Dad missing his own kids while he was on the campaign trail. After all, Michael wasn't that much older than me. Somewhere between the primaries and election race, Dad sort of "adopted" Michael.

I guess it was our fault—my brothers' and mine. Certainly the three of us had done our best to stay out of the preelection madness when we could. My brother Charlie, one year my junior, avoided politics as much as possible, just like me. But he'd been more successful than I had in his avoidance techniques. Charlie had a very satisfying life in Vermont, where he ran an Internet software business that he'd built from scratch and that was making money out the wazoo. Thanks to his cyber fortune, he was living the life of a comfortable Net hermit. But even if he were dirt poor and destitute, there wasn't enough money in the world to bribe him into playing the candidate's son during the campaign.

The only time he willingly left his self-imposed hibernation was when Dad asked him to make an appearance. And then Charlie'd grumbled constantly how he'd rather be back home with his computers. But he didn't fool me; I knew how much Charlie loved Dad and how he'd do anything Dad asked him to do. Then again, Dad respected Charlie's need for privacy and didn't ask my brother to violate it too often or too much.

Dad even knew not to suggest that Charlie live in the White House.

But my younger brother, Drew, didn't have the same freedom.

Drew was only fifteen, so he couldn't have tagged along on the campaign trail because of school, no matter how he felt about it. Lucky stiff. Of course, now that we were in the White House, Drew wasn't feeling too lucky. He'd had to change schools and currently had the distinction of being not only the new guy in class, but the President's son as well.

Poor kid. I tried to give him an outlet to vent at, to be a safety valve for him, but he's at that age. . . . Could you imagine having to suffer through driver's ed class with two Secret Service men in the backseat of your car?

And think about a teenaged boy asking a girl for a date with a couple of grim-faced security types hovering in the background.

As I said, poor kid.

As for me, during the campaign, I used graduate school as my excuse not to tag along with Dad, but because I worked part-time as an NPS wire service photographer, our paths crossed frequently enough for him to be happy. NPS liked it because, as the candidate's daughter, I had access to photo ops that few other photographers could even dream of.

Except for Michael Cauffman.

Michael had taken some candid shots of Dad during the early part of the campaign—shots that had ended up on the front of several magazines, most notably *Time* and *People*. The photos had captured Dad's dedication to duty, as well as providing an uncannily accurate look at the man I knew and loved.

They were good shots . . . *really* good shots.

Okay. Maybe I *was* jealous of him. For more than just his sappy grin and what I assumed was his satisfying life in an antique-free apartment without armed guards.

His expression was definitely sappy when he nodded toward the door. "So let's go outside."

I phoned ahead for a security escort. It's not quite like calling ahead for a pizza, but close. The family floor is the only real bastion of privacy we have in the White House. Once we leave that area of the building, the family members are escorted by Secret Service agents. So once Michael and I left the private quarters, we picked up two agents. They went by the names Perkins and McNally. I hadn't gotten brave enough to ask them their first names, but top money said they were Bulldog and Spike—at least, that's what I called them behind their backs.

The gang of us stumped downstairs, avoiding the public areas by ducking behind security screens, and headed toward the infamous Rose Garden, despite my earlier protests.

Michael's words rang in my ears: *Ya gotta give the public what they want* . . . I suppose he had a point.

I was glad the two Dawgs led the way; I kept getting turned around, wandering into the wrong part of the . . . house. Forgive me, but I'm still having a hard time thinking of this over-ornamented goldfish bowl as a house, much less a home.

Or, heaven forbid, *my* home . . .

Home was where I grew up, the place where my family and I lived until I left for college. Or, once I became an adult, home meant my apartment in Colorado, which had just made the transition from austere to having that indefinable warm, lived-in feeling when Dad asked me to move with the family to Washington.

Long story short, I did, and now I was stuck on the

wrong side of the lens on a possible photo op from hell.

Talk about a cold day in hell . . .

But once outside, I realized the weather wasn't really bad for February in D.C.—clear blue skies and a bite in the air. However, everything was pretty much covered in snow because we'd had a really good snowfall the day before. You usually see pictures of the Rose Garden in full bloom and sporting such flowery descriptions in the captions as ". . . a floral symphony crafted by master gardeners, often adorned with even more tulips than roses." But I had to admit the place was awfully grand-looking, even all covered in snow. Back in Colorado, snow was considered the great equalizer, covering everything with the same white blanket. Here, even the snow was ornamental. Rather than masking the beauty of the garden, the snow magnified it.

But after a half hour of fresh air, my admiration for snow-flocked beauty diminished fast. What had seemed a bearable cold at first now had a real meat-locker feel to it.

I sighed.

I seemed to do that a lot since I moved into the White House.

"Hold your breath," Michael ordered. "You're fogging up the shot."

I nodded because answering would simply make the frosty cloud hanging around my head even worse. But then my teeth began to chatter, spoiling the close-up.

He lowered the camera. "You're doing that on purpose."

"If I c-could stop, I w-would. I didn't g-grow up here in the cold, cruel North like you. I don't do . . . cold. Not well at all."

He rubbed one gloved hand briskly against his pants leg, a gesture I didn't miss. Evidently, Superphotographers could get chilled, just like the rest of us poor mortals. It was comforting to know that.

"You can't fool me with the cold, cruel North stuff. You used to live in Denver."

Rats. Caught.

"Well . . ." I hedged. "You're cold, too. You're shivering," I noted, trying not to grin. Presidents' daughters weren't supposed to take comfort in the suffering of others. It made for bad press. "Why don't we stop? Don't you have enough shots?"

He contemplated the scenery while he slapped his gloves together briskly to warm his hands. After a few moments, he said, "Nah . . . just a few more."

With his fingers evidently thawed, he began to position me, using the weak winter sunlight to its best advantage. I might not have staged the shot quite like he was, but I had to admit to myself that he was higher up the food chain than I was, careerwise. Probably talentwise, too, but I wasn't ready to admit that.

Besides, I was still learning. Why, I might just catch up with the boy genius, any minute now.

Suddenly, I noticed that his lens wasn't pointed exactly at me. Mind you, I don't have to be the center of attention all of the time, even most of the time, but I did think the purpose at the moment was to get shots of me. If I was going to suffer in the freezing cold for Michael's sense of art and composition, he could at least make the effort to aim his camera somewhere in my direction.

"Excuse me?" I raised my hand and waved. "I'm over here, remember?"

He continued to focus somewhere five or so feet to the left of me. "Hang on for a minute." He stepped closer, almost pushing me aside to get a better angle. Suddenly, I wanted my own camera. I recognized the look on his face; I'd seen it on the faces of a hundred other photographers. That intense interest, the sudden attention when something was happening—something interesting and possibly very photographic.

I craned over his shoulder, trying not to jostle him. Call it photographer-to-photographer respect. "What is it? Where?" I squinted against the glare of the snow, not seeing anything of any particular note. What did the man have? X-ray vision?

He freed an index finger to point toward the snow-covered hedges that ran along the west colonnade. Just beyond the walkway was the Oval Office. I figured maybe he was pointing toward the window or the glass door leading inside.

"What?" Panic ran through me as I squinted again. "Dad?"

"No, beneath the boxwood . . ." His voice trailed off. I could hear him swallow hard.

"What?" I reached up for his camera but knew his grip would be iron-tight. I couldn't blame him; I wouldn't have given up my camera if I'd framed a great shot in my lens, either.

I peered toward the boxwood hedge that peeked out over the bank of snow. Nothing there. In front of the hedge, smaller shrubs laid out in a sort of rickrack pattern were covered in a blanket of white, with bare crabapple trees emerging from the snow mounds, their branches like gnarled fingers. I shivered, not knowing whether to blame the cold or my overactive imagination.

Shielding my eyes, I tried to block the glare from the snow. Finally, I thought I saw something dark at the base of the hedge.

A squirrel, maybe? I was being upstaged by a bushytailed rodent? Somehow, I doubted it.

Michael turned to me, his face drained of color. "Oh, shi . . ."

Now I was really alarmed. "What?"

He looked beyond me and made a motion. A split second later, Perkins and McNally, my two Secret Service Dawgs, were beside us. Michael pushed me toward them. "Take her inside. And get your boss out here. Quick."

Perkins was already doing his protect-her-at-all-costs shtick, hustling me toward the building while McNally played rear guard, scanning the area, watching our backsides, and talking into his wristwatch or the radio up his sleeve or something Dad always calls their "Dick Tracy–Flash Gordon wrist communicators."

The Secret Service guys ushered me—a nice way to say they *pushed* me—into the building, choosing the closest entrance. Once we passed through the security check ("Hi, I'm Eve. Remember me? I live here"), we rushed straight to my father's office, where, as luck would have it, he was taking a break.

Standing at the window, Dad was little more than a

silhouette against the glare of the snow outside. I could see a steaming mug in his hands. Hot chocolate, I'd bet. After three weeks, the most closely held secret in this administration is the fact that my Dad hates coffee.

What would the American public say if they knew?

He glanced over his shoulder and gave me a wave. "Hi, doll." He pointed toward the cluster of men who stood on the other side of the box hedge, their attention focused on the ground beneath it. "Looks like there's a little excitement outside."

Suddenly, I was glad there was bulletproof glass between my father and the outside world. I stepped beside him and saw Michael, who was still out there, standing off to one side and snapping pictures like mad. My jealousy soared to new heights. Something was happening and I wanted to be in on it. I was torn between running upstairs and getting my camera and possibly missing some of the drama, and staying there in the Oval Office and witnessing firsthand whatever intrigue might unfold.

Curiosity got the better of me, and I decided to stay where I was and watch. It helped that I saw two agents suddenly block Michael. They made unmistakable gestures that suggested they didn't want him taking any more pictures. I had a sneaking suspicion he was lucky they didn't rip the film out of his camera right then and there or dig into his bag and get the cameras he had stashed there. He trudged toward the building with his camera tucked in his arm, the lens conveniently pointing toward the growing cluster of men. Although I couldn't hear it, I was sure the shutter was clicking as Michael took purloined shots during his forced retreat.

What red-blooded photographer wouldn't?

I turned my attention back to the police, who'd arrived along with some other guys who looked like paramedics. Everyone was bundled up so much that it was hard to figure out who was who. But what I did notice was that everybody was hanging back, not trampling all over the snow in the vicinity of the dark shadow. Somehow, I didn't think it was reverence toward the plants hidden beneath the snow that made them so careful.

So far in my career, I've been sent on a variety of assignments as a photographer, covering everything from the beautiful bodies walking the world's catwalks to not-so-beautiful bodies found dead in abandoned cars. The way everyone moved out there looked to me like the way cops tried not to disturb a potential crime scene. I didn't like it.

I nudged Dad. "Why don't you call someone and see what's going on?"

He shook his head. "I don't want to bother them in the middle of whatever they're doing. It looks important. They'll tell us soon enough." He turned to the Dawgs. "Right, guys?"

Spike stood next to us, apparently ready to hurl himself between us and the window should the need arise. Bulldog guarded the door, holding a conversation with his watch. They both gave curt nods, knowing they'd been asked to find out exactly what was going on—fast. I had to hand it to Dad; he was really getting the hang of this presidential power thing.

But me? I wasn't as diplomatic. Straight to the point—that was much more my style. I turned to Bulldog. "C'mon . . . don't you know anything yet?"

He shook his head and continued his soft conversation with his arm, only to stop when someone knocked on the door. He stiffened, then glanced at Dad, who nodded. Then Bulldog cautiously opened the door.

Michael stumbled into the room, his face still pale and his camera trembling in his bare hands. He was panting as if he had run all the way after being ejected from the scene outside. Come to think of it, he probably had run, once he'd gotten inside the building. He'd have known that we in the Oval Office would have a decent ringside seat to whatever was going on out there in the Rose Garden.

Dad stepped forward, bracing Michael, who, I'll admit, did look a bit unsteady on his feet. "Good God, Mike, are you all right? What's happening out there?" He reached up to take the camera from the photographer, but Michael still had a death grip on it. I figured his unbreakable grip was a sure sign he probably had some very good shots of whatever had transpired outside. In the same situation, I don't know if I'd have been so willing to give up my camera, either.

Even to the President.

Michael looked down and saw clumps of melting snow falling off his shoes and onto the rug with the presidential seal on it. A large chunk landed on the eagle's beak. That seemed to shake him back into some semblance of control.

"Oh . . . sorry, sir." He bent down, picked up the melting snow clod, and, after a moment's confusion, stuffed it into his coat pocket. Then, as if suddenly cognizant of where he was, he rushed toward the window, almost pushing me aside in the quest for a better view. "Can you see it from here?"

"Not really." My father joined us, not nearly as pushy as Michael. "And I'm not sure what 'it' is. What did you see while you were out there, Mike?"

"It must have been there all night long. It was pretty much covered up, buried in the snow."

" 'It,' " I repeated. " 'It' as in what?" Somehow I already knew the answer. I restructured my question. "Or is it 'It' as in who?"

Dad looked shocked. "Who? You mean . . ."

Michael gulped, then nodded. "Yes, sir. A dead body. A man. Under the snow. I noticed . . . what I thought was a hand when I was taking shots of Eve out in the garden. When I got closer, I was sure. . . ." His voice trailed off.

We all turned simultaneously toward the window, straining to make out a corpse on the ground. The most we could see were the grim faces of the men tending to the body.

"Are you sure it . . . he was dead?" I asked, not liking the quivery tone in my voice.

"I didn't hang around to take his pulse." Michael looked as if he suddenly remembered where he was. "I mean, he looked dead to me"—Michael flushed—"but I don't have much experience in that department. I do portraits, celebrity stuff—I never had the city beat."

My father said nothing, but I noticed him twisting the ring on his right hand. It had been a present from a man whose life Dad had saved in Vietnam. I knew what was going through his head; he'd seen more than his share of death as a young man and wasn't all that anxious to view it now, especially not in what amounted to our own backyard.

Dad walked across the room to a small credenza to the right of the fireplace. From its recesses, he pulled out a bottle and a glass.

"Brandy," he said, pouring about two fingers into the glass. "For medicinal purposes, of course. To warm the body, as well as the soul. Even though all the medical experts tell me it doesn't work, I still find it comforting in extreme circumstances." He handed the glass to Michael, who gulped its contents all in one grateful swallow.

"Thanks, sir." The liquor seemed to help him control the worst of his shakes. He sat down on the couch, on the end next to the fireplace—a fireplace I wished was more functional than decorative at the moment. It wasn't just Michael who felt half frozen. I couldn't stop shivering, either.

Michael drew a long, deep breath, as if he couldn't get quite enough oxygen into his system. "I saw his face," he said.

Both Dad and I stared at each other.

"Did you recognize him?" Dad asked.

Michael nodded, but said nothing else.

"Well?" I prompted.

He closed his eyes. "It looked like Mr. O'Connor."

"O'Connor?" I repeated. "Burton O'Connor?" I said. Dad and I stared at each other. "The head usher here?"

Michael nodded. "Yeah, him."

Dad glanced at Bulldog, who listened intently to his forefinger, then nodded. "About the body, sir. They're saying it's probably been there since late yesterday afternoon, judging from all the snow on him."

Dad and I again shared an incredulous look.

"But that's impossible," I blurted. "We saw Mr. O'Connor at breakfast this morning. All of us—Dad, Drew, and me. He wanted to discuss decoration changes on the second floor with us."

Michael looked confused. "But I'm sure that's who I saw. I mean, that's who it looked like to me—and I don't make mistakes about faces. That was Mr. O'Connor."

Dad released a sigh. "Couldn't be. Not unless he has an identical twin brother."

Two hours later, we learned that Burton O'Connor did indeed have a twin brother.

Now a very dead one.

That night, Dad didn't have any formal functions to attend and the free world was relatively quiet, so we all ate dinner together in the formal family dining room. I'd call it fancy, but that's like calling the Lincoln Memorial slightly larger than life-sized. The first time Drew saw the room, he ignored the Sheraton table, the Turkish carpet, the Steuben glassware, and immediately zeroed in on the roast turkey perched at the end of the table. It was only after he'd finished his third helping that he looked up and spotted the words carved in the fireplace mantel on the east wall.

'We have met the enemy, and they are ours,' " he read aloud. He leaned back and patted his stomach. "God bless America."

Even though we'd filled out a questionnaire about

our food preferences, the chefs hadn't quite anticipated how much food they needed to prepare for our family of four. It had been a while since the White House had hosted a teenaged boy as one of its residents. In the last few administrations, if the presidents had had any teenaged kids living there, they'd been girls, and their eating habits were worlds apart from my kid brother's unlimited appetite.

Put simply, my brother Drew was doing his best to eat the White House kitchen empty—and it's a big kitchen. To do him justice, the kid was in the middle of a growth spurt, but we simply couldn't keep him fed. The staff ended up preparing dinner for ten just to feed the four of us. And even then, thanks to Drew, there was precious little in the way of leftovers.

Good thing, too. I'm not sure who eats the White House leftovers, and I don't really think I want to know.

Drew had just finished polishing off a mountain of mashed potatoes when there was a polite cough originating from the hallway. It was Peter Seybold, the head of the Presidential Protection Division.

He looked past me and straight at Dad.

"I'm sorry to disturb your meal, Mr. President, but I need to speak to you. You asked for a full report on this afternoon's incident as soon as one was available. The Metro Police have delivered their initial report."

That's right, the Washington, D.C., Metro Police, not the Secret Service, even though the body was found on the White House grounds. The jurisdiction boundaries around here are totally crazy. As someone explained to me the second day of my life in the fishbowl, the Park Police have the sidewalks, the Metro Police have the streets, and the Secret Service have the eighteen-acre White House complex. But of the three, only the Metro Police have an investigative arm that can handle homicides.

And evidently, when you find a dead body in the Rose Garden, you're allowed to jump to conclusions and think homicide.

Dad got Drew to leave the table with the usual "Don't you have homework?" excuse. Drew shot me a look that said, "You *are* going to tell me everything later, aren't you?"

I winked.

"Come on in, Peter." Dad waved the man over to the table.

Seybold stood there stiffly until Dad nudged a chair in his direction, told him to sit, and asked him if he wanted coffee. They keep it around for the President as a matter of national policy, I think, which was fine with me. Dad might not drink the stuff, but I do. Seybold looked as if he'd never been invited to sit at the presidential supper table before. Maybe he had, maybe he hadn't, but maybe the best thing was for him not to make any assumptions until he learned otherwise. People were still tiptoeing around Dad, trying to get a read on him and figure him out for themselves.

"So, tell me," Dad said, "do you have news about the body?"

Seybold gave me a pointed look, as if he was reluctant to say, "Not in front of the civilian," to the President, but was unable to proceed until he'd done his duty by at least hinting at it.

Dad shrugged. "Eve needs to stay. She was there when the body was found. I think she deserves to hear everything about this situation."

Seybold sat rigidly in the chair. "Yes, sir, Mr. President." He cleared his throat, then plunged ahead. "The deceased's name is Sterling O'Connor. As his appearance indicated, he is indeed Burton O'Connor's brother—an identical twin, in fact. According to Metro, preliminary autopsy reports show that he died of a heart attack." He glanced at his coffee cup and took a small sip, as if he were required to drink whatever the President poured for him.

"No foul play?"

"None whatsoever, sir. Just an unfortunate heart attack. The coroner said it was highly likely that O'Connor was dead before he even hit the ground. It was a massive coronary."

There was visible relief in Dad's eyes. I knew he'd been thinking what I had: Had the heart attack killed the guy? Or had he suffered one, fallen, and frozen slowly to death just outside our window? At least this way it had been quick and the man hadn't suffered. And we couldn't have saved him.

"Also, we don't believe he was out there for very long. We know when he went through the gates. The agents stationed there identified him by sight as our Mr. O'Connor. The duty officer said that the man waved a pass at them, but they were so used to the head usher coming and going at all hours that they let him in without really looking at it. For what it's worth, the security breach and those responsible have been suitably dealt with." He wore an appropriately grim expression.

He continued. "We believe the deceased was coming to visit his brother. Our early discussions with the living Mr. O'Connor indicate that he'd arranged a pass for his brother, who had expressed the intention to— forgive me, but this is verbatim—'check out what the new administration has done to wreck the place this time' in the near future. We are not sure, however, how the dead man ended up in the Rose Garden." He paused, as if marshaling his thoughts.

"Our current working assumption is that he was feeling ill and not watching where he was going. With all the blowing snow, the cameras and sensors weren't operating at peak performance. If he staggered into the garden and died immediately, that might explain why our routine surveillance didn't catch him. There's a nasty downdraft coming off the roof there, and we always have big snowbanks forming in that area of the garden whenever we get hit with snow. If he succumbed to his heart attack shortly after he entered the grounds, which was just after our regular patrol, a drift could have covered him from sight almost immediately, and the next patrol would have seen nothing amiss."

I don't know if Seybold talked like that all the time or only when he was trying to cover his rear. Dead bodies that go undiscovered on the White House grounds didn't reflect well on the new administration or the Secret Service sworn to protect it. A new president might want to make some changes, starting at the top of the security chain, which in our case meant Seybold. But I could tell by the look on Dad's face that he thought this explanation sounded reasonable. Plus, if the man was dead before he hit the ground, no patrol could have saved him.

"How's Burton taking it?" Dad asked, pushing the sugar and cream toward Seybold.

Seybold relaxed slightly, having gotten over the first hurdle fairly unscathed. From what I've heard, the previous president had liked to yell first and ask questions later, and Dad's more laid-back approach had caught the entire White House staff a bit off-guard.

Seybold spooned some sugar into his coffee. "He's doing as well as can be expected, sir. As you might suspect, being twins, they were very close. Burton's already begun the process of making funeral arrangements."

"Poor man. Is there anything we can do? Of course he can have all the time off he needs . . ."

Seybold shrugged. "Knowing Burton, he'll be back to work immediately. When his wife died a couple of years ago, he was back here, full steam ahead, in two days. He told me that he found the work to be therapeutic, that it helped him get his mind off his grief. He does tend to throw himself into one-man projects when he's upset, which can play havoc with this place, but whatever it takes to help him deal with the death."

"Indeed."

Normally, Seybold would have excused himself, but he didn't, which was a sure sign something else was up. Dad noticed it, too.

"Is there anything else?"

Seybold's left eye twitched. I tucked that bit of information in my mental file cabinet: *Seybold—eye-twitch—something bad.*

"It's Mr. O'Connor's personal effects, sir . . . Mr. Sterling O'Connor, that is. He had the usual: wallet, checkbook, cell phone. He also had an empty medicine bottle, evidently something he took for his heart condition. The police gave all these things to Burton with the exception of one item."

"What item?" Dad and I asked simultaneously.

Seybold glanced at me as if he'd forgotten I was there. He began to hedge, as if he didn't want to discuss this "one item" in front of me.

Dad smiled at him. "Peter, you'll learn soon enough that Eve will know everything going on around here, not because she's nosy, but because she's very observant. Plus, I tell her everything, anyway. Think of her as my personal adviser. Anything you have to tell me, you can say in front of her. It'll go no further."

I smiled, especially about the "nosy" line, because in private my father used that word to describe me all the time.

Seybold colored slightly, then reached into his pocket and brought out a scrap of paper. It was a torn piece of a photo. "He had this on his person. Luckily, the lead investigator realized the possible political implications and turned it over to me as a matter of national security."

Dad motioned for me to come over and I stood behind his chair, peering over his shoulder. It was a black-and-white glossy photo of a man and a woman. You could see most of her naked body and enough of his to understand which position of the Kama Sutra they were trying. The picture had been torn so that you couldn't see the man's face, but I had a feeling, from the composition, that given the entire photo, the man's features would be fully in view. It was smutty, sure . . . but a matter of national security? I didn't understand.

"You were afraid it would upset Burton to know his brother had pictures like this?" Dad asked.

Seybold shook his head. "No, sir." He pulled a small, square magnifying lens from his jacket pocket and handed it to my father. "If you'll look at the rug and this part of the table."

Dad and I stared at the photo, using the magnifying glass. I wanted to run to my room and get my photographer's loupe, the one that I use to examine my own pictures, but I resisted the urge. They might not let me back in. Besides, this time maybe I didn't need it. We could make out the pattern of the rug and the delicate carvings of the chair leg in the background. It rang a bell.

"It's a rug and a table. So why am I looking at it?" Dad asked.

Seybold cleared his throat. "That's the right front leg of an 1846 walnut side chair."

My supper started doing flip-flops in my stomach. I was pretty sure I recognized the flower pattern in the rug from my first official "The White House *Really Is* Your House" tour.

I looked up at my dad. "It's the Lincoln bedroom."

CHAPTER TWO

A little background, first. Although my father is a widower and I'm the oldest child and, obviously, female, I'm not the First Lady.

Thank God for that.

And thank God for my aunt Patsy, who fills those very big shoes. High heels are traditional for that job, and she wears them well. As for me, I don't do heels if I can help it.

Aunt Patsy has been an important part of our lives from the moment we were born. She's my father's sister, widowed young when Uncle Herbert lost control of his car and drove off into Lake Pontchartrain while on a business trip to New Orleans. They'd had no children, so Charlie and I, and later Drew, became her surrogate kids. Then, when Mom died, Aunt Patsy stepped into the maternal role for real.

So when Dad started talking about running for office, it was natural for him to ask Patsy to act as official First Lady should he be elected President. But I did appreciate that he approached me first about the position and its responsibilities, even if we both knew I'd turn it down at the speed of light. I must admit that Patsy seems to be enjoying her official duties, and I'm thrilled for her. The only problem with the arrangement—at least from my limited point of view—is that I have nothing much to do.

I dropped out of graduate school for the last two semesters because I realized my life would be in chaos for a while, what with the campaign and—fingers crossed—whatever else might follow. Once Dad won the election, I knew it would take time to get used to life in the public eye.

Even before Dad won, a former First Child called to explain to me—that is, to warn me—about the Glass White House syndrome. She told me that my privacy would be a precious commodity that I'd have to work hard to keep intact. A photographer myself, even I have to admit that presidential children are an obvious photo op.

Of course, I knew I'd have to attend the obligatory State Department dinners, learn to deal with Secret Service tagalongs, remember that any careless word or action of mine would be magnified by the press, the whole mess. But those things hardly take all my waking hours.

At least I didn't need to deal with graduate work

while trying to figure out how to ease myself back into some semblance of a normal life in this very abnormal world. But I still have every intention of picking things back up at school. Maybe this summer, if I can get the right classes.

I also took a leave of absence from my position in Denver at the wire service because I knew I needed to be with my family. Maybe somewhere in the back of my head, I'd toyed with the notion that I had a chance of talking Dad into letting me be the official White House photographer. But the first time I saw him and Michael laughing together during a shoot—and then saw the resulting pictures—I knew I had some stiff competition for the job. Plus, I knew there would be a strong anti-favoritism backlash if Dad actually gave me the job. I could just hear the outcry of "Nepotism!" if he appointed me. I doubt Dad's political opponents would admit that the President's daughter might be perfect for the position, even if she did have the talent.

And trust me, I do.

So I ended up with no official job in the Cooper administration other than Unemployed First Daughter Leech. And I'm lousy at it.

Dad keeps playing the "my personal adviser" card, which I appreciate, but I can't help but realize it is his way of trying to make me feel like I belong here—that I have an important role to fill. Twenty-five is awfully old to still be living at home and sponging off your father.

Especially when he lives in the White House.

So I was looking for something real, something fulfilling to sink my teeth into, when I talked and wheedled and rationalized myself into being part of the investigation concerning the photo found in Sterling O'Connor's possession. Dad fought the idea to start with, but I can be persuasive when I try. Eventually, I won and the party line was that I was Dad's personal representative. If there was anything in that picture that smacked of impropriety committed by someone in his administration or even in any of the previous ones, he wanted to know immediately.

In detail.

In the end, the pros tolerated me, I guess because they thought that if they discovered bad news, I'd have a better chance of breaking it to Dad without repercussions than they would. You can fire a Secret Service agent or somebody from the FBI, but being a daughter is pretty much a job-for-life deal.

At least that was the argument I used when I informed Peter Seybold about Dad's plans for my inclusion in the investigation. Mr. Seybold evidently hadn't learned that Dad didn't come from the "shoot the messenger" school of reactionary governing.

Or that I wasn't above using a man's ignorance for my gain when my family's well-being was at stake.

He stood stiffly, staring at me with dispassionate eyes. "Miss Cooper—"

I held up my hand to stop him. "Please, first, it's Eve. And second, I know all your objections. Don't worry. I'll keep my mouth shut—except to Dad. I'll stay in the background, and I'll simply take pictures to document the investigation—"

"It's not an investigation," Seybold corrected. "It's an independent fact-finding mission, being conducted with the permission of the deceased's next of kin."

"Let's not mess with semantics. It doesn't really matter what terms you use. I've got a solid security clearance. I know you have copies of it in your files. And I've got experience—I've covered enough stories involving police investigations . . . er, fact-finding missions in Denver to know what to do or, and this is even better, what not to do in and around a crime scene and its aftermath."

His face darkened. "Don't go wishing for trouble. This isn't a crime. It's probably nothing. We're not going to even mention the word 'crime' in association with this inquiry. Is that clear?"

I shrugged. "What two people do in the privacy of their Lincoln bedroom . . ."

Judging by the look on his face, Seybold didn't share my sense of humor.

So we set off—we, in this case, being Seybold, my two Secret Service Dawgs, and me. To my belated amazement, I realized it was my first real trip outside of the White House grounds since I'd arrived there in all pomp and circumstance for the inauguration.

Ah, yes. The inauguration hoopla. It'd been a rip-roaring celebration, a wonderful introduction to the Washington social scene, what with all the parties that lasted into the wee hours. However, when someone says Washington has balls, he's not usually talking about the fancy-dress type. More often, he's thinking big brass ones.

The parties only last a short while. The rest of the time, it's a tough town and a lonely one, too. After the inauguration, my social life stopped.

Cold.

As we climbed into the car, I realized that since our family had moved into the White House, I hadn't been on a date. I hadn't gone to a girlfriend's house, either, since most everybody I knew well enough to inflict myself and the Dawgs on lived back in Denver. Since I'd moved to the White House, I hadn't gone shopping, or made a movie run to the cineplex, or even taken a trip to the local Blockbuster. I hadn't set foot in a fast food place, either. As far as that went, I wasn't even sure where the nearest McDonald's and Blockbuster were.

God, I couldn't believe how isolated, how sedentary, how housebound I'd become.

But now I was sneaking out in the dead of night, camera in hand, and it was just like the old days back in Denver when I worked for the wire service. The only difference was, back then, I drove myself to the investigations, arriving in a Mustang that tended to overheat in the summer and had to be babied in cold weather.

Now my Mustang was in storage and I was flying along in a bulletproof limo with government plates. The man behind the wheel was wearing at least one gun, and I had an armed Dawg riding shotgun. Literally. Evidently, my other Dawg was in another vehicle, riding point or cleanup or shotgun or some other such inexplicably named position. There were cars in front of us and cars behind us that were part of our little cavalcade. All in all, it was quite a production.

I hoped it wasn't typical procedure for a First Daughter jaunt outside the White House walls. Otherwise, I could see that my social life was likely to be severely curtailed for the next four years. Who wants to inconvenience so many people just to get a little shopping done or meet a friend for lunch?

I attempted some small talk with the Secret Service agent beside me. My companion's answers were even smaller than my talk.

"You're . . . McNally?" I asked rather hesitantly.

He wore no expression as he corrected me. "Perkins."

"Oh, sorry." I tried for the stupid laugh. "But probably not as sorry as Mrs. McNally, eh?"

He didn't crack a grin. "He's not married, ma'am."

"Oh. Are you?"

He kept his attention on the road, looking for potential terrorists, kidnappers, foreign agents, domestic dissidents, and any other unsavory folks who were apt to stop us and cause potential havoc.

"Yes, ma'am."

The second "ma'am" exhausted my patience. "Listen, can you stop with the 'ma'am' business, please? I know it's probably in the Secret Service rule book or something like that, but it's making me feel weird."

He hesitated. "Okay."

I smiled. "Thanks." After a moment, I picked up the previous thread of conversation. "Got any kids?"

"Two. A boy and a girl."

Heck, I thought. In for a penny . . .

"Got any pictures?"

Without taking his eyes off the road, he reached into his back pocket with a fluid move, pulled out his wallet, and flipped it open to reveal a family portrait of him— smiling, no less, with his wife and two kids, a boy who

looked like his mother and a girl who looked like neither of them.

I cooed appropriately over the children, which
wasn't hard because they were pretty cute, and remarked that his wife looked like a friend of mine who
lived in Texas.

All the while, Perkins kept his attention on our sur-
roundings, never even looking at his wallet or at my
examination of the picture. "The wife has family in
Texas," he said in a carefully modulated voice. "Maybe
they're kin."

"Maybe so."

That was the sum total of our animated conversation
as we crossed over the Potomac into Virginia and hit
U.S. 1 for the short drive south to Crystal City.

Sterling O'Connor had lived in one of the high-rise
apartments clumped there, and we'd been given permission by his brother to take a look at his house—
and the appropriate key and codes. I'm not sure why
they waited until after eleven at night to start the
search. Maybe they thought the press had long since
folded up their card tables and wouldn't notice our car-
avan leaving the White House. Fat chance. Having
been a newshound of sorts myself, I figured it was a
good bet that we had a media tail, but sure enough, no
one was following us.

Maybe the Dawgs actually knew their stuff. For
Dad's sake and his safety, I hoped they were infallible.

We entered the glass-front lobby, but I didn't pay
much attention; I was deep in thought. So exactly what

did we hope to find in O'Connor's apartment? The torn photo had given us no clue as to either subject's identity. But though I lacked any real facts to work with here, my imagination readily filled the void. I created several plausible scenarios in my mind.

Maybe the man in the picture had been Sterling O'Connor himself. Maybe he had a bad habit of carrying around glossy photos of himself *in flagrante delicto*. Men have done stranger things. That was my most hopeful scenario, one that would end things silently and with no scandal for my father.

Perhaps Sterling had shown the picture to the wrong person, like the woman's husband, which might account for the fact it'd been torn. I could imagine an enraged husband reacting that way to a photo of what he considered a personal and private view of his own wife. If we found the missing piece of the photo at O'Connor's apartment, maybe we'd have more to go on. Maybe if we found other pictures, ones from the same photo session, we could identify the people.

Then again, maybe Sterling had been blackmailed and had ripped the picture out of the blackmailer's hands. Maybe the shock from the event later caused him to suffer a heart attack on the White House grounds.

Then again, maybe *he* was the blackmailer, and the ripped photograph had been the prize in a struggle with his intended victim. I hoped, for the White House's sake, that wasn't the case. Our head usher wouldn't be happy if we proved his brother had such unfortunate morals and motives.

Then maybe . . .

Uh . . . did I mention that I have an overactive imagination? Or even worse, a hyperactive one, according to Aunt Patsy.

But I managed to keep my promise to Mr. Seybold. I didn't expound aloud on my wild theories. All I did was tag behind him as he entered the elevator, and I kept my opinions and my comments to myself as we went to the ninth floor. I even remained quiet as we trooped to the apartment door and met up with another set of plainclothesmen. I figured they weren't Metro Police since we were out of their jurisdiction. So who were they? Secret Service, FBI, or Arlington PD?

All I know is that I didn't feel comfortable asking, but I had my suspicions that Seybold was keeping everything in house, so to speak. Why complicate things by having to coordinate silence among multiple agencies? Like he'd said, it wasn't an investigation; it was a fact-finding mission. And evidently, facts were found using some tools that were strikingly similar to those investigators used. I watched one of the agents carry in a small black bag, which, once inside, I learned held an assortment of fingerprinting equipment.

For folks who didn't run investigations, these guys sure brought a nifty collection of investigative equipment to this noncrime scene.

Standing inside the small foyer, Seybold handed me a pair of surgical gloves that I duly pulled on, no questions asked. I watch cop shows on television, just like everybody else. To my surprise, Seybold waved the agents back and nodded at me.

"Let's let her do her stuff first."

I'd brought a digital camera as well as a thirty-five-

millimeter SLR, so I started with the digital, taking
careful photographic records of each room in the apartment, presearch, for reference, then switched to the
thirty-five millimeter, taking care to get a lot of good
angles on the lighting.

A couple of years ago, at my first crime scene, the
supervising detective almost jerked my arm out of its
socket as I started walking into the middle of the room
for a photo. From that moment on, I learned to walk
carefully along the fringes of the room, watching where
I put my feet to make sure I don't disturb any visible
evidence on the floor, like blood spatters or footprints
or depressions in the carpet surface, and not touching
anything.

At all.

So I knew enough in this case to walk along the
edges of the room to get the reverse angles. But as I
did so, I couldn't help but find my mind racing ahead,
making some assumptions based on what I saw in the
room.

Sterling O'Connor must have been the antithesis of
his brother, Burton. Whereas our Mr. O'Connor dealt
with White House antiquities with obvious love and
reverence for their age and value, this Mr. O'Connor
had a thoroughly modern apartment, complete with a
large flat-screen TV, a high-priced stereo system, and
a computer with every peripheral known to man. My
brother Charlie is our resident family computer geek,
and this setup almost rivaled his in terms of having all
the latest technological gizmos.

Computer geek may be too harsh of a term; Charlie's
a highly successful Internet entrepreneur who special-

izes in computer security and runs a multimillion-dollar business out of his isolated home/compound in Vermont. It's quite galling to have a baby brother, even if only younger than me by one year, who has achieved such success in his chosen field, while I'm still struggling, trying to find my place in the world . . . any world.

Oh, well, back to the story.

The plan was simple, in theory. Once I cataloged each room with enough photographs, the team of agents would begin to systematically search that room. Then I would hang back, to be their independent witness and to record hidden evidence, should they find anything.

Yeah, right. Me, as their corroborating witness. The President's daughter—who was, of course, totally objective.

Trouble was, I knew I'd be objective. But why would anyone else beyond the family think so?

The living room was clean except for some extremely pornographic magazines one agent found under the sofa cushion. When the man pulled them out, he had the decency to blush to the tips of his ears. The fingerprint guy lifted some latents from the first couple of pages as well as the centerfold, then made a dirty crack about wondering if he'd be able to get a saliva sample, too.

I think he meant to be funny, but Seybold pivoted and we could all see fiery bolts in his eyes. I knew he was about to land hard on the guy for spouting such a crude comment in front of my delicate, First Daughter ears.

I decided to intervene.

I kept a straight face. "Maybe you ought to check for semen, instead."

That was even cruder than his statement, but it was highly effective. It did what I wanted it to do: it took the heat off the fingerprint guy and maybe suggested that I wasn't a complete stiff at a crime scene. No pun intended.

Seybold's posture eased and he turned off his fire-breathing-dragon look. Evidently, he'd suffered from the same misconception as a good percentage of the press corps: that I was some sheltered flower who had only seen life through a rose-colored lens filter.

Heck, I'd lived in the real world. I even had some of the scars to prove it. In my opinion, a person has not experienced true life and death until he's done a photo shoot at a major city's ER on a Saturday night. I'd spent a lot of nights doing just that at Denver General.

During a full moon.

And with the Broncos losing.

The fingerprint guy waited until Seybold was called away before shooting me a grin. "Know what? You're all right."

I grinned back. It wasn't hard. He was fairly cute. "For a president's daughter, eh?"

Hoo, boy . . . big mistake.

The young man's face drained of all color. "Oh, crap," he whispered. "That's who you are?"

I didn't know whether to be thrilled that he didn't know who I was and yet thought that I was competent, or fearful that I'd just watched a man talk his way out of gainful employment. I didn't want him to lose his job over something like this, so instead of turning back and seeing if Seybold was within earshot and ready to shoot first and not even ask questions, I started laughing.

"Honestly, I can't believe it, myself. I look in the mirror and all I see is the same old Eve as before. I figure, Dad's the one who got elected. I'm just some of the baggage that came with him."

I braced myself to glance back at Seybold as I indicated my cameras and the bag of lenses I had slung around my neck. "I'm trying to make myself useful here, boys," I said, hoping my laughter didn't seem forced. "You know, maybe work off a little of my room and board. Justify the air I breathe."

Unlike a moment earlier, Seybold wore no discernible expression; look up the phrase "poker face" in the dictionary, and you'd have seen a picture of him. Evidently, he could scream at his own people without a second thought, but he didn't quite think he had the right to yell at me.

But somehow I think he agreed silently that I was indeed excess baggage.

"Why don't you photograph the bedroom?" he asked flatly.

I knew I was being dismissed. As I left the room, I stopped and faced him. "Don't give him a hard time," I said to him in a low voice. "He didn't do anything wrong." I paused. "And I'm really trying to do everything right here. I'll do my best for you, and my best is damned good. You have my word on it."

Seybold didn't answer me, so I simply continued with my assignment, getting everything I needed to photograph the bedroom.

No use fretting, better off forgetting, as Aunt Patsy would say.

I walked down the hallway to the bedroom to document it, photographing carefully as I went. Once I was finished, I stepped back to let the agents do their stuff. I was pleased to see that the fingerprint guy was still among the living, evidently still in possession of all his fingers and toes, and only a little singed around the edges.

When Seybold's attention was turned elsewhere, the fingerprint guy managed a half smile and whispered, "Thanks. I still have a job. It would have been a toss-up if you hadn't put in your bit there."

"Good," I whispered back. "I was hoping I helped."

I headed to the bathroom for the next session of photoreconnaissance. Of course, the inevitable happened.

Dad might not like coffee, but I do, and I'd fortified myself with a couple of cups of it before I came—for the caffeine jolt—and now the call of nature was whispering rather insistently in my ear. However, I knew better than to give into the urge. I'd read enough mystery books, seen enough television, and had once heard a real-life detective royally chewing out a patrolman for using the bathroom at a crime scene and possibly flushing away valuable evidence.

The last thing I needed to do was pull a bone-headed stunt like that. I was on thin ice as it was, just being me. So I took my pictures, trying to ignore my growing discomfort. Pulling back the mildewed shower curtain, I took a shot of the tub, noticing some unusual holes that had been drilled into the tub's tile surround, about two feet apart on either end and at about waist height.

Odd.

Very odd, in fact.

I made sure to get a clear shot of both walls, using a ruler to show the relative distance between holes.

As I turned to leave, I spotted something behind the door. At first I thought it was another door, maybe that of a linen closet, but it turned out to be nothing more than a wide plank, evidently being stored there. I pulled out my folding rule and, sure enough, the plank was just about the same length as the tub.

My mind raced ahead.

Put a couple of screws, nails, or some type of shelf pin in the holes that had been drilled, and you could rest the plank on them, making a waist-high shelf.

Or worktable.

I went back to the tub and examined the area above the shower rod, discovering two of those retractable clotheslines like you see in hotel bathrooms. Did O'Connor have so many delicate hand-washables that he needed two? Or were they a convenient place for other things he needed to dry?

Like freshly printed photographs.

Also, in the ceiling, where you might expect to find a heat lamp, there was a fifteen-watt red lightbulb.

Red for color, not for heat.

Bingo.

"Hey . . . uh . . . Mr. Seybold?" I didn't really want to start at the top, but he was the only man in the apartment I knew by name.

One of the other agents stuck his head in. "He's on the horn. What's wrong?" His face darkened. "You didn't . . ." He pointed to the toilet.

"No, of course not." *Although I'd love to . . .* "But I've found something I think he needs to see."

He looked downright dubious. "What?"

I crooked my forefinger to encourage him inside the bathroom. "I'm pretty sure Mr. O'Connor used this as a darkroom." I pulled a pencil from my jacket pocket and used the eraser to reverse the wall switches, turning off the light bar over the lavatory and turning on the "heat lamp."

Red light reduced the room to shades of scarlet and black. I restored the regular lights, then walked over and pointed to the holes in the tile.

"Here's where he hung his work surface, which is stored behind the door." I used the pencil point to snag the ring of one of the retractable clotheslines. "And here's where he hung his photos to dry." Then I pointed to the cabinet under the sink. "Ten to one, you find developing chemicals under there."

The agent used one gloved fingertip to open the cabinet door just far enough to see inside, but not show me. After a long moment and after making an even longer face, he opened cabinet wider, revealing that it was empty.

No chemicals. No equipment. Not even a towel or a bottle of Drano.

His expression revealed nothing.

Did they hire these guys because of their ability to camouflage their feelings, or is it something they taught them in Secret Service school?

Or maybe someone had Botoxed this one's entire face.

I sighed. "I promise you it's a darkroom," I repeated. "I'm sure it is."

The agent motioned for me to follow him to the living room, where we found Seybold flipping closed his cell phone. The man stared at us.

At me.

"What is it?"

All he lacked was an added *"now?"* in an exasperated voice to remind me of my aunt Patsy during the worst of my rebellious teen years (though, for the record, those years were pretty tame by most standards).

The agent thumbed over his shoulder. *"She* thinks she's found evidence of a darkroom. In the bathroom. But there's nothing there that I can see." The words were innocuous enough but the attitude suggested that I was in the habit of hallucinating such things.

To my surprise, Seybold strode toward the bathroom, which meant he either believed I saw something of interest or wanted to shut me up by showing me the error of my ways. The other agent and I fell in close behind him.

I felt compelled to defend my observation. "There may be nothing there now," I said, "but I know there was something there not so long ago.

"Something," he repeated darkly as he stepped into the bathroom.

The three of us couldn't crowd in there with him, so the other agent graciously stepped back and allowed me to follow Seybold. I suspect it was a calculated move to put me in the direct line of fire when the boss turned around and let loose a volley.

Seybold opened the cabinet door and stooped down to peer into the empty space. "Nothing here."

I scrunched in beside him. "No, but look at those rings." I pointed to the three dark oblong rings on the wooden floor of the cabinet. "Three rings, three solutions—developer, stop, and fix. The rings are the right size and shape for the usual half-gallon bottles." I started building up steam as my faith in myself amplified. "You can analyze the stains and check the chemical profiles." I sniffed the air. "I can even smell some of the residual odors from the solutions."

Seybold sniffed as well. "I don't smell anything."

I stood up straight. "You don't work with this stuff almost every day. I do. I'm a professional photographer."

He hesitated for a moment, then nodded. "Point taken."

I almost jumped for joy because someone was finally listening to me, but then he ruined it by saying, "But what's the significance of a darkroom?"

I forced myself not to say "Duh . . ."

"Mr. O'Connor had a piece of a potentially important and possibly incriminating photo in his possession when he died. Did he develop the print himself? It's possible since it appears he had a functional darkroom in here some time in the very recent past. Maybe the most important question raised by the existence of a darkroom is whether he dismantled it himself or if someone did it for him. And, if so—"

Seybold held up his hand to stop me, then used the

same hand to motion to the agent standing at the door to leave and close it behind him.

The man complied.

If I were the guy, I'd have stood with my ear against the door and listened to the ensuing conversation. Of course, I don't know what kind of oaths they make the Secret Service guys take about that kind of thing. I bet there's a section on the subject in their job description.

Seybold lowered his voice. "Don't go jumping to conclusions. We have no evidence of any improprieties. As far as we know, O'Connor died of natural causes. No foul play. That picture could have been nothing more than a memento of a special night with a special woman."

I nodded. "Or it could have been a blackmail attempt."

So much for not spreading my opinions around.

Seybold raised a graying eyebrow and adopted an expression that almost bordered on mild amusement as he looked at me. "Blackmail? Do you know something I don't?"

"N-no, sir," I stuttered, "but I do know that we have to look at all the possibilities. And as ridiculous as that blackmail theory might sound to you, I won't be the only one who comes up with the idea. You know how it is in politics. They're more apt to remember the accusations than they are the resolutions. If we want to control this situation, then we have to be the ones who bring up any unsavory issues—along with the evidence to disprove them. If someone comes up with a scenario we haven't anticipated, every second of delay between the question and the answer means that that many more people remember only the question. And assume guilt."

He stared at me for a long moment. "How old are you again?"

I knew what was coming. I'd get the old line about how he'd been a Secret Service agent for as long as I'd been alive and he knew far more about the business than I ever would and to leave such things to the professionals.

I steeled myself for the onslaught. "Twenty-five, sir."

He laughed, but it wasn't a "The young think they know everything" sort of snorting laughter. It was something less biting, even warm.

His smile grew more genuine. "If I'd known as much about this politics business as you clearly do when I was your age, I would have gone a lot farther." He paused, then gave me a good once-over. "You thinking about following in your father's footsteps?"

"Politics?" I shook my head. "Absolutely not, sir. You don't have to worry about a Cooper dynasty. We leave that to the Roosevelts, the Kennedys, and the Bushes. So far, neither of my brothers are interested in the family business, and that goes double for me."

He brushed past me, reached for the door, and made a comment that I couldn't quite make out over the sound of the door's squeaky hinges. It was either "Good God!" or "Good thing!"

I couldn't tell which.

He changed his search philosophy after that, though. Instead of relegating me strictly to photo duty, he pulled me in to help his team look around. Our mission was to think like the blackmailer O'Connor might or might not have been. We were looking for photographs, cameras, exposed film, negatives, cash, bank records, anything that might suggest he wasn't the upstanding citizen his brother—and the federal agencies who'd cleared him before hiring his brother—said he was.

It was an odd feeling, looking through a dead man's things. One reassuring item we did find was an assortment of heavy-duty prescription medicines for heart problems in his master bathroom. Most of them were low and a few were even empty, as if he'd been hitting them pretty hard lately or maybe had been too busy or too broke to refill them. So the heart attack was likely to have been just what the doctor said—due to natural causes, not foul play. But those empty bottles worried me.

Maybe blackmailing was a more stressful occupation than our victim had thought.

One of the agents started going through O'Connor's computer, looking for graphic files and suspicious e-mail. At one point when I walked into the room, he shifted as to block the screen from my view.

"Find something?" I asked.

He blushed. "Possibly. But it's nothing you really need to see."

I could read between the lines. "Porn?"

He nodded, hit a few keys, then sat back down, un-blocking the offensive screen, which was now mini-mized. "And lots of it." He made a face. "Most of it seems to be in his Internet temp files from various web-sites he seemed to visit—a lot. But none of them was sent to him by file transfer or originated in this com-puter. He wasn't actually keeping any of the stuff, and if he was making it, I'm not seeing any signs of that, either." The young man sighed. "I don't think we're going to find anything here. This guy didn't seem to have anything other than a basic working knowledge of how to get on the Net and how to access his e-mail. I can't find any signs of advanced ability."

He was starting to report to me like he would a superior. I didn't know whether I should be encouraged by that or not.

I struggled for the right response so I could get back to my own job. "Well, back to the grind, I guess?"

In this room, with that little minimized picture on the screen of the computer behind him, it was a bad choice of words. I could see the young man thinking, As in bump and grind?

He blushed again. "Guess so."

By this time, the call of nature had stopped whispering in the back of my brain and was screaming to be acknowledged. But before I could use the blasted toilet in this apartment, it had to be searched. Computer Guy was knee-deep in "porno .gifs and .jpgs," Fingerprint Guy was dusting various objects in the living room, Seybold was back on his cell phone in deep discussion with somebody back at base, and the other guy (I was too lazy to nickname him) was rooting around behind a pile of boxes in O'Connor's walk-in closet.

It was up to me, I guess.

I pulled my latex glove up my arm as high as it would reach and stuck my hand into the toilet bowl, thankful the water and porcelain looked clean. I felt around to see if anything was lodged just out of sight in the drain.

Nothing.

I took off the tank lid and peered inside. Nothing. Craning my head, I pushed close to the wall to see behind the tank. Nothing.

No . . . wait . . .

There was a piece of duct tape stuck to the back of the tank. Had it once been used to hold something in place? I felt along its flat edges.

Whatever had been there was now gone.

However, the tip of my gloved forefinger caught on something along the top edge. Unable to see, I pulled back and relied on a sense of touch to identify whether it was merely some exposed adhesive grabbing the latex or something else.

It was something else.

A nearly invisible string.

I bent down and spotted the slender piece of monofilament fishing line extending from its anchored position on the back of the tank, over the rim, and into the tank itself. I followed the taut line into the cold water down past the black ball valve to the pipe, where it disappeared.

Something was being hidden in the toilet. I also noticed that the chain that connected the handle to the ball valve had been disconnected. Evidently, someone, maybe O'Connor, didn't want to accidentally flush his hidden treasure down the toilet. And since there was the other bathroom off the master bedroom, he could afford to make this one essentially inoperable.

"Hey, guys, uh . . . somebody, come here," I called out. "I think I found something."

They crowded in the door, but only Seybold stepped in. "What is it?"

I ran my finger gently down the fishing line. "This goes all the way down to below the ball valve. I think there's something hidden down there."

Seybold assessed the situation and came to the same conclusion as I had. So it was time for action. First, we bailed as much water out of the tank as we could, then he reached down and gently lifted the valve, letting only a trickle of water go out; a hard rush of water and we might lose the object in the inner part of the toilet. A little patience and we might get it out the easy way.

With most of the water drained, Seybold took over the operation, which was fine with me. If anything went wrong, it was on his shoulders. Also, I'm not fond of fishing about in plumbing at the best of times.

Seybold let out a few choice words, the gist of which was that the object in question hung right below the mouth of the drain and was caught on something, and it was up to me and my smaller fingers to free it. If I couldn't do it, it was time to call in a plumber, which might need more explaining than Seybold wanted to make right now.

White House plumbers have such a bad reputation . . .

Pointed jokes aside, and despite my dislike for the task, I gave it my best shot. After maneuvers I still don't like to think about, eventually I got what we wanted out of there.

I held up our new treasure with a flourish. "Ta-da!"

It was a film canister.

CHAPTER THREE

I wish I could say I developed and printed the film under the watchful eye of Seybold and his cohorts, further proving my prowess as a photographer and my worth as a member of the investigative . . . fact-finding-mission team.

No such luck.

Seybold pretty much ripped it out of my hands, and I never saw it again. All I got was a "Good job" from Seybold, and a wink from Fingerprint Guy, who then immediately blushed. Had I been any other female in the known universe, I think he might have asked for my phone number.

Just call the White House switchboard and ask to speak to Eve. . . .

Did I mention that not only had I not left the White

House in over three weeks, but that I'd not had a date in almost twice that long, either? Fingerprint Guy wasn't my type, but I bet he'd go to McDonald's with me. . . .

I ignored the little plaintive voice in the back of my head that was insisting that a super-sized order of french fries and a chocolate shake would free my soul. Instead, I joined the others, who were stepping up their search, going through magazines and books, looking for more prints. However, try as we might, we found nothing else that seemed to be of any possible interest.

Finally, at around 4:30 A.M., Seybold called a halt to the search and we piled in our cars with our booty and headed back. We even drove past a McDonald's, but it was closed and I was too tired to care—though I did make a mental note of its location.

I was exhausted. My caffeine load had given out about an hour earlier and I was really dragging. If there had been any tabloid reporters around, I'm sure the headline beneath a close-up of my bloodshot eyes would have read "First Daughter Sees First Light After All-Night Partying."

I wish.

I'm no party animal, but I'm no saint, either. I've been known to enjoy a beer or two, even three sometimes, at a local pub, hanging out with friends from work. But it seemed as if I no longer had that luxury. I had to coordinate any and every place I went with my Secret Service detail, and they hadn't yet grasped the concept of spontaneity.

But if I thought I had it bad, I knew Drew had it worse.

When I was fifteen, Dad had been well on his way in his political career, but it hadn't really affected us like it does now. Dad did the traveling and we stayed home. The press pretty much ignored us, except for official ceremonial events. Aunt Patsy made sure we had a normal childhood with all the rights, privileges, and activities thereof. When I was a freshman in high school, like Drew is now, I was in the band and told myself it was the real reason why I hadn't gone out for cheerleading, not because I had no talent whatsoever in the "sis-boom-bah" field. Charlie, a year younger and in junior high, was already displaying his predilection for computers over humans, but he tolerated us carbon-based units when he had to. Ten years younger than me, Drew was in kindergarten and oblivious to anything but Ninja Turtles and Matchbox cars.

But now, ten years later, things had changed. At the beginning of the year, Drew had transferred into some ritzy private institution called The Altamont School, where he knew exactly nobody. Plus, he had the added burden of being the only freshman in school with— count 'em—not one but two bodyguards sitting across the hall, ready to dog his every movement. He didn't like it. The worst moment, at least for me, was the first day when he'd come home practically heartbroken and exploding with news.

"Some school," he'd complained. "I asked about football, hoping that maybe I could try out for next year's team."

"So?" I'd asked.

He made a face. "They looked at me as if I was

crazy. Evidently, Altamont doesn't even have a football team!"

Which I knew meant no pep rallies, no homecoming bonfires, no cheerleading squads, no drill team full of scantily dressed cuties for Drew to eye.

I put my arm around him. "I'm sorry, Drew."

He pulled away. "Oh, no, not yet. It gets better." His grimace had turned into a sneer. "Their big sport is— get this—lacrosse!"

Oh, joy . . . *that* was going to impress the girls back home.

I knew we couldn't let this one small problem distract us from the fact that Drew would be getting a great education. Up to the Christmas break, he'd been going to public school in Denver, and in January, we'd anticipated merely shifting him into a public high school in D.C. Then we learned that he couldn't continue his studies in both Latin and Japanese in any of the public high schools in D.C., so private school became the best option. And who knows? He would probably get a far better education than the ones Charlie and I got in public school back in Colorado. But then again, Charlie's education hadn't kept him from getting into MIT. And I'd had my pick of universities, too, not to mention a couple of decent merit scholarships tossed my way.

So, in my opinion, Drew was getting a mixed bag, thanks to Dad's new job—a unique set of experiences, living in the White House, where the staff fed him like a king and picked up after his typical teenaged-boy sloppiness, and possibly a better education than he'd have had if Dad had lost the election, but all at the cost of what we both considered a normal, everyday life. The one we'd always expected we would have.

I guess the trick to surviving the ordeal was in not letting him figure that last part out.

But that was going to be difficult, because the kid was smart. Really smart. And matters were made worse for Drew by the fact that, though both Charlie and I had had a full-time mother substitute in Aunt Patty during those critical teenaged years, he was going to have to do this pretty much alone. Patsy already had a full slate in front of her with all the First Lady things—lunches, speeches, travel, press, etc.

But we'd been smart enough to anticipate that there would be changes. After Dad won the election, we all started sorting out our pre-planned roles in the Cooper administration. Patsy admitted early on, once it became clear that Dad had a real shot at the presidency, that she was worried about overextending herself. She believed that Drew still needed a full-time mother figure. Her biggest argument was that Drew shouldn't be shortchanged and given less attention than Charlie and I had been at that age. But, she also realized she'd be pulled in every direction with her First Lady duties if Dad won.

So the obvious solution was for me to volunteer to play pseudomom for Drew, taking over some of the mothering responsibilities when Patsy had to be elsewhere. It was the core of the reason I was here in D.C. playing "Leech off Dad."

Those duties included making sure Drew got up, ate something resembling a reasonable breakfast, and headed off to school on time with his completed homework in his backpack. As Dad put it, some duties just had to fall to family, not government aides. I agreed. I wouldn't want to inflict early-morning Drew on any hired hands if I didn't have to.

It definitely wasn't a pretty sight.

So even though I didn't get to sleep until 5 A.M., I still had to rise dutifully at six-thirty to make sure Drew was up and getting ready for school. And don't suggest I buy him an alarm clock for Christmas. They don't make a machine loud and obnoxious enough to override Drew's own loud and obnoxious early-morning attitude that isn't a weapon of mass destruction.

After I rousted him out of bed (a process normally requiring a cattle prod and a wish for some C-4 explosive), I wandered down the hallway to the kitchen.

Yes, we have our own kitchen, a rather ordinary-looking one, which is a welcome relief in the midst of the pomp and circumstance and antiquity in the rest of the private sections of the White House. Aunt Patsy even outfitted it with decorations from the kitchen of the house I grew up in, so it almost feels like home. If I had a choice, I'd opt to eat all our meals in here, rather than in the family dining room, which smacks of too much formality for me. Let's put it this way— we probably have more in common with Barney Fife than Duncan Phyfe.

At least we are able to eat breakfast here every morning, pretending for a half hour or so each day that we all live a normal life. Dad, in particular, needs that sense of normality before heading to the Oval Office each morning to assume his role as the Leader of the Free World.

Dad wasn't in there just yet, so I draped myself in a chair at the end of the table and poured my coffee with two very unsteady hands.

"You look worse than stoned," Drew offered with his usual amount of brotherly solicitousness as he entered.

"Thanks. I feel lousy."

"Rough night last night?" he sneered. "What was it? The booze or the drugs?"

I tossed a piece of toast at him. "Shut up and eat. I'm only up because you haven't mastered how to use that technological wonder called an alarm clock."

He made a face.

"And no more cracks about drugs or booze," I added. "Someone might actually take you seriously."

He whipped out his Palm Pilot, a Christmas gift from Charlie. Charlie'd given me one, too, and although I'd been slightly miffed that Drew and I had received the same present despite our age difference, I was starting to appreciate mine.

Drew pretended to write on the screen. "No more cracks . . . about crack. Got it. Any more Presidential Progeny Proclamations?"

"Hurry up or you'll be late," boomed our father's voice. "And I'm not writing you an excuse if you are."

Drew made a face, somewhat similar to the grimace he always greeted me with when I woke him. "Aw, c'mon, Dad. Do you know how much I can get for a genuine presidential signature?"

Dad settled at the other end of the table and rolled his eyes. "If I start hearing anything about my autograph on a school absence excuse slip going up for sale on eBay, you're going to be *so* grounded."

Drew crossed his arms and legs and kicked the table leg in the process. My coffee sloshed and I made a grab for it. I needed every precious, eye-opening drop.

"Grounded from what?" he grumbled. "I can't go anywhere, I can't see anybody . . ."

He meant one body in particular. Despite his status as the new kid in class, Drew had already picked out and made the initial moves on a girl. The boy works fast. Her name was Cammie, and I hoped to God she'd hooked up with him because she liked him for him, not because he was the President's son.

Drew hadn't run into that sort of stuff much, whereas Charlie and I had learned our lessons about hanger-ons the hard way, years ago back when Dad was still a congressman.

I'd have to drop Charlie an e-mail about the situation and let him broach the subject in a brother-to-brother manner with Drew. Charlie was good at that sort of stuff because they were close, despite the nine-year age difference and the several hundred miles between D.C. and Charlie's Fortress of Silicon nestled in the mountains of Vermont.

Drew stuffed a piece of toast in his mouth and gathered the various articles he'd dropped around his chair—his backpack, his CD player for that oh-so-long 1.5-mile drive to school, and his new coat.

He waved in our general direction and ran out the door, still crunching his toast.

"Got your homework?" I yelled after him.

"Yeah, yeah . . ." Drew's voice faded away along

with the pounding noise of his footsteps as he ran farther and farther from us.

I stared at my dad, who is always much too chipper in the mornings for my taste. "Well, Ward, I'm worried about the Beav," I said.

He looked over the sheaf of reports that awaited him every morning—the state of the free and not-so-free world in a hundred pages or less. "How so, June?"

"New girlfriend. Senator's daughter."

"Which one?" He paused to sip his hot chocolate. "Senator, I mean."

"Kitchener. She's Cammie, his youngest."

Dad nodded. "Tall guy, turns red at the drop of a hat." He shuffled his papers. "Actually, Kitchener's quite nice. No reason to believe his daughter won't be, too."

I'd seen a picture of her and she was a knockout. It made me worry even more. Pretty girl. Teenaged boy. Raging hormones.

I gulped.

And the Lincoln bedroom . . .

I shook that thought out of my mind and promised to yell at myself later for coming up with such a hideous idea.

"Have you talked to him lately about . . ." I hesitated. "You know . . ." My voice trailed off. Surely he knew what I was talking about and wouldn't make me actually say the words.

Dad gave me a blank stare. "Huh?"

Darn it, was he going to make me say it? Aloud?

His blank expression turned into a grin. "You mean

the birds and the bees and cross-pollination? That sort of father-and-son-talk thing?"

I sighed. There ought to be a law about not having to talk about your kid brother's sex life—or hopeful lack thereof—with your father. Especially at my advanced age.

"Especially the cross-pollination bit," I answered.

He put down his papers and attacked his breakfast with unusual gusto. "Don't worry. We've been talking about it since he was eight."

I sighed. "I know. But that was merely a preemptive strike. He wasn't likely to do anything when he was eight. We're now in his prime time. I think he needs a reminder call about what he should and shouldn't do."

"What who should do?" called out a voice from the door. Aunt Patsy stood in the doorway, dressed in her usual early-morning running outfit.

Dad dropped his napkin on the table, pushed back his chair, and met her in the middle of the room, giving her a big hug. "Hey, sis. When'd you get back?"

She hugged him back, then dropped into a chair at the table. "Last night in the wee hours." She tipped back the lid to the silver pot and peered inside. "You didn't leave me any hot chocolate, did you?"

He pushed his mug toward her. "Here, take mine." He settled at his place, resting his elbows on the table and his chin on his hands just like an eager kid. "So? How was the trip?"

She took a long sip from the cup as if she needed the sugar and the caffeine to jump-start her storytelling muscles. "It was fine. Fun, in fact. The audience was really interested and I think we locked in some solid support for the foundation."

Aunt Patsy heads up the Carolyn Cooper Cancer Research Foundation, named after my mom, who died of lung cancer when I was twelve. The tragic thing was that she'd been a lifelong nonsmoker raised in a family of smokers. According to the doctors, it was the secondhand smoke that probably got her. She'd been entirely too young to go like that, so Dad and Aunt Patsy started the CCC to help fund cancer research. Now, with Patsy serving as First Lady, she planned to use her new position to help pull in some big funding for the foundation.

After all, every First Lady so far has had her pet charity.

Patsy gave us a smile decorated with a faint chocolate mustache. "I have a meeting with two Silicon Valley CEOs next week. I hope I can talk them into a matching fund program for their employees. And considering their astronomical salaries, they can afford to be generous."

Dad shook his head. "Don't forget the cost of living there is high. They'll have about the same percentage of disposable income as people elsewhere in the country."

Patsy drained the cup, tapping it so as not to miss any lumps of chocolate clinging to the bottom. "True, but ten percent of a hundred thousand dollars is still more money than ten percent of a thousand."

He nodded. "Point taken."

"Make sure you talk to Charlie before you squeeze them." I pushed the plate of toast closer to her. "I bet he either knows the CEOs or someone else high up in their organization. He can help you identify any soft spots in their hard silicon hearts."

"I caught him online this morning and he's going to do some research on them for me."

"Good." Dad stood up and brushed nonexistent crumbs from his pants. "I'd better go clock in. America wants a full-time President."

"Wait," I called out. "Don't you want to hear what happened last night?"

"What? Where?" Patsy looked confused.

He dropped back in his seat. "Burton O'Connor's brother dropped dead of a heart attack in the Rose Garden yesterday. Eve went along with Seybold's men to check out the guy's house."

Patsy looked at me, even more confused. "You? But why?"

I took up the tale. "He had part of a photograph in his possession. Judging by what was left, it looked like a man and a woman screwing their buns off in the Lincoln bedroom."

Confusion gave way to amazement. "A photo? Of them . . . ?" She made the universal sign for two people rutting like dogs.

Did I mention that Patsy is one really neat lady?

She looked more intrigued than shocked. "Recently?"

I shrugged. "We don't know. And we haven't identified the folks in the picture yet. That's why we went to O'Connor's place last night—the brother, not Burton—to see if we could find anything else to explain the picture." I yawned. "I only got back"—I consulted my watch, which I'd never taken off—"two hours ago."

Patsy made a face. "No wonder you look exhausted. Why don't you head back to bed?"

"Not yet, my girl." Dad leaned forward. "First you tell us what you found."

"Elliot James! Give the child a break."

When Aunt Patsy uses your middle name, you're dead.

She continued to scold the Commander in Chief of the Armed Forces as if he were a recalcitrant schoolboy. "Leave the girl alone. Look at her, she's barely able to keep her eyes open."

I held out my hand to stop her. "I'll sleep better if I can get this off my chest." I turned to Dad. "We think Sterling O'Connor used the bathroom in his apartment as a darkroom, but we didn't find any developing or printing equipment." I leaned forward as well. "But I did find a roll of film, hidden really well—in the toilet tank. Mr. Seybold is having it printed so we can see what was so important about it that it had to be hidden. He said he'd be by to see you this morning with the shots and any recommendations."

"Intriguing, and just a bit scary, too." Dad glanced at his watch. "I have back-to-back meetings today . . . just like the last twenty-eight days before this. I don't think this looks likely to blow up in my face just yet. So you get some sleep, then meet with Seybold. I'm keeping you as my official representative concerning this situation until I tell you otherwise."

"Official?"

He nodded and gave me a smile. "You'll continue

to do great. Don't worry. Keep me posted."

Great. Right.

Seybold showed up a half hour later, right as I was falling asleep on the couch watching the *Today* show. I hadn't even had time to start that nice recurring dream about Matt Lauer.

As soon as I saw Seybold, I had a sneaking suspicion he was pissed at having to deal with me, official representative or not. But to his credit, he regrouped and gave me the Official Face.

The Official Face is a White House phenomenon I was just learning to recognize. It was a professional frown that included elements of vague concern and unidentified determination. You know—an expression with those little pinched lines where the nose and eyebrows meet. Plus, there was a slight air of pomposity thrown in for good measure, which I supposed was a by-product of working in both a high-stress and high-profile area. It made even the most idle aide look incredibly busy as he strode down the corridors with noticeable purpose in his steps.

So I knew that Seybold's expression didn't necessarily mean anything . . . until he laid the enlargements on the coffee table.

Okay, I'm not particularly squeamish, but I'm no voyeur, either. I tried to examine the photos carefully, looking at them in terms of composition and detail, not because they were of two people in the throes of some heavy-duty-Kama-Sutra-position-number-twenty-something sex.

I could see the event was definitely taking place in the Lincoln bedroom.

I could see the man's face clearly in several of the shots, and it was neither Burton nor Sterling O'Connor. I didn't recognize the man at all. The woman was a different matter, however—not because I recognized her, but because none of the shots had caught her face. In each case, you could see her only from the rear, her very naked rear.

Seybold pointed to one particularly clear shot, tapping it with his forefinger, and said the three most frightening words I'd heard in a very long time.

"Is this you?"

I stared at him, my stomach churning like a Ferris wheel and my heart trying to catch a ride. "Absolutely not."

He remained expressionless. "Prove it."

What did the man want me to do? Strip right then and there and let him make an inch-by-inch comparison? The guy had some balls—

Ooh . . . bad choice of words.

I sighed to myself. And he was exactly the sort of tough, ballsy guy I wanted protecting my father's interest. If he had enough cojones to accuse the First Daughter of something—of anything—like that to her face, then nothing and nobody would be likely to slip under his radar.

I stared at the picture, trying to look for any identifying marks on her body that would prove I wasn't her. The woman had a figure I'd kill for. She was— ahem—evidently a natural blonde, about my height, and she had no identifying marks on the parts of her we could see.

Inspiration struck. She might not have any identi-

fying marks, but I did. Enough of them to put me in
the clear. I turned around and lifted the right rear tail
of my shirt, displaying a small mole above my waist.

"Does she have this? I've had it all my life." I knew
I could prove it because there was a picture behind my
Dad's desk in the Oval Office of me at age six, doing
what he called a Betty Grable pose in my two-piece
bathing suit. The mole was clearly visible in that shot
as well.

He pulled out a photographer's loupe and used it to
magnify the clearest shot of the nude woman's back-
side. We could both see that she had no moles on that
part of her anatomy. And if his people had developed
the film and then made the print directly from the neg-
ative, nothing had been airbrushed out.

He looked up and caught my eye, displaying only
the mildest look of relief. "Sorry. I had to ask."

I shrugged. "I'd have been disappointed if you
hadn't." Well, not really, but it sounded appropriate for
the moment. And I couldn't blame him for being thorough.

I picked up the loupe and used it to study an enlargement of the naked man. (Get your mind out of the
gutter. I was studying his face. Most of the time . . .)

"Have you identified this guy? You've got several
clear shots of him."

Seybold shook his head. "Not yet, but it won't take
long. We keep detailed security records on all the
guests who stay here overnight."

I selected one of the enlargements that caught a bit
of the window. Using the loupe, I stared at the visible
corner of windowpane. "I'm not so sure these were

taken at night. It looks as if the photographer used mostly ambient light with low-light film." I pointed to the window. "If he'd used a flash, you'd see a reflection here in the glass because it's in a straight line with the photographer's position." I offered him the loupe. "See?"

He took it and examined the shot. "Which means the photo might have been taken during the day . . ."

"Exactly."

He pushed the loupe back toward me. "Notice anything else?"

I pored over the photos, trying to look for things like reflections of the woman's face in background items such as the highly polished furniture, anything that might help to identify her.

"Sorry. Nothing jumps out at me." I swallowed my pride. "I'll tell you who you ought to ask—Michael Cauffman. He might see something I missed."

"We tried his apartment early this morning, but he wasn't there. If you see him here, send him to my office immediately. I want his opinion of the photographs."

"What's your next step?" I asked.

"We'll try to identify the man in the picture, then determine what connection he might have to Sterling O'Connor. Perhaps you were right when you suggested O'Connor was not a souvenir collector or a victim here, but a blackmailer instead. It would explain why he had the film hidden that way in his bathroom."

"And why he suddenly has no photography equipment in a room where it clearly used to be a fixture. He decided to hide the evidence." I paused for a moment. "You didn't find any cameras in the house, did you? I don't remember seeing any."

"No. I sent a full detail over there after we left. They didn't turn up anything else—no cameras, no film, no photographs other than the expected family and vacation shots. Also, no pawn ticket stubs, no charitable organization receipts, no rental receipts—nothing to explain where his equipment might be. But the lab did turn up a nice latent print on the inside lid of the plastic film canister. It was of a right thumb, and it belonged to Sterling O'Connor."

So what would make O'Connor suddenly dismantle his darkroom, get rid of all his equipment, and hide some compromising film in his toilet? Fear of discovery? Maybe the blackmail victim decided to fight back, and instead of O'Connor being the criminal, the roles of the game had been reversed and he'd been a victim of sorts.

My overactive imagination started coming up with more and more preposterous scenarios concerning undetectable poisons, Mafia mistresses, and other totally absurd concepts that reeked of wild conspiracy theories or Hollywood on a bad day.

I shook my head, trying to free myself from the grip of some truly harebrained ideas.

Seybold began to look uncomfortable, then after a moment's hesitation, he spoke. "I . . . appreciate your help last night." He gathered the photos and tapped them into a neat stack. "And today, as well. You have a good eye for detail."

"A photographer's eye," I offered.

"Indeed." He looked as if his collar were a half-size

too small. "I'll keep both you and your father informed during this continuing discovery process."

Continuing discovery process—a neat euphemism for criminal investigation, don'tcha think?

I started to ask a question, then thought better of it.

Seybold noticed and stopped, crossing his arms. "Is there something else?"

Aw, heck, go for it, I figured. "I . . . I thought I might speak to Mr. O'Connor . . . er . . . Burton, that is. Maybe I could get some information about his brother."

Seybold waited for a moment, then, to my surprise, nodded. "My people have talked to him, of course, but you might be effective. He might tell you something that he wouldn't tell one of my people." He raised an eyebrow. "Just don't mention the film we found, or these pictures. So far he only knows about the torn photo we found on his brother's body. Let's keep it that way for now."

I snapped him a salute worthy of one of the Marine guards outside. "Yes, sir!"

I don't think he was amused.

Twenty minutes later, I stood at the door of the chief usher's office. One Dawg stood beside me and the other had hurried around to guard the other office door that led to the entrance hall.

Before I moved here, someone had described the chief usher's office as the nerve center of the White House. It didn't take me long to discover how true that was. Burton O'Connor had survived five administrations so far, and I was hoping ours wouldn't be the one to run him off. But I'd have to admit I wouldn't want to work in the same place where they'd found my brother's dead body.

No matter how obnoxious Drew—or Charlie—could be.

I'd used the back staircase to reach Mr. O'Connor's office, which was located on the State floor. The door was open as usual. I knocked on the frame, not quite feeling like I could just walk in.

"Uh . . . Mr. O'Connor?"

He looked at me. Although he appeared to have aged twenty years in the last twenty-four hours, his smile was genuine as he stood. "Miss Cooper, what a delightful surprise!"

"Please, it's Eve."

He nodded. "As you've told me before." He managed to put a twinkle into his grin. "I'm afraid the formality is a holdover from the previous administration."

I knew just what he was talking about. Dad's predecessor had had four children, two stepchildren from his wife's first marriage and two of their own from his current, second marriage. It was the typical story. The older kids—aged nineteen and twenty-two—resented the attention the younger ones—aged four and five—got, and all that supposed inequity made for a not-so-happy First Family. I have it from several very good sources that the oldest daughter made life miserable for the White House staff, making demands that would make a rock star think twice. One of her ironclad peccadilloes was being addressed formally at all times by those people she called "my servants."

I met her once. My opinion? Bit of a bitch. Later, I heard that her code name had been changed early on from Glass Slipper to Broom, and somehow I think it was a matter of some astute Secret Service agent finding a *B* word with a witch connotation. Best of all, she reportedly never caught on to the subtle reasons behind the reference.

It certainly explained why people were still tiptoeing around me. It didn't help that we were both blue-eyed blondes, either. But I figured it wouldn't take long for the comparison to serve me well. I wasn't her, I would never be her, and once everyone realized that, they could breathe normally again.

So far, my code name is Apple—evidently, the White House staff had caught on to the Adam and Eve stuff, too. But it could be worse. If they called her Broom, they could have called me Vacuum . . .

I smiled back at Mr. O'Connor. "Do you have a moment, sir? I'd like to talk to you about something."

He reached over and tugged an empty chair across the red carpet, closer to his desk. "Absolutely . . . Eve. Have a seat."

I glanced at the door, which remained open to the stair and elevator landing. "May I?" I asked, reaching for the knob.

"Certainly."

I winked at the Dawg stationed there, closed the door, and took the offered seat. "First, let me offer my condolences for the death of your brother. I'm so sorry for your loss."

He reached over and patted my hand, very much like my grandfather used to do. Not surprising, I supposed.

Though he wasn't quite as old as my grandfather, he had the same sort of Old World manners and cultured air about him.

"That's very kind of you, Eve. You don't know what it means to me to have you and your father demonstrate such concern and care for me."

I allowed him to continue holding my hand. I guess I missed my grandfather. "I don't understand why you even came here today, sir. You could have taken a day off and everyone would have understood completely."

He released a small sigh. "Your father said the same thing, but I insisted." He looked around and shrugged. "This is my life. I almost feel as if the White House is *my* home." He colored slightly and added a small smile, letting me have my hand back. "I suppose I shouldn't admit that to anyone, much less the President's daughter."

"You've been here longer than any of us, sir. I'm glad to know someone feels at home here. I haven't settled in yet."

He leaned forward, his concern for me masking all other emotions from his face. "Is there something lacking? Is there something the staff and I could do to make it more hospitable for you?"

"Good heavens, no." It was my turn to blush. "Everyone has been wonderful. I have everything I could possibly need. I'm still amazed at the beautiful fresh flowers in my room every day." Nor had I gotten used to coming back to my room and finding a fresh vase of flowers every night, as if day-old ones wouldn't do for someone of my stature.

Sure . . .

"Your father told me daisies are your favorite," he said, drawing even more strongly on his Old World, grandfatherly charms.

"They are. Thank you." I drew a deep breath. "But my problem isn't the"—I stumbled over the word— "*house*. It's more me getting used to living here."

"You mean the difficulties of trying to live in a museum?"

"That's it exactly." I nodded. "It's . . . I can't say creepy, because this isn't a creepy place. It's old, sure, but it's beautiful. Elegant, even. But I'm not used to living in such overwhelming splendor." I ducked my head and, for some reason, felt comfortable enough to make a confession I'd not made to anyone else. "Honestly? I've never even stayed in a hotel this nice. I was brought up in a middle-class neighborhood. Our idea of elegance was using matching place mats at Thanksgiving. I can handle formality when I have to. I know which knife to use at what time during a formal state dinner, or what not to say to a head of state. The folks in protocol here have filled in any gaps and seen that I'm well trained. But I'm just not comfortable with the idea of living like this all the time—or for the next few years, anyway."

O'Connor leaned back in his chair. "It can be quite an adjustment for the presidential family members. Some adapt better than others. But in all honesty, you've done better than most. You and your brother are observant, nondemanding, and appreciative—and the staff has begun to realize that . . . ." His voice trailed off, probably curtailed by his own good manners.

I finished his statement for him. "That we're not the

same type of offspring as our recent predecessor's?"

Ever the gentleman, he smiled, but merely said, "The McClaren offspring were unique in their needs."

Translation: they were Goldie Bitch and the Three Unbearables.

I smiled, too. "Well, let's put it this way; if either my brother or I start to take any of this for granted, you have every right to read either of us the riot act, especially my brother. As Aunt Patsy says, I'm pretty much congealed as a person—I am who I am—but Drew . . . he's still molding. I don't want life with people at his potential beck and call to turn him into . . ." What should I say? A bastard? A spoiled brat? I found the perfect title. "Into a McClaren."

O'Connor stuck out his hand. "I don't think it'll ever come to that, but you have my word." We shook on the deal. He stood, but when I didn't rise as well, he sat back down.

"Is there something else?"

We'd finished the calculated small talk. Now I had to pull out the real reason for my visit. "Yes, sir . . . it's about your brother."

He looked appropriately confused. "You know . . . knew my brother?"

"No, sir. I never met him. But unfortunately, I was outside having my picture taken when his body was found. So I was a witness, you see."

Pain etched several lines in his forehead. "My poor dear, you must have been so frightened." I was surprised to see that his concern for me seemed stronger than his sympathy for his brother. That might possibly change shortly.

He continued. "Sterling had a bad heart, an ailment left over from a childhood disease that he caught but I managed to dodge. We always knew it was only a matter of time before it caught up with him. We were so much alike in some ways and so very different in others." His look grew vacant. "They said he had his medicine with him but that the bottle was empty. He was usually quite good about keeping up his prescriptions and keeping emergency medications handy. If only . . ." His voice trailed away.

I swallowed hard. "I know that the medical examiner said that his death was instantaneous. I suspect he might not have had time to even reach for his medicine." It was time to plunge ahead with the real reason for my visit. "I don't know if the police told you about the item they did find in his hand, when he . . . passed on."

O'Connor's posture changed, and I couldn't tell if it was because he was growing defensive or not.

He paled a bit. "You mean that . . . distasteful picture he had in his possession?"

I nodded. "Yes, sir."

"Mr. Seybold was the one who brought it to my attention. I'm sorry you had to see that. I'm afraid that my brother and I were also diametrically opposed in temperament when it came to women."

I raised my hand to dismiss his obvious concern. "No apologies, please. You're not responsible for your brother's actions."

He lifted a gray eyebrow. "Just as you're not responsible for your brother?"

"But Drew's still a child," I replied.

O'Connor sighed and leaned back in his chair. "In some ways, especially when it came to women, my brother was just as much a child, too. In all honesty, I'm not surprised to learn that he might have taken advantage of my good nature to pose as me and sneak a woman into here. I'm ashamed but, unfortunately, not really surprised." He leveled me with a stare that cut through me, passed through the window behind me, and traveled across the North Lawn. "Eve, does this conversation have something to do with Mr. Seybold's investigation?"

I gave myself permission to lie, telling myself it was for the right reasons.

Most liars tell themselves that. A defense mechanism, I guess.

"I know he is conducting a preliminary investigation but I don't know all the details. He did ask me something about the photography issues because of my background in it and your brother's obvious interest in taking pictures."

Mr. O'Connor looked mildly surprised. "He believes my brother was behind the camera rather than in front of it?"

I've seen the pictures, I wanted to say. *Trust me, it wasn't him.*

But instead, I shrugged. "You'd have to ask Mr. Seybold. Maybe the important question to ask is whether *you* believe your brother could have taken this picture."

His leveling glare weakened until he was staring vaguely into the distance. "I don't really know. Sterling has never been interested in photography. In all honesty, he wasn't good with a camera." He heaved a large sigh. "He was always holding it crooked and cutting off the tops of people's heads. I always tried to make sure I was the one taking pictures whenever we were together."

"But you do believe he could have played up your similarities and gotten in here, posing as you?"

"Normally, not without the proper passes." His face darkened. "But I can think of more than one time in the recent past when he might have used my ID and gotten into the White House posing as me and not been stopped."

He paused but I said nothing, hoping he'd continue to fill the silence. An old trick, but it works.

"It was late at night, and I was home, sick in bed. I realized that I'd left an important personal paper in my office. Sterling offered to come here and get it for me. He told me he could use my ID, walk in, get whatever I needed, and nobody would be the wiser."

O'Connor stalled, turning his attention to a paper clip that he tortured into an ungainly shape. I bet we were both sharing the same thought: Did Sterling know he could pull off such an impersonation because he'd done it before?

O'Connor tossed the bent paper clip into the trash, as if trying to throw away such an unsavory concept as well. "I told him that it would just have to wait until the next day. Then I fell asleep." He colored slightly. "The medication, you know. But evidently, Sterling went ahead with his plan. When I woke up the next morning, my security pass, my wallet, and the papers I'd needed were laying on the bedside table."

Motive might still be up in the air, but I'd nailed opportunity. I pressed on. "What about during the day? Would he attempt to impersonate you in the daytime?"

He shook his head. "He wouldn't have had access to my pass and IDs. Plus, even if he did, he would have run into too many people whose names he didn't know. He could never have pulled off such a masquerade." His focus sharpened. "Are you always this inquisitive?"

I tried a disarming smile. "My dad thinks so. Just ask him. But right now, it's not so much me being nosy, but more like feeling that I need to know everything that's going on so that I can protect my father. I'd just as soon be able to tell him that any unsanctioned trysts in the Lincoln bedroom happened under someone else's administration, not his." I glanced at the calendar beside O'Connor's desk. "Dad's had roughly four weeks in office. I'd like at least four more before we get hit with the first real scandal."

O'Connor nodded. "Indeed . . ." He paused. "I see your point. Is there anything else, Eve?"

I was pleased that he hadn't backslid to "Ms. Cooper" or, worse yet, "Miss Cooper." "No, sir. And thank you for being so frank with me."

I rose and walked toward the door. Maybe I felt a bit guilty for questioning him. Maybe I could give him something in return. I pivoted and said, "Uh . . . one last thing."

He offered me a pale smile. "Isn't that what Detective Columbo always said before he nailed his witness to the wall?"

So he did know he was being grilled. So much for

my soft touch. "I'm no detective, sir," I said, knowing it was much too true. "I just wanted to warn you that Drew is contemplating getting new, aggressive blades."

He looked puzzled. "Aggressive what?"

"Blades." In light of his look of continued confusion, I added, "Roller blades. In-line skates."

His face lit in recognition. Now I wasn't speaking Greek to him.

I continued. "These particular blades would be specially designed so that he can grind. That's where the skater jumps on top of handrails or pipes and slides down them."

I could tell by his aghast expression that he was already entertaining a mental image of Drew performing this stunt in one or two key locations in the building. His look of shock was almost comical.

I hid my smile, unwilling to laugh at his obvious discomfort. "You might want to lay down the law *before* he gets the blades, and tell him exactly where he can and can't use them. His common sense stretches only so far when he goes blading. Maybe you could have someone install a low pipe somewhere on the grounds away from the house so he could have a safe place to skate and not be subject to temptation."

"Safe . . ." he repeated blankly, as if not able to reconcile the use of the word with the mental picture filling his head.

I touched the tip of my nose with my forefinger. "Forewarned is forearmed."

He looked definitely distracted. "Indeed, Eve. Indeed. Thanks."

CHAPTER FOUR

The Dawgs and I hadn't climbed up one entire flight of stairs when someone grabbed my arm. I turned around to discover the person accosting me was Michael Cauffman. I glared at my rearguard, giving him the *Aren't you supposed to protect me from people like him?* stare, but the agent offered me a smirk in return.

What a time for the Secret Service to get a sense of humor.

Michael spoke between strained gasps of air as he matched me step for step. "Hey, what's this I hear about you going on a photoreconnaissance mission with Seybold?"

I pulled out of his grasp. "So what? Remember, you're not the only professional photographer in the White House."

I expected the usual *Who, me?* denial, but to my surprise, Michael's look contained no smugness, not even a smidgen of feigned shock. "I never said I was the only one," he said. "I've seen your stuff. It's good."

I stopped cold, in midstep, and gaped at him. I'd never expected anyone, much less him, to make such an admission. In public, no less.

Michael had the audacity to ruin the moment and laugh. He used his fingers to frame the shot. "Now there's a rare pose. 'First Daughter, Speechless.' "

His jibe broke the mood. "Shut up," I growled as I continued up the stairs, taking them a bit faster, if only to see him puff harder for breath. After we rounded the corner, I stopped on a landing, with him almost plowing into me. I turned toward him and gave him my best smirk. "You know, maybe you ought to think about getting some exercise. You might build up some stamina."

He held on to the handrail, his face slightly red as he gulped several lungfuls of air. "I do exercise," he said between gasps. "Ran six miles this morning."

"Yeah, sure." I started up the stairs again at an ambitious speed, trying not to hide the fact I was starting to struggle a bit to catch my own breath.

"Slow down," he complained as he trailed me by several steps. "And tell me how last night went. Did you find anything?"

"Not here." I almost added, *The walls have ears,* which was probably truer than I'd like to believe.

Actually, I did want to talk things over with him. I'm no fool. I have some practical experience as a photographer, but I wasn't stupid enough to believe that I knew more than he did. I wanted to share a couple of my theories, especially the one about shooting in natural light versus flash, and see if he agreed with me.

I led him up to the door to our private quarters, where we ditched the Dawgs, then up another floor to the third floor, where I live.

Dad and Aunt Patsy had agreed with me that I needed privacy because I was an adult, and to support that theory, they'd insisted that I take rooms on the third floor while they stayed on the second with Drew. I appreciate having what essentially is my own pseudo-apartment, with a bedroom, a sitting room, and a mini-kitchen. There is also a music room on the same floor that I'm eyeing for possible transformation into a darkroom. But I know I might have to fight Drew for that space, since he tends to like his music loud and obnoxious and the music room is soundproof. The household's peace of mind might benefit best if the room remains a music room, one where my brother can happily blast his brains to liquid without bringing the house down around our ears.

When it came to my entertaining "guests," as my father and aunt had carefully put it when explaining the arrangement to me, my mini-kitchen would allow me to fix basic munchies but not much more, since it consisted of little more than a bar fridge, microwave, toaster, and hot plate—somewhat like the setup I had in my first college dorm.

Since neither man nor woman can live on munchies alone, I still took meals with my family, though that had as much to do with enjoying their company—and the talents of the White House chefs—as it did with the lack of an oven up here or the appropriate "guest" to use it on. But, primitive kitchen facilities aside, it was nice to know I had a private place in the middle of an extremely public house. Assuming I ever dated again, it might come in handy.

If truth be told, Michael Cauffman was actually my first guest, if you could call him that. As we walked down the hallway to my quarters, I was thinking of him more as a cohort in crime.

I led him into my sitting room, waved him toward a seat, and stopped to dig around in the refrigerator. "Diet Coke okay?"

"Sure, thanks." He settled himself on the couch. "Tell me what happened last night."

"First, you tell me how you found out about it." I handed him the can and sat down in the chair next to him.

"Your dad. He knew I'd be interested since I found the body."

Okay. I suppose that meant I had official presidential permission to fill in the rest of the story. Which was good, since I wanted to pick Michael's brain. "Okay, then. Here's what happened. At Dad's request, I joined a security detail late last night that went to Sterling O'Connor's apartment in Crystal City and searched it, top to bottom, stem to stern. I went along both as Dad's representative and as the documenting photographer."

He straightened perceptibly. "You got the shots? Can I see them?"

"Heck, *I* haven't seen them." I shook my head. "Seybold took everything. My film, what we found, everything."

Actually, Seybold hadn't taken everything, though he didn't know that. I'd used two flash cards in my digital camera, duplicating most of the key shots on the second card. A real photographer can't just cave in to the authorities. It goes against everything we believe in. But then again, I didn't have anything on the second disk that wasn't on the first, so I hadn't held anything back.

Technically . . .

"We did find one thing particularly interesting," I added. "At one point in time, O'Connor had his bathroom set up as a darkroom."

Michael nodded. "And where there is a darkroom, there's bound to be film—"

"—a roll of which I found carefully hidden in the toilet."

He made a face. "Gross."

"In the nice, clean, and probably, thank God, never-used toilet," I added. "Seybold came by this morning with enlargements made from the film, saying he'd tried calling you, hoping to get your opinion of them, but you weren't in."

He made an "I told you so" face. "Like I said earlier, I ran six miles this morning."

"He said he wants you to stop by his office and look at them."

He took a gulp of his soda. "Then I'd better hightail it down there. Gotta admit I'm curious. I want to see the pictures."

On the whole, I was trying to forget them. "Let me know when you're through." I finished filling him in on everything that had happened last night. After summing it up, I said, "I have some ideas about the shots. I want to meet you in the Lincoln bedroom and show you something."

He wiggled his eyebrows at me. Clearly he was thinking of the content of the pictures Seybold was waiting for him to look at. I threatened Michael with my not-so-empty can of soda.

"Grow up and get your mind out of the gutter. You know what I mean."

He pretended to duck. "Okay, okay. I'll call when Seybold's through with me."

Michael didn't call me back for an hour, which meant that either Seybold was too busy to see him and had him cooling his heels in a waiting area, or that the two of them had found far more than I had in the pictures. I was hoping for the former.

Just as I was about to give up and allow myself to fall to sleep, the phone rang.

It was Michael. "Meet me at Abe's?"

"You got it."

Ten minutes later, we stood in the Lincoln bedroom. Funny how a few shenanigans by past residents and guests had turned this otherwise dignified room filled with some very nice antiques into something that was more suited as a punch line to a dirty joke.

I resented that, because it was one of my favorite places in the house. The room was done up in shades of yellow, white, and muted green, fitted out with walnut and rosewood furniture that had an air of sturdy elegance. I guess it had to be sturdy, to withstand some of the more unsavory rumors that had circulated through there in the last couple of decades.

Today it looked cheery and bright, with the heavy drapes pulled back to allow the winter sun to fill the room with warmth and light.

But when I looked around, I couldn't help but shiver for some reason. At least, this *had* been one of my favorite rooms, until I'd seen a certain stack of contraband glossies. It was hard for me now to look at parts of the room without superimposing a mental image of a couple in the throes of something I couldn't quite bring myself to describe as passion.

Michael lifted his camera and took a shot. "From Den of Antiquity to Den of Iniquity."

I deliberately jostled his arm, spoiling his shot. "Don't joke about it." I pulled out the enlargement I'd coerced out of Seybold and walked over to the far corner of the room. I could feel the intensity of Michael's stare over my shoulder as he stood behind me, studying the picture I held.

He whistled. "Well, we meet again, eh, beautiful?"

I sighed. "Grow up."

He snickered.

"Mentally, I mean."

He pushed aside his laughter and reached for the picture, his interest switching from puerile to professional in the wink of an eye. He studied first the photo, then the room, then he handed the photo back to me and reached into his ever-present bag and pulled out a digital SLR camera.

I immediately began to salivate. But I didn't have three grand sitting idle that I could sink into a camera like that. And by the time I could earmark that much money, a newer, more expensive model would be out, one with more bells and whistles.

Ah, technology . . .

Michael hoisted his camera up. "Let's see if we can match this shot." He took several exposures, adjusting his position each time in an effort to recapture the angle and setting of the original photograph.

After a moment, he stopped and thought, then he nodded toward the table. "Okay, so you play the woman. Stand over there." He nudged me into position with clear verbal directions, using the photograph as his guide. Finally satisfied with my basic position, he looked into the viewfinder and added, "Perfect. Now take off your shirt."

I guess we were lucky that no one had wandered past the door as he made that remark. Or when I shot him a one-fingered salute in response.

"Now I understand where the phrase 'Watch the birdie' came from," he said in a low voice.

The camera jiggled a little as he laughed, but to my relief, he didn't immortalize that particular pose. "Two inches over to the left."

I shifted my hand, finger still outstretched.

"Eve? I need your help."

We began to work in earnest, with me playing reluctant model. After a dozen changes to my position, I ended up standing with my back to the camera in the exact same pose and location as the woman. Michael would shoot a picture, we'd compare it with the original, then we'd make our adjustments accordingly. We weren't worried at the moment about shadow angles, since they'd be dependent on the time or season the original photo had been shot.

That'd be a concept I'd sic Charlie on later.

Finally, we'd established the most likely place for the woman to have been positioned, as well as where her photographer would have likely been standing. The odd thing was that in order to get the angle right, Michael had to crouch down with his camera about four feet from the floor.

"He was either a short photographer," he remarked as we compared the digital display with the photograph, "or he used a tripod."

The digital shot of me was as perfect a match to the original as we were likely to get—I wasn't about to undress to make sure the pose was completely accurate.

"Okay, I'm in the right place now, so let's try it again," I ordered. "This time with the flash."

He looked confused. "We don't need that. There's plenty of natural light for a good image."

I turned and scowled at him. "Humor me. Take the same shot but with the flash." I knew full well that there'd be a reflection of the flash in the reflective surfaces of the room, but I still needed it documented.

He fiddled with the camera's controls and dropped down to the same crouch as before and I returned to my position. Once I was back in place, he took the shot. Since my back was to the camera and I was facing the window, I noticed an unmistakable glare reflected in the pane.

When we examined the camera's digital display, sure enough, it showed a telltale flash of light in the glass. There was also a harsh shadow trailing behind

, something that definitely didn't exist in the actual photograph.

"Look"—Michael stabbed the print with his forefinger—"no shadow. No reflection. Therefore, no flash."

I studied the photo. "Unless they had an elaborate light setup. Reflectors, remote lights, the works, right?"

"Sure, but do you honestly think someone lugged all that equipment into the White House without anyone in security noticing it, and then had enough uninterrupted time to set everything up in here?" He paused to draw a theatrical breath. "And then fooled the victim into stepping in front of such an elaborate set with a camera, knowing the shots would be used for blackmail? I don't think so."

Michael laughed and supplied his own answer. "No way. Try this." He began to pace around the room in a small circle, almost talking to himself.

"Sterling O'Connor uses his remarkable likeness to his brother to get John Q. Public and his girlfriend into the White House and they decide to have a midday booty call in the Lincoln bedroom. Maybe it was even a three-way, and Sterling was bright enough never to get any recognizable parts in front of the camera."

I made a face. "It's my turn to say 'gross' now."

Michael continued pacing and talking. "Anyway, Johnny Q. probably wants a permanent reminder of this momentous occasion of bagging someone in the Lincoln bedroom. Or maybe O'Connor took the picture himself. Or assume he didn't. The two visitors shuck their clothes, set the camera on autotimer, and go for it. Later on, they send O'Connor a copy and threaten to rat him out to his brother unless he pays big bucks.

Or maybe he has an attack of conscience. E̶ the stress is too much for him and he keels ᴏ̶ᴠᴇ̶ʀ ɪɴ tɦe Rose Garden."

I had to admit his theory sounded fairly plausible. Except for one small . . . "Problem," I said aloud.

Michael stopped in midstep. "What?"

"Security. How'd Sterling get in here during the day? Our Mr. O'Connor admitted to me this morning that he knew of only one occasion where his brother used his ID to get into the White House, and that was in the middle of the night."

Michael whistled. "I bet Seybold is having a fit over that."

I felt a fine blush crawl up my face. "I haven't told him yet." At Michael's look of astonishment, I added a quick, "But I bet Mr. O'Connor tells him. Soon."

"He'd better. It'd look better coming from him than from you ratting him out." Michael scratched his temple. "Okay, so there's one ID and two faces that match it." He stopped, obviously caught up in his thoughts.

An idea lit his face. "What if, for some reason, our Mr. O'Connor lost track of his ID during one of his days off? Sterling could have grabbed it and come here in the daylight to impersonate his brother and arrange for the nooner."

It was nice to know he was following the same path of logic I'd already wandered down. I shook my head. "No. According to Mr. O'Connor, his brother didn't know enough names, faces, and facts to fool all the folks he might run into during the day. But late at night? The wee hours of the morning? The only people Sterling O'Connor would have to deal with would be security guys who didn't deal with him on an everyday basis. They'd know him by sight, check his ID, but probably not realize it was someone else masquerading as him. After all, the two men *were* identical twins."

Michael dropped down to the edge of the bed, his face more contemplative than confused. "So if logic dictates that Sterling O'Connor could sneak in here only during the night, posing as his brother, then he probably didn't take these pictures himself."

"Right. Yet he had the undeveloped film in his possession." I sat down beside Michael. Even though we'd proven my no-flash theory, any sense of success slowly faded under the realization that I'd eliminated our most convenient explanation for how these pictures got taken. "We know he was involved, but we still don't know how. Or why. Or with whom."

We sat for a moment in silence.

Finally Michael spoke. "Okay, try this out for size. During one of his late-night visits to the White House, he stops off and, posing as Burton O'Connor, makes arrangements for someone to get a visitor's pass. No, two visitor's passes. He hands them off to a buddy, who uses them later, during the day, of course, and the buddy and his companion find the Lincoln bedroom, close the door, take a couple rolls of souvenir shots, then hightail it out."

"A couple of rolls?"

He nodded, his face growing more animated. "At least. You found one roll undeveloped in his apartment. . . ." His voice trailed off, evidently waiting for me to have the appropriate epiphany.

I complied, unable to push away the excitement that

was building in my own veins. "And he had a developed print in his possession when he died. Therefore, there's at least one more roll of film somewhere which has already been developed."

"Exactly. So where are the shots? Evidently, Sterling doesn't have them at his home, or you and Seybold would have found 'em." He closed his eyes and leaned back until he was sprawled across the bed. "All he had was the one print. Was someone trying to blackmail him with it? Did he come to the White House to confess all to his brother?"

I debated leaning back myself, but Michael managed to hog the entire bed. Plus, it really wouldn't look so hot if someone walked by and saw us like that. We were trying to prevent a possible scandal, not create a new one.

I stood up to pace the flowered carpet. "Two identical twins, two rolls of film, two apparently uninvited visitors to the Lincoln bedroom, and one torn print. What does it all add up to?"

Michael rolled over and propped himself up on one elbow. "Besides a headache? It sure adds up to enough stress to give a vulnerable man a fatal coronary." He made a show of grabbing his chest, groaning, and slumping back onto the bed.

After a moment, he cracked open one eye. "Now, as to whether Sterling's stress was caused by guilt, excitement, greed, or shame, we don't know. Someone could be trying to blackmail him with the picture, or he could have been trying to blackmail someone else, or he could have just wanted to slip into the room and relive the fun. We simply don't know."

I stopped pacing, turning my pent-up energies to a thorough reexamination of the enlargement. The woman had a model's figure, impossibly small in all the right places and impossibly big in all the others. Maybe she also had a model's instincts when it came to the lens. Maybe she'd deliberately kept her face out of the frame.

Had she been smart or merely lucky?

In either case, the man in the photo hadn't been as lucky. I'd also wheedled from Seybold one of the enlargements that had caught the male subject in profile.

I stared at the man's face, which was starting to look familiar to me if for no other reason than I'd been staring at it in lieu of lower sights.

Certainly the authorities would figure out who he was. . . .

They did.

Unfortunately, so did the press.

CHAPTER FIVE

Someone at the *Post* waited until the final edition had reached the presses before leaking the lead story to the White House. It was between two and three in the morning when Seybold got the news that their front-page headline was BALTIMORE AD EXEC CAUGHT BARE . . . HANDED IN LINCOLN BEDROOM.

But Seybold opted not to wake Dad or me until 6 A.M. His rationale was that the people in the burbs weren't reading about the story over their morning coffee because they received the earlier, home edition, which he'd learned didn't include the new headline and accompanying picture. Only the final edition boasted the story.

But once those suburbanites saw the paper machines on the street corners and in the Metro stations, and noticed the different layout, with the picture prominently displayed above the fold and visible in the paper machine window, something nasty was going to hit the fan.

Twenty-nine days into office and our first scandal. We'd lasted longer than most administrations, I guess.

Dad sat at the breakfast table, ignoring his food and glaring at the paper that an aide had delivered directly from the *Post*'s printing plant in Maryland.

Ah, those presidential perks . . .

Dad was perplexed, upset, and mad as fury, and I don't think anyone begrudged him his scowl or his bottle of antacids. He'd even switched from hot chocolate to hot tea, which is never a good sign.

Luckily, Drew seemed to understand that his usual banter would not be viewed favorably on this morning. He ate in silence, excused himself with an unusual display of manners, and headed out. However, he paused at the door and gave me a quick nod as if to say, *I need to talk to you.*

I joined him at the door and instinctively stepped out of Dad's earshot.

He glanced toward the door, keeping his voice low. "This is bad, isn't it, Eve?"

I shrugged. "It's not good, but it's not *real* bad. At least it wasn't a picture of Dad in that bedroom."

Drew made a face. "Now, there's an image I don't want hanging around me all day." He grew quiet and I could hear the gears turning in his head. I knew what he was thinking, and I knew he was searching for the right way to ask it. I decided to give the kid a break.

"No, it's not me, either."

"I didn't say it was," he retorted automatically, as if the "little brother" confrontational gene couldn't be denied a prime shot. He swallowed hard, his voice dropping to a whisper. "I never thought it was . . . but it's good to know for sure."

I silently turned to the side, lifted my sweater, and showed him the mole at my waist. "Proof. That's not on the photos. Even the Secret Service agrees I'm clear."

He nodded. "Thanks. The primitive screwheads in my class are sure to say something stupid."

"The primitive screwheads . . ." I echoed in total agreement as he walked down the hall and turned the corner.

Wasn't it hard enough to be a freshman in high school without knowing the hot topic in the papers, and therefore in school, would be how someone had been taking nudie pictures in the house where you live? Poor kid . . .

"Eve?"

I turned around and saw Patsy, coming from the opposite direction, paper in hand.

"Have you . . ." Her voice trailed off as she saw my face. "Oh . . . you've seen it already. How's your dad?"

"He's drinking tea."

She wrinkled her nose. "That bad, eh? Is it my turn to sit with him?"

I nodded. "If you don't mind."

"Time for a shift change, then." She paused to give me a hug before entering the dining room.

Thank God for Patsy. Not only had she been a surrogate mother to all of us, she understood Dad better than anyone I knew, me included. It wasn't that he needed anyone to watch him; he needed someone to be there as a sounding board as he worked through issues or discussed problems aloud. More often than not, Patsy and I bore the brunt of that responsibility first thing in the morning.

His closest staff members, those who had been with us for a while, understood how he operated and would take over soon enough during the course of the day. But traditionally the breakfast table remained unsullied family time, and that meant when things got tough, we became Dad's first line of defense.

However, with Patsy taking over, that relieved me to conduct my own investigation. I imagined that Seybold was already fighting off initial accusations from various sources—though probably not Dad—about a security leak within his organization. Rather than going back up to my rooms, where I knew I'd find a dozen messages waiting from people I'd worked with at the wire service—friends begging for gossip, former bosses clamoring for confidential information, bare acquaintances hitting me for a scoop—I instead went straight to Seybold's office in the Eisenhower Building.

Luckily for me, he believed in clearing the air at the earliest possible convenience. I didn't step a foot into his office before he closed the door behind me and stared, arms crossed. "Have you spoken to anyone about the pictures or our investigation of Mr. Sterling O'Connor's apartment?"

"No one other than my father and Michael Cauffman, and him only because I knew you and Dad had spoken to him."

"You have friends in the wire service," he said, more as a statement than a question.

No doubt one of the bright boys under his tutelage had been checking the White House switchboard for incoming calls, not to mention cell phone records. God bless Caller ID. "I do have friends and acquaintances in the wire service, but I haven't contacted them, nor have I returned any of the calls or e-mails that I know they've left for me in the last few hours. You're welcome to check it out."

"I have already. So I believe you." His pinched features got more pinched. "Then the leak didn't come from the White House."

"I'd like to point out, neither did that picture, unless you've been holding out on me."

He nodded. "I know. That particular pose isn't included in the roll that we developed. And it doesn't match the pose in the shot O'Connor had on him when he died."

"May I look at that picture again, sir? The one Mr. O'Connor had?"

Seybold shook his head. "The original has been entered as evidence, and I don't want it handled any more than necessary." He reached into his lap drawer. "But we did make copies. Would that do?" He handed one over.

It would, and it did. It took me only a few minutes to confirm that not only was the newspaper photo not the same as any of the shots we had, but that the camera was in a different position, shooting at a different angle. More important, O'Connor's photo looked as if it had been taken at the same session as our shots, using the same stationary-camera position—roughly four feet off the ground.

It was probably from the missing roll of film.

When I told Seybold my conclusions, he grunted and nodded. "My men said the same thing."

I studied the man in the photo. The paper had identified him as Roger J. Stansfield. "So what do we know about this Stansfield guy?"

Seybold tapped a large file folder that sat in the center of his desk with a professional black-and-white PR shot paper-clipped to the outside. I stared at the photo, seeing only the barest resemblance between his staged smile here and the look of tawdry ecstasy he'd worn in the more candid shots I'd looked at so recently.

Seybold opened the file. "Big-time ad executive, heading up one of the larger and more successful firms in Baltimore. Married with four children. Wife is also a partner in the firm."

Stansfield didn't look like the sort of man who would get caught in midtryst. Judging from his "Look into my eyes . . . would I lie to you?" expression, he looked more like the kind of guy who liked to do the catching. In all honesty, he looked like the sort of guy who collected bits of information about his competition and wasn't afraid to exert a little pressure if the situation warranted it.

In fact, if faces were any indication of character, a man like him would be a lot more likely to use those photographs for blackmail rather than being victimized by them.

Okay, that's a lot of inference from one lousy portrait shot, but he really did have a snake-oil-salesman look about him. Can I help it if I believe in first impressions? I'm a photographer. It's an occupational hazard.

I turned back to Seybold. "Has this businessman made any statements yet? Explained what he was doing here?"

"His lawyers say he'll be holding a press conference to make a statement at ten o'clock." Seybold turned another page. "However, we show no official record of him visiting the White House in this administration. I've had the archives searched and there's no record that he's ever stayed overnight here. And we've established no connections between him and either Sterling or Burton O'Connor."

Seybold's phone rang and he shot me an apologetic grimace and answered it. He paused, covered the mouthpiece, and said, "I'll be briefing your father at eight-thirty. Hopefully, I'll have more then."

I understood this was a dismissal and backed toward the door. "The sooner the better," I whispered. I slipped out, closing the door behind me to discover Perkins and McNally waiting patiently. They snapped to attention.

At least they don't salute me.

As we trudged back home, Perkins was the one who broke the silence. "They know anything about this Stansfield guy yet?"

I was surprised by his question, but pleased that he was starting to warm up enough to engage me in conversation. "Nothing yet."

McNally grunted. "Can't believe the *Post* printed that picture."

Perkins and I spoke simultaneously. "It's newsworthy." We stopped and stared at each other. "Bread and butter," we said in the same rapid-fire tones.

Then to my surprise, both of them released a snort of laughter and we started on our way, the mood lightened considerably.

It was a neat moment. Sure, both of them were assigned to protect me at all costs, even to the extent of taking a bullet for me, God forbid. I firmly believed either of them would do it, should the occasion arise. But for the first time, I felt the beginnings of a connection with them, as if I was something slightly more than just this month's assignment.

It felt good.

When we got inside, I dropped them off at the door leading to our private quarters and told them I'd be up there for a while. I continued upstairs to my quarters, where I previewed my phone messages. I discovered the machine contained a few messages from friends and a bunch more messages from business acquaintances wanting my "unique" insight.

Can we say "career-making inside scoop"?

I hit "erase" and cleared the whole lot of them. I'd call my friends back later. But right now, there was only one person I wanted to talk to, and that was my brother Charlie.

I dialed his number, waded through his latest answering machine message, which was laden with sound effects, and finally got the beep.

"Charlie, it's me. I know you're screening. Pick up."

There was a noticeable click and the brief squeal of feedback. "Hi, Eve, I'd ask what's shaking, but I can feel the aftershocks all the way up here. How's Dad?"

"Quiet . . . of course. So what do you have on this Stansfield guy?" I asked, knowing that my brother would have already completed a significant amount of research on the man, rooting out all the data that could be legally squeezed out of the Internet.

I won't mention his ability to tap into places that might violate major federal regulations.

"Nope, no land line. I'll e-mail it to you. I didn't catch Drew online this morning. I bet he's pretty upset."

"Sorta. He didn't quite come out and ask, but he was worried that it was me in the picture."

Charlie's laughter made the line crackle. "You?" he managed between gasps. "Not bloody likely."

Charlie's slip into Brit-speak was all the assurance I needed. He'd had a roommate at MIT who was from London, and whenever Charlie used one of Nigel's phrases, it meant all was right in the world. Well, maybe not all over the world, but it meant Charlie never seriously thought I was the woman in the picture.

"You don't have to sound quite that positive," I complained in secret relief.

"You don't go for forty-year-old smokers working on their second million, their second childhood, and their second marriage."

"Sounds like you've been busy." This was one of the times I really appreciated having an insatiable hacker for a brother. "You sending the files soon?"

"Even as we speak. Let me know if you need anything else. And if there's anything I can do from here."

"I will. I think Drew's going to need a bit more attention than anyone."

I could hear Charlie's sigh over the phone.

"It's rough being fifteen, but add to that starting a new school?" He made a shivery "brrr-ing" noise. "Glad I moved out of the nest." He paused and added, "And I'm really glad you moved back in. Dad and Patsy need you."

"I know."

"And Drew really needs you."

"I know," I repeated.

We seldom got this maudlin during calls, which only showed how much both of us were perturbed by the situation.

I drew a deep breath, willing myself to return to the topic du jour. "Okay, Stansfield is making a statement at ten. If any new crap hits the fan on this end, I'll call you with details."

"Thanks, Eve. And I'll keep digging into the man's background. Maybe I can find something you can use. Catch you later . . ."

I hung up. Turning to my computer, I checked the "In" folder and saw a glut of mail, knowing a good bit of it was friends checking in to see if we were okay. Charlie had designed magnificent computer systems for the four of us—Dad, Patsy, Drew, and me. With all the latest software, courtesy of Charlie's company, we could cruise the Net in anonymity and keep up with friends without going through the White House equivalent of a fire wall.

I checked my "Charlie" folder, and there sat several e-mails, all with attachments. I settled myself down and began to read the files.

Roger "J"-for-Jenkins Stansfield was one of the part-

ners of Brassman, Conyers, and Stansfield Advertising
in Baltimore. These days, Brassman and Conyers were
dead, and Stansfield and his soon-to-be-ex-wife owned
majority shares in the business. Their company was
housed in one of the renovated red-brick buildings near
the harbor area. High-rent district. Their clientele var-
ied from major food manufacturers to major motion
picture studios—literally "from soup to nuts."

I didn't say that, Charlie did. It was a direct quote
from some notes he added to the file. Lately, Charlie
has developed a real distaste for Hollywood that he's
never quite explained to me. I wondered if he finally
wrote that screenplay he's always threatened to write
and it got shredded.

I won't pry and then, one day, he'll tell me. That's
how we do things.

I turned back to the file, where I learned about Mr.
Stansfield's extensive travel, here and abroad, his pro-
clivity for fast cars, his strained relationship with his
children, his ongoing and acrimonious disassociation
with his first wife, Jensen Seager Stansfield, and
background on Alice Conyers Stansfield, his soon-
to-be-second wife, who, not long ago, had been a
second-runner-up for Miss Maryland. Charlie included
a picture of the prospective trophy wife with her
runner-up bouquet, complete with a loser's forced
smile.

I hated her instantly.

He included a shot of Jensen and Roger, the happy
couple arm in arm at a movie premiere in New York
City, and a shot of the much happier and soon-to-be-
former Mrs. Stansfield.

Both women were brunettes, which doused my hopeful idea that Mr. Stansfield had merely been doing one of the Mrs. Stansfields in the Lincoln bedroom.

I pushed back from the computer and tried to dovetail the information Charlie had with what Seybold had told me. How far back had Seybold looked into the White House visitors' records?

Our three weeks in residence?

Or three months, covering the postelection, preinauguration period?

Or three years? Thirty?

Selfishly speaking, if the assignation occurred before Dad came into office, then I didn't see how the public could blame anything on our administration. But the American public has a short attention span when it comes to details. A dirtied White House has to be cleaned in public, even if the stains are proven to be old ones. Truman said it best: When it comes to the White House, the buck stops at the President's desk. These days, that's true whether he's guilty or not.

I continued to brood over what I knew about the players involved but came to no real conclusions. Shortly before ten, I emerged from the family quarters and picked up my Dawg detail. McNally was there, but Perkins wasn't, replaced by a tall woman who gave her name as Gates. I turned to McNally. "Perkins decided to take the rest of the day off?"

He shook his head. "No, ma'am. His wife called. She's sick."

I looked appropriately shocked. "Nothing serious, I hope."

He betrayed only the slightest amount of emotion. "She had a miscarriage this morning."

Now I was really concerned. "Oh, no! I didn't even know she was pregnant. Is she going to be okay?"

McNally lifted one shoulder. "She wasn't far along. The doctors say there should be no lasting damage."

I paused, not quite sure of the protocol in such a situation. I figured the best thing to do was simply ask. "Would it be okay for me to send a card or flowers?"

"You don't have to, ma'am," McNally offered.

Well, duh. I knew that. "I know I don't *have* to," I explained. "I just want to know if you thought it'd be okay with the man and his wife if I did. I don't want to intrude into your private lives or anything like that, but I figure we're all going to get to know each other soon enough."

Gates seemed to understand. "I'll find out when she's going home from the hospital and give you their address. I know she's got lots of flowers right now, but some later on at the house would be nice."

I nodded. "Good idea. You can carry home only so many vases in the car."

"Yes, ma'am."

I stopped. "Okay, I had this talk with Perkins, I'll have it with both of you. I know you guys have rules to follow, but I'm not a ma'am. I'm practically never Ms. Cooper. I'm simply Eve. Will you get in trouble if you call me by my first name, at least when it's just us?"

McNally seemed unsure, but Gates offered me an almost human smile and said, "Not at all. I'm Diana and this is Mac."

He offered a half smile as if to acknowledge his name, albeit reluctantly.

She continued. "And it's Gary and Anita Perkins. I'm sure they'd be pleased to receive a card or flowers, whichever you'd like to send."

Thank heavens. Someone clear on the concept! I wondered if I could request that Diana Gates be assigned to me all the time.

"Great, Diana. I appreciate it. I'll wait until they get home."

I wish I could say that this new agreement meant we chitchatted like old friends as we walked down the stairs, but their primary responsibility was to maintain my security, so we didn't talk much. But it wasn't an eerie silence like before, just a mutual one.

Instead of going directly into the Oval Office, we went to Dad's secretary's office. I hadn't gotten to know Jeanne Seales well yet, but I had a feeling I was going to like her a lot. In her middle fifties and graying, she was the perfect complement to Dad in terms of operating style. She kept him on task, managing to keep the paperwork flowing without being pushy, safeguarding him from unwanted distractions, but not playing judge and jury. She fully understood that his family ranked high on his list of priorities, but she also knew we understood there were times when we had to sit and wait outside because he was busy.

She'd even established a good relationship with Drew, understanding how important it is for a boy to see his father, *right now*. A couple days ago, before all this trouble started, Drew had admitted to me that Jeanne'd offered him some "really great" advice about what to give Cammie—the new girl in his life—for her birthday. I ignored the fact that I'd given him almost identical purchasing advice a week earlier.

Jeanne was a warm, strong, and disciplined woman, who at the moment was red-faced and speaking into the phone with a louder tone than usual. "Sir, with all due respect, you will have to talk to the Scheduling Office and put your request to them. . . . No, sir, I can't . . . no, sir, I won't. The Scheduling Office, yes, sir. Only them. Yes, sir . . . thank you, sir." She hung up with a little more force than necessary and looked up at us. "Rookie senator. Doesn't know the ropes yet." She gave me a critical once-over. "We're all having quite a morning, aren't we?"

I nodded. "We've had better." As I felt her gaze linger a bit longer than necessary, I felt compelled to add, "It wasn't me, you know. In that picture."

Her gaze softened. "Of course it wasn't. If I'd thought it was, then you and I would have had a long, long talk first thing this morning."

I believed her. I really, really didn't want to be read the riot act by this woman.

"Thanks," I said and I meant it.

She nodded toward the door leading to the Oval Office. "I think he'd like you with him when that press conference starts."

Press conference? "Dad's decided to do a press conference?" I said, shock making my stomach twist in anticipation.

She shook her head, her gray curls bouncing in an uneven rhythm. "No, but this Mr. Stansfield has. Maybe they ought to rename him 'Grandstands-field.'

This press conference is nothing but a bunch of grand-standing. After all, he has to explain why he had his blurry fanny splashed all over the front page. Count on him putting a lot of spin on the details."

"Once an ad exec?"

"Always an ad exec," she supplied. She pointed toward the door. "Better hurry, Eve. It's almost ten."

Dad was sitting on one of the couches, staring at a TV that someone had brought in on a rolling stand. When he saw me, he patted the couch next to him. "Come on, he's about to start."

I expected the room to be full of advisers and such, but it was empty. "Where is everyone? I thought at least Seybold would be here."

Dad heaved a sigh. "I sent them out. I'll get their assessments and reviews soon enough. I just want to hear what the man has to say without being interrupted or getting a running commentary."

That was my none-too-subtle clue to keep my remarks to myself during the broadcast.

The local programming faded into a "Special Bulletin," which, thankfully, was local and not national. I knew that if Stansfield had anything truly scandalous to say, the networks would cut in, replay the conference, and then have a heyday with their long-winded analyses.

On the East Coast, the morning news machine had essentially shut down, but the further west you went, the earlier it was, and the morning news shows were still in full swing and on the air. The rest of America might not have awakened to the picture of Stansfield's naked butt as the lead story in their morning paper, but their morning news shows could cover every iota of detail should it become truly newsworthy.

God forbid . . .

Stansfield stepped in front of the cameras, looking slightly ill at ease but somewhat prepared. "Ladies and gentlemen, my name is Roger Stansfield, and I'm afraid this morning you were all treated to a prominent view of my worst side." There was the appropriate amount of tittering and smothered giggles from the press corps.

"I'm here today to say that I am a victim twice over, a victim of the press for printing such a personal and private photo without my permission, and a victim of a far worse crime . . ." He paused artfully, then looked up from his notes, his face creased with concern and sadness.

"The crime of blackmail."

The buzz of conversation swelled for a moment and he was hit with a barrage of flashes from a dozen cameras.

"As you know, I am the head of a very successful ad agency here in Baltimore. Our clients include some of the top manufacturers in the U.S. and abroad. It was my hard and dedicated work with one of my clients that resulted in an invitation for an overnight stay at the White House. My behavior there was, let's say, not particularly dignified, and that picture is unfortunately proof of my indiscretion."

He shifted his weight, almost as if signaling a different direction. "Six weeks ago, I received a picture similar to this in the mail. It came from an anonymous source. It had with it demands that if I did not pay a certain amount, the pictures would be released to the press. I paid. And then a second demand came. And then a third. Each time I paid these demands, this blackmail, until I literally spent every personal dime I had. But it's true what they say about there being no honor among thieves. I paid them every cent they asked for—and they still released the picture."

A tear rolled down his cheek, prompting a dozen flashes. If I'd been there, it's a shot I would have taken, too.

"I'd like to take this time to apologize to my business partners, my wife, my family, and my friends for having let them down. I regret my behavior while at the White House. I thought that by paying these extortion demands, I was bringing a private end to an unfortunate situation. I never dreamed how wrong I would be."

The man's face grew red and his voice rose as he looked away from his notes and seemed to speak from his heart. "But I'm here today to say—no more money. I don't care how many other pictures you might have. Print 'em all. I don't care. You won't get another penny out of me. You've destroyed my marriage, shredded my dignity, and caused perhaps irreparable damage to my business. I've already lost my biggest account because of it. I—" Someone standing beside him reached over and placed a hand on his arm as if to remind him where he was. He drew a deep breath, then released a shaky sigh. "I'm sorry. Let me turn this over to my attorney, and let him take any questions. Thank you."

With head bent, Stansfield stepped away from the podium and another man took his place. He had "Expensive Lawyer" written all over him, but I couldn't figure out how, if Stansfield was broke, he could afford the hefty retainer someone like this would require.

Can we say "lawsuit?"

"Please excuse my client." Expensive Lawyer paused and his face softened as he added, "And my friend. I've known Roger Stansfield for over ten years and I know how much of a trying time this has been for him. He's understandably upset. No man should have to pay such a public price for a private indiscretion." His calculated moment of personal connection and reflection ended and he suddenly became Media Super Lawyer. "Let me take some questions."

Hands flew up and a dozen voices blended together in a cacophony of queries. The attorney leaned in as if trying to distinguish one question from the rest. It was a trick I'd seen done at other press conferences. Pretend to hear the question that you're prepared to answer and deliver your message.

"Which account? I'm not at liberty to identify them, but I will say they are a large, well-known tobacco manufacturer."

I knew that Charlie had included a list of the advertising firm's most prominent accounts, so it would take me and any reporter worth his salt thirty seconds at most to figure out exactly which account was involved.

"When? Mr. Stansfield visited the White House shortly before Thanksgiving and received the initial blackmail photos the first week of December."

This time the question rang out loud and clear. "Who's the woman in the picture with him?"

"The young lady? We aren't ready to identify her. We've been in contact with her and she's received no blackmail demands. So we feel as if it's our duty to protect her identity from the public, not to mention the press. I will say she had no connection to the advertising client or to Mr. Stansfield's company."

"A hooker," I muttered aloud.

Another question rang out above the rest. "Was the visit to the White House a payment of sorts for services rendered to a tobacco manufacturer that is a client of Mr. Stansfield's firm?"

The lawyer grew stone-faced. "No comment."

The same voice rang out again, "Isn't it true that Mr. Stansfield brokered a large soft-money donation from the tobacco industry to President Cooper's campaign, and Cooper arranged the stay with the previous administration as a way to pay these interests back with a gratis visit to the White House?"

"No comment."

That dialogue was a setup if I ever heard one, and I was steaming mad. But Dad . . . he just sat on the couch, staring at the television screen, his face blank. I knew him well enough to realize he wasn't in shock or anything like that.

He was thinking.

Long and hard.

And planning.

Stansfield leaned back into the picture, whispered something into his lawyer's ear. The man waved off the rest of the questions and called a somewhat abrupt end to the press conference.

Dad didn't move a muscle.

I got up quietly and went to the door that led to Jeanne's office. Judging by the look on her face, she'd been listening to the press conference, too. I motioned for her to come into the room and she automatically picked up her pen and paper.

We both knew Dad's silence was merely a mental ramp-up to action. Somewhere behind that expression-less face were plans for a major assault strike, including the steps he needed to find all the holes and lies in Stansfield's story and the strategies he'd use to collect the evidence that showed he'd never taken a penny from any tobacco manufacturer.

When your beloved wife, the mother of your chil-dren, dies at age thirty-five of lung cancer attributed to secondhand cigarette smoke, you have some lines that you just don't cross.

And that was one of them. . . .

CHAPTER SIX

The next few days were sheer torture.

Not only did Dad have to contend with all the fallout from the Stansfield press conference, but the World Powers That Be decided it was the perfect time to test the new U.S. President's mettle by seeing if he could multitask—deal with domestic difficulties along with newly manufactured ones overseas.

I'm not naive enough to believe that this occurrence was strictly coincidental. What better way to test a new President than to throw something at him when he has messy personal problems dogging him at home?

I think he surprised everyone except his closest advisers (and, of course, his family) when he managed to handle everything, making a strong statement about a recent outbreak of violence in the Middle East, offering humanitarian aid to a small island nation threatened by an impending volcano eruption, and putting troops on standby to support a border patrol initiative.

At the same time, he was delving into his own campaign finance records, trying to disprove the accusation that he'd ever received any financial support from tobacco lobbyists.

But the "nameless" tobacco company, Balfour Industries Inc., supplied bank records that showed they paid the advertising agency far more than the amount billed for services rendered. In turn, the agency showed cash withdrawals for that exact difference and receipts from the campaign's chief financial officer for that amount, marked "donation." Nowhere did it mention the tobacco connection.

I sat in on one meeting between Dad and his chief campaign finance officer, Margaret Bloom. I would have bet from the tip of her stiff brown curls to the toes of her sensible shoes that she could explain the discrepancy.

But she couldn't.

"We do show contributions from Brassman, Conyers, and Stansfield, but the amounts we have in our records are totally different from what they say they gave." She pulled out her computer readouts with the donations circled. "Plus, as you can see, there was no obvious connection to any tobacco company. These appeared to be perfectly normal donations, and they were within the limits of current guidelines for political contributions."

Dad studied the paper. "Margaret, how can something like this happen? Stansfield's supposedly got re-

ceipts and canceled checks showing donations for ten
times this much." Any accusation of financial irregularities was made many times worse by the fact that
one of Dad's key platform planks had been campaign
reform. This was going to look ugly in the press, no
matter how fast we got to the bottom of it. Add to it a
bunch of naked pictures taken in the Lincoln bedroom,
and it was going to send the media into a feeding frenzy
that would make swarming piranha look civilized. But
it didn't look like answers were going to be forthcom-
ing any time soon, judging by the look on Margaret's
face.

She sat there, stiffly. "I don't know how this happened, sir. All of our financial records are under constant scrutiny during the campaign."

"You know what the public is saying, don't you?"

She grew red in the face. "That we kept two sets of
books." It was a statement, not a question.

He nodded. "Margaret, I can't allow that kind of talk
to remain unchallenged." He reached out and took her
hand, patting it, not in a condescending way, but in a
"bad news is coming" way.

"You know I don't doubt your veracity, or that of
your committee, but I must put an end to any specu-
lation of wrongdoing. I *must* bring in an independent
auditor to go over the books."

I watched her knuckles whiten as she grasped his
hand. But her calm voice belied any disbelief or dis-
appointment she might be suffering. "Yes, sir, I understand."

It was only one of many meetings I sat in on. Typically, I stayed in the background, kept my mouth shut

and my ears open. If anything, these incidents only served to remind me how much I dislike politics.

Now, don't get the wrong idea; that doesn't mean that I dislike what my father does for a living, or disapprove of the way he does it, but simply that I couldn't do anything like it myself.

This was a prime example of a situation where I would have thrown up my hands, packed my stuff, and headed into the wilderness to live forever on dandelion salads and trout—anything to be someplace where the accusations weren't nearly as loud or as obnoxious as they were here in D.C. The idea of becoming a wilderness photographer and moving to some far-flung place was starting to sound quite enticing to me.

But my dad had the right idea. This was no time to run away from controversy. After the financial meeting, I went back to my suite and mulled over Ms. Bloom's information. Either we had indeed kept double books at the campaign headquarters, or somebody on either the receiving or the giving end was dabbling in a little receipt kiting.

To make matters more complicated, when Seybold reexamined the White House archives for the visitor-pass records for the months of November and December, he still found no evidence that Roger Stansfield had ever visited the White House.

Ever.

Yet we had proof in black-and-white that he was there. Definitely there, in the flesh, so to speak.

So who was lying?

It appeared as if it was us, or at least the McClaren administration on behalf of us. The popular opinion was that the Stansfield visit was arranged postelection and prior to inauguration because it allowed a lame-duck administration to "pay it forward" for its successor's sake.

However, anyone who knew President McClaren at all would have known that the man would have gnawed his own foot off rather than take a step that would help my father. During one weak moment, I even contemplated the idea that McClaren might have set this whole thing up, just to complicate things for Dad. But that gave the former President a lot of credit for initiative and foresight, both things he reportedly lacked.

But what really upset me was when one of the town's lesser papers came up with a preposterous theory that implied that Sterling O'Connor died, not of natural causes, but in a covert hit carried out tracelessly by a White House goon squad, trying to eliminate all witnesses to the scandal.

I like fiction as much as the next person, but not when it is presented as the "unvarnished truth" about my father and his administration. I was ready to fight fire with fire, and even went as far as to ask a few veiled questions about the so-called reporter who'd trumped up that set of lies. I found out he was a conspiracy theorist. Folks who knew him told me he delighted in causing discord in an otherwise orderly society.

The jerk.

Once the truth came out, as I knew it had to in the end, maybe I would make it my special task to see how much I could upset that reporter's orderly world, I thought. Mind you, I'm not a vindictive person, but I do have my limitations as to how much out-and-out lying I will tolerate. Nobody attacks my family with a trumped-up frame job and gets away with it—and I wasn't alone when it came to that. My brother Charlie, if properly motivated, I knew, could cause all sorts of havoc in the offending reporter's life, cyber or otherwise. That reporter would never know what hit him. . . .

Okay, okay . . . We all knew I wasn't going to do anything rash or even vindictive. I wasn't even going to unleash Secret Weapon Charlie on anybody. Despite his abilities, he's not the vindictive type either. Or not very, anyway. Just dreaming about the proper way to get even, and contemplating the potential results, was as far as I ever went—though I wasn't willing to answer for Charlie. He always had a few tricks up his sleeve, not that you'd ever catch him at it. But I believe what Dad says, that you should always endeavor to work on a higher level than your tormentors.

And speaking of my dad, he took his own advice. But it hurt to watch him get more and more frustrated every day as the evidence of corruption mounted and he had to handle it secondary to his primary job of being the country's leader and Commander in Chief. It was a helluva way to end his first month in office.

And Drew wasn't helping things at all, either. For the last few mornings, he'd been more uncommunicative than usual. I didn't know if it was the unrest about the tension around the house or something else bothering him. Ever since he was a little kid, he's seemed to take great pleasure and, perhaps, great solace in habit. And he'd retreated fully into habit—eating the same things every morning, saying—or grunting—the same things at the breakfast table, and listening to the same CD as he stomped around, trying to find the books and homework he habitually misplaced.

Typically, when he arrives home from school, he heads straight for the White House kitchen, where the cooks know to have a cheeseburger waiting for him. Me, I'm partial to their fries and it's already become a real test to see how long I can go without them.

But as I passed Drew in the hallway, I realized that instead of sitting down in the kitchen, leisurely eating his snack, he was munching it as he was making a beeline for the Oval Office, and presumably for Dad.

Drew stopped long enough to plant himself in front of me, gulping down the last bite of his burger. "He's here, right?"

I shrugged. "Don't know. I guess so." I took a minute to give him my best glare, the one he sometimes called "the X Ray" for its uncanny ability to see through crap—specifically his crap. "What went wrong at school today?"

"Nothing." Drew stared at his size-twelve shoes, then up at me. "Really. Nothing at all."

Two "nothing"s from Drew always added up to Something—usually a big Something at that. I ran through a mental checklist of Things That Can Go Wrong and settled on the obvious. "You didn't bust that algebra test, did you?"

He placed his hands on his hips and mimicked me, in both voice and gesture. "You didn't bust that algebra test, did you?" he said in a hideous singsong voice that sounded nothing like me. Then Drew straightened, making sure to call undue attention to the inch-and-a-half difference in our height.

Have I mentioned lately how galling it is to know that your little brother is taller than you?

Said "little" brother made a highly unattractive face. "Have some faith, will ya? We haven't gotten the grades back, but I know I aced it." He paused and added a fairly sincere, "Really."

Okay, one down. I returned to the mental checklist and ran down the other possibilities:

> *You hate your teacher.*
> *Your teacher hates you.*
> *You forgot you have a major project due.*

My stomach soured as I slipped back into those hazy memories of being a panicked student. Did feelings like that ever really go away? Would I ever be able to dodge those sit-up-in-bed-in-the-middle-of-the-night night-mares? The ones where you suddenly think you have a major exam, but have forgotten to go to class all semester long? Or you can't remember where your class is? Or worse, you remember to show up, but do so nude?

Or maybe worst of all, I worry that nobody else in the world is haunted by these types of dreams and that's the real nightmare.

I swallowed hard and decided it was time to give up guessing. "Then you want to see Dad because . . . ?"

Drew dropped the attitude as well as his head. He made an extensive study of his shoelaces. After several false starts, he finally blurted out, "You see, there's this program tonight at school and . . ." His courage weakened and his voice faded away.

"And . . ." I prompted.

The tips of his ears began to turn red and his voice lowered to a whisper. "I sorta promised we'd be there. Tonight."

"Tonight," I repeated faintly.

He nodded.

" 'We' as in you and me and Aunt Patsy?"

His whisper grew hoarse. "And Dad."

"Drew . . ."

I tried not to sigh aloud, but I couldn't help it. Dad had too many problems pressing down on him at the moment, too many people wanting his time and his attention. Add to that the recent Lincoln bedroom unpleasantness in the news . . . Did our father really need his younger son to spring a school function on him with only a couple of hours' notice?

I would have expected, even accepted a sense of oblivion out of Drew before, but not now. Not since we moved here and inherited a whole new set of responsibilities and rules. All of us. Drew included. My little brother knew full well that Dad's movements outside the White House had to be carefully orchestrated. Dad couldn't just drop the affairs of state and gallop off with almost no notice to some school program . . .

Even though education had been one of the major planks in his campaign platform . . .

Even though Drew was his last child in school . . .

The only one who grew up without a mother . . .

I stopped for a moment. Maybe a field trip was exactly what Dad needed—a chance to forget he was the

President and to slip back into the role of father, even if it meant sitting in a folding chair in a smelly school gym and trying to understand what was being said over a really bad sound system.

Maybe that was exactly what Dad needed.

A dose of the good ol', bad ol' days.

I placed my hands on Drew's shoulders and gave him my most reassuring smile. "Know what? This couldn't be better timed. I think Dad could use a night away from this place and all the people in it."

I pulled him closer. It was time for Drew to benefit from some wisdom from his older sister, who had been there, finagled that. "So this is how you need to approach him. . . ."

A half hour later, I was back in my room, just settling down at the computer with the intent to answer some e-mail, when I got a call.

It was Dad.

He sounded rushed. "Eve? You have any pressing duties tonight?"

"No, sir."

"You do now. Drew just sprang the news on me that we have to attend some sort of school play. Tonight. And if I have to go, you have to go."

I laughed. "Is that by presidential or paternal decree?"

"Both. Call it payback for all the times you pulled the same sort of no-notice thing on me when you were in high school. I remember one particular time when—"

I interrupted him, unwilling to sit through the story

of the School Play From Hell. "Please, Dad. I've apologized for that a thousand times at least.

"So I can expect nine hundred and ninety-nine more from Drew, I guess." He snorted with something that sounded a lot like laughter. "The motorcade will leave at six-thirty. Be there."

"Yes, sir."

I smiled as I hung up. It was nice to know that Drew took stage directions well.

It was a short drive from the White House to Drew's school. Once inside, it took only a few steps down the carpeted hallway for me to come to the stunning conclusion that The Altamont School bore little resemblance to the public high school I attended. I don't think even the teachers' lounge had carpet in my school, much less the places where students tended to congregate. Rather than sitting in folding chairs placed somewhere on the foul line in the gym or even worse, in the metal bleachers, we were ushered to some rather plush seats in a prime location in the school's auditorium. It was the equivalent of the President's box, I suppose.

And that's when I learned exactly how well Drew could follow stage directions.

The program started as expected, with the headmaster standing center stage and droning on about the school's students and their academic achievements. But a minute into his speech, there was a disruption at the back of the auditorium. In true American public fashion, we all turned around to see what was going on. I watched the nearest Secret Service agent stiffen and adjust his earpiece as if getting instructions from someone. Then, to my surprise, he relaxed.

Something fishy was going on . . .

A student stood in the back of the auditorium, his hands cupped around his mouth. "Free the Altamont Five!" Parents looked around, panic-stricken. A rumble of whispers rippled across the crowd.

Patsy leaned over toward me. "What did he say?"

I repeated the demand to her in a whisper, adding, "What or who are the Altamont Five?"

She shrugged. "I have no idea."

Another student stood up in another part of the auditorium. He jumped to his seat and shook his fist in the air. "Yeah, free the Altamont Five."

Then, to my amazement, Drew, who had been sitting sedately beside me, suddenly sprang to his feet. "Yeah, freedom for the people." He batted away my hand as I instinctively grabbed his jacket. He made a hurried *Wait!* gesture to me.

Something was definitely fishy.

"Down with the administration!" he continued in a theatrical shout.

I smelled a rat. And lucky for the audience, so did the Secret Service. Instead of hustling Dad and the rest of us out of the auditorium, they remained in their places. Maybe the person on the other end of their earpieces knew something they weren't telling us.

A moment after the fourth and fifth rat stood, shouting what I now felt sure were scripted lines, someone struck an opening riff on an electric guitar.

The five rats, Drew included, broke out in a song, something about not needing "no education." In my opinion, the members of Pink Floyd weren't in danger of having their positions usurped. Several bars later, a couple dozen students rose from their seats and joined in, all winding their way to the stage, where the head-master pretended all sorts of outrage as he was swallowed up by the crowd. As the students continued singing various songs about school, and dancing with obviously choreographed moves, the audience went from shocked to amused to clapping along with the medley of tunes.

As one of the songs drew to an end, the headmaster reappeared, now dressed as a greaser—black leather jacket, slicked-back hair, and tight jeans, and they all sang about not knowing "much about history."

Dad leaned over and whispered in my ear, "Things sure have changed a lot since I was in school."

I stared at the headmaster, who didn't look much older than me. He was cute, well built, and probably had every teenaged girl and half the female teachers madly in lust with him.

I tried to mask my obvious interest. "I never had a teacher or a principal who looked like him." I watched him move to the music. As I recall, none of them danced like that either. I leaned over to my dad. "I want to go on the record—the next time Drew has a parent-teacher conference with the headmaster, I volunteer to go."

Patsy nudged me in the ribs. "No way, sister," she whispered. "You'll have to fight me for him."

Dad shushed us. "Quiet, you two. Someone will overhear you."

Patsy and I tried not to giggle.

As it turned out, what the parents had been told was to be an academic awards program was a musical variety show in disguise. Although Drew had attended the school for only six weeks, he'd been there long enough to win a decent part in this subterfuge, probably based on the fact he had a surprisingly good baritone voice for a fifteen-year-old, was a quick study, and was always willing to be a ham in public.

Who knows? He just may be the only politician in our family's next generation.

The program turned out to be the perfect panacea to Dad's lingering sense of frustration. As the students performed a second number, I sneaked a look at my father, watching him laugh and clap in time to the music. I hadn't seen him smile in a while and it felt good.

Of course, once the program was over, the parents were invited to an informal reception where the room soon polarized into two groups—those who were almost too eager to take the opportunity to meet the presidential family, up close and personal, and those who hung back and whispered and pointed. I'm used to that sort of thing, but Drew wasn't, and as the night wore on, I couldn't help but notice his growing sense of frustration. However, to Drew's credit, he did manage to rein in any real urges he might have had to confront a couple of classmates who were part of the whispering and pointing crowd.

He remained understandably quiet on our drive back to the White House, sulking quietly as Dad and Patsy carried on a conversation about the evening's events that was a bit too animated. It was as if they had both sensed Drew's discomfort and had jointly decided to ignore it, but not ignore him. As we all trooped up to the family quarters, Dad and Patsy both gave me the look that said, *You are going to talk to him, aren't you?*

I gave them a furtive nod and invited Drew up to my room for a Coke. He waited until after Dad and Patsy had conveniently disappeared when he stopped me.

"It's okay. I don't need 'The Talk.'" He added a sigh and pulled a face that reminded me why I was glad to have my teenage years behind me.

"Dad warned me last year that stuff like this would happen once we got here." Drew's face darkened. "But some of those guys . . . I was beginning to think they were my friends."

"Some of them are. Not everybody who was talking about us was saying bad things. I bet there were as many people defending Dad as condemning him."

Drew crossed his arms. "You didn't hear some of the things I heard."

I wanted to ask "Like what?" but I knew it wouldn't help. I wanted to help bleed off Drew's stronger emotions, not feed them. But the real trick was figuring out how to do that without simply dismissing them.

So we talked. First, about the difficulties of making new friends, then about life in the fishbowl, and then we danced around the topic of Dad's troubles and how it affected the two of us directly and indirectly.

After about an hour of talk, we'd downgraded the tone of our conversation to merely chitchatting. When Drew yawned in midsentence, we both agreed we were talked out. He admitted he felt better, which had been the task at hand, at least from my perspective. He gave me a rare kiss on the cheek and headed downstairs to his own room.

Okay, I probably should have felt some sense of accomplishment, having played the parental advice card as well as I apparently had. Drew had gotten lots of stuff off his chest and I'd received definite assurance that my little brother was likely to remain a sane, well-functioning member of society. It's every "third" parent's dream, right?

Then why did I feel so lousy? I may have bled off some of Drew's emotions, but I had a feeling I'd instead absorbed them myself.

Why did I want retribution? Better yet, resolution? Why did I have to spend so much time damage-controlling when I'd much rather be out there doing the damage to the guilty party?

The guilty party had a lot to answer for—and I had every intention of making sure that the time would come when those answers were made painfully public, and the guilty party paid in full.

Have I mentioned that I hate it when my family is targeted? Feeling better, I walked off to find my own bed.

CHAPTER SEVEN

I couldn't stand by and simply do nothing.

That's just not my way.

I knew my dad was innocent, and if I wanted to make sure the rest of the world knew that, then I'd have to start my own investigation. Unofficial, yes. Effective? Who knew? But it would at least give me something constructive to do. And I couldn't come up with less than my father's advisers had so far.

So I began with the one concrete clue we had. If the pictures proved that Stansfield was in the White House, then that's where I needed to start. After all, photographs fell within my own area of expertise, so to speak, and I might have a shot of finding some discrepancy on a photographic level.

But I knew my limitations.

So I called Michael, and he agreed to be my cohort in crime—or, at least, investigation. I'm not ashamed to say he knows more about photography than I do. When it came to helping Dad, my self-esteem willingly took a backseat. Plus, to Michael's credit, he didn't give me a hard time about turning to him; he knew how upset we all were and I think he honestly wanted to help.

So we made plans.

We met in the Lincoln bedroom, and this time I was armed with a black-and-white glossy enlargement of the front-page photo, thanks to a sympathetic contact at the paper. When I'd approached Mr. Seybold with my plans to initiate my own investigation, he turned out to be surprisingly supportive and gave me a clear copy of the partial photo found in Sterling O'Connor's possession.

"I trust these won't end up plastered across a tabloid's front page," he said in his best "We'd have to kill you in that eventuality" voice.

I responded with the appropriately deferential and respectful, "No, sir. They will never leave my possession."

Seybold responded with a hearty, "Good," then turned back to his duties.

So a half hour later, when Michael arrived, we didn't have to waste any time.

I held up both pictures up for our examination and comparison. "I want to do what we did before—figure out the camera and people placement. We know these were taken from a different position than the others." I had a couple of the other pictures from the roll I'd found, also on generous loan from Seybold.

Michael studied the pictures, shifting two of them side by side. "Obviously, but what will that prove?"

I shrugged. "I have no idea, but we have to start somewhere."

He held up the photo from the paper, comparing it with the room. "Okay . . . she was standing there." He pointed to a spot across the room. I dutifully slipped into that position, adopting a similar pose. He set up two cameras on one tripod, mounted side by side: a digital and a small autofocus camera, the same type you see around the neck of every tourist in D.C.

"Why that one?" I asked, pointing to the small camera. I'd figured he would bring his professional rigs because of the quality picture they would produce.

"Because I talked to Seybold and found out that the pictures weren't taken on regular thirty-five-millimeter film, but with APS film. If we're going to re-create this, let's do it right."

I thought back to the canister in the toilet tank. Of course it wasn't round, but elliptical. I didn't know why the significance had escaped my attention.

"Good idea," I managed to say without grumbling. I didn't mind *me* knowing that he knew more than I did. However, I did mind *him* knowing. . . .

He gave me directions for position, based on the picture, and continued to shift his own location, moving farther back and raising his tripod until he had to stand on his tiptoes to see through the viewfinder.

Finally, he backed into the bed.

"Okay, this is getting weird. Why would the camera be on the bed? This high up?"

He slipped off his shoes and climbed up onto the bedspread.

"Wait." I ran over and closed the door. "If Mr. Wallerston sees you, the shock might kill him." Carl Wallerston was the White House curator, the one who had given Patsy, Drew, and me our first lecture on the history of the White House and its priceless antiques. I hadn't minded him giving Drew the evil eye and talking about his responsibility to "do no harm" but I had gotten my panties in a wad when he segued into a general "Today's kids don't respect the past" lecture. That was the first incident where I realized my McClaren predecessor had left a bad legacy for fair-haired First Daughters.

Luckily for me, I'd been able to make points with him by answering one of Drew's questions about a piece of furniture in the Blue Room before Mr. Wallerston could begin his laborious recitation. I'd been smart enough to bone up on White House furnishings the night before, courtesy of the Internet.

Wallerston had looked surprised but pleased at my accuracy and assumed it meant I was actually interested in antiques.

Sorry, not this girl.

Although my plan had worked for that moment, it still continued to backfire, because whenever I see the man, he delights in giving me his latest long-winded lecture about all things antique.

The poor man would have a coronary if he saw Michael standing on the bed, even in his sock feet.

"It's still not high enough," Michael complained.

I gave him a critical once-over that he couldn't help but notice.

"What?" He checked immediately to see if his fly was closed.

"How tall are you?"

He shrugged. "Almost six feet tall."

I raised an eyebrow. "How many inches short of six is 'almost'?"

He sighed, then wrinkled his face in a grimace. "I'm five-ten and a half."

I abandoned my "pretend I'm the naked anonymous woman" pose, went to the tripod, uncoupled the digital camera, and handed it up to him. "Try this and hold it higher, as if you were six-six or so."

I ran back to my place.

Michael aimed the digital, then carefully raised it about a half foot higher with the lens still aimed at me. After he took the picture, he climbed down and we jockeyed for position around the small display, comparing the image stored there with the actual picture.

"Still not high enough," he complained.

"I don't understand," I said as I turned to brush the wrinkles from the bedspread, erasing all evidence of his crime against antiquities. Evidently, some of Wallerston's lectures had sunk in whether I liked it or not. "Neither of the shots from this second camera position included a clear view of the woman's face. And we had the other entire roll, shot by shot, just as they were taken."

Perplexed, I sat down on the bed, adding a new set of more socially acceptable wrinkles to the bedspread. "What are the chances of her not being caught in at least one frame from either camera position?"

"Pretty slim." Michael sat down beside me. "So because of that, do we assume the camera wasn't on autotimer and had a human operator?"

"A third person?" I suddenly had visions of a voyeuristic, seven-foot-tall photographer folding himself into the four-foot position from the first roll of film and then climbing up on the bed to take shots for the imaginary second roll. It was so absurd that I began to laugh.

Michael scowled at me. "What's so funny?"

I tried to shake the image from my thoughts, but it refused to go. "Nothing, just a sudden mental picture of the center for the Boston Celtics standing on the bed saying, "Lean to your left, darling, I can still see your nose."

Michael grinned. "Yeah . . ."

But the mental image, however silly, jogged my thinking process. "Why her?" I blurted out.

Confusion replaced Michael's grin. "Why her what?"

"Why protect her face and not his? Seems to me that the person with more to lose in this situation would be him."

"Unless she's not the nameless, faceless person we thought she was."

After a moment's silence, we both said, "Willa McClaren."

We stared at each other.

She was the perfect culprit: uncooperative, unliked, and unimpressed by rules and regulations.

I spoke first. "I have absolutely no problem believing that she used whatever position she had to, to sneak someone into the White House and then pose for staged pictures just to upset her father and his administration."

Michael nodded. "That fits the tales that folks around here have been telling on her. Evidently, they called her the First Bitch behind her back."

"And one unlucky soul had the misfortune to call her that within her hearing," added a solemn voice. Seybold stepped into the room from the open doorway leading to the Lincoln sitting room. We'd neglected to close that door.

We gaped at him, surprised as much by his sudden appearance as his revelation.

He stepped into the room and surveyed our equipment. "I suspected she was the blond in the picture long before I thought of you, Eve." He offered us a rare smile. "I suppose, in light of the current events, that I should be grateful to find you two with all this equipment and with your clothes on."

Michael and I turned and gaped at each other, belatedly realizing we were sitting on the bed next to each other.

A famous and, at the same time, infamous bed.

We both sprang up, stepping instinctively away from each other and both uttering a juvenile, "Ooh . . ." Even as I shifted, I realized it was a silly reaction; we'd been doing nothing. We hadn't even contemplated doing anything. We hadn't been playing any sort of man-woman games, but simply tackling a perplexing problem by working together.

"Don't worry, I know what you two have been doing," Seybold added in a reassuring voice. "And I appreciate having two photographers looking at this from a unique and knowledgeable perspective."

"So is it true?" I asked, once I caught my breath. "The pictures are of Willa McClaren?"

He closed the door to the sitting room. "Forgive me if I say I wish they were. It would be a very convenient solution to our entire problem." Seybold shook his head. "But no, they weren't of Miss McClaren." He stepped closer and lowered his voice. "This is confidential. I expect it not to leave this room."

We both nodded and I had a feeling Michael's curiosity was as piqued as mine.

"During the entire month of November, Willa McClaren was in a drug rehab clinic in Switzerland. The cover story was that she'd gone there to a cooking school and broken her leg while skiing. As it happens, she didn't even return to the White House until after the first blackmail attempt had been made." Seybold sighed. "As much as she would have been a suitable solution, both personally and politically, we can't hang this one on her. She's not the woman in those pictures because she wasn't anywhere near the White House during the time in question."

I sat back on the bed, feeling like a child who'd been taken on an excursion to the toy store but forced to leave empty-handed.

"Are you sure?" I said, trying not to whine.

"Positive. It was the quietest month the White House had experienced in eight long years." He turned and scanned the room. "Have you two made any other discoveries?"

Michael motioned for him to come over and indicated the pictures sitting on the foot of the bed. "We've determined that the roll of pictures you found in O'Connor's toilet were all taken from one location, one central position. That suggests the camera was on a tripod."

I chimed in. Why let Michael have all the glory? It had been a joint assumption, deserving a joint delivery. "But we're pretty sure the camera wasn't on autotimer because the chances are pretty rare of getting twenty-four continuous shots of the two of them and never getting her face in the frame. And we have the processed film to prove that, too. The pictures had to have been taken by someone."

"Not just someone. A professional photographer," Michael added. "These two other pictures seem to have been taken from a different spot, but here's where it gets downright strange." Michael pointed to a spot right above the tall, ornate headboard. "They seem to have been taken from right there. The camera had to have been more than seven feet higher than the level of the mattress. I can't re-create the shots because I can't get high enough."

"Then the camera was on a tripod? On the bed?" Seybold's face folded into a frown. "That seems . . ." His voice trailed off as he obviously contemplated the mental image.

"Stupid," I supplied.

"I was going to say 'awfully awkward' or 'excessive' or even 'extremely likely to produce blurred images under the circumstances' but I think 'stupid' would suffice in this case." He stared up at the headboard as well. "You honestly believe Stansfield and his . . . escort were accompanied by a third person—someone with photographic know-how who took two sets of pictures from two divergent positions, one of them while dangling from the ceiling?"

"That about sums it up," Michael said with a sense of frustration.

But I didn't share this conclusion. The position on the floor—I could understand that. But on the bed? And so high? It just didn't make sense.

Something about the whole concept bugged me. I nudged Michael aside and climbed up on the bed again. I had to satisfy the little voice inside of me, the one that watched too much television, had seen too many movies, and read too many books. I held on to the headboard and used it to anchor myself as I craned my head to see between the bed and the wall.

I heard a voice. The little voice that whispered about impossible political conspiracies and spy technology gone amock.

Okay, so I was desperate.

"Uh . . . Eve? What are you doing?" Michael crossed his arms as if to say, *I've already been up there. What do you expect to find that I didn't?*

Seybold stared at me as well, as if I'd lost my mind.

"I'm checking to make sure there's not a hidden camera in the headboard." It had sounded so much more reasonable when said by the little voice in my head. Nonetheless, I searched for wires, holes, anything that looked odd or out of the ordinary in the dark polished wood. Nothing hiding in the elegant carved wooden flowers and leaves.

Not even any dust.

Score one for the housekeeping staff.

From my lofty position, I couldn't help but notice the chandelier hanging from the center of the room. It was a multilayered-wedding-cake sort of affair with several rings of crystals dripping from the center shaft and then more crystals dangling from each globe-topped arm. A bit ostentatious for my tastes, but it did fit the room with its high ceiling and luxurious furnishings.

High ceiling, yes, I thought. But was the ceiling high enough?

I attempted to bounce ever so slightly on the bed, not to live out some unfulfilled childhood fantasy, but in order to get some height advantage.

"Have you gone nutzoid?" Michael reached up, trying to snag my arm. "Get down from there before you hurt yourself."

"Or break the bed," Seybold added. "It's irreplaceable. Trust me, you're not, in comparison."

"Don't—you—see?" I said between bounces, trying to maintain my balance while framing the shot with my hands. "The chandelier."

"It's a nice chandelier," Michael said in a "Let's not upset the crazy lady" voice.

I stopped jumping, realizing I couldn't get enough of a vertical leap to succeed. I bent down and grabbed Michael's arm. "You come up here. You see."

He stood his ground. "Not me, sister. No way. That's an invitation to a tabloid headline. 'First Daughter and White House Photographer Break Bed in Lincoln Bedroom.' "

Why was he being so dense? I climbed down. "You get up there, then. And this time, go as high as you can and take the shot." To his credit, he didn't ask why. I suppose he'd already decided that I was totally nuts.

But he wouldn't think so for long.

Dutifully, Michael climbed up and held the camera over his head, using the full length of his arms to get the maximum height on the shot. Then he got down from the bed and handed me the camera.

"And this is supposed to prove what?"

I studied the display screen. Sure enough, the lowest ring of crystals from the chandelier was centered in the top of the shot. Comparing it with the photo we were trying to duplicate, we'd succeeded in finding the right angle with respect to the furniture. But our picture from the same angle included the telltale light fixture.

Michael crowded me, trying to see the screen. "Wait . . . the angle's right, but we got the chandelier in the shot." He looked up, puzzled, then turned his attention to the glossy photo. "But how come they didn't?"

Seybold joined our happy little throng and we passed both the camera and the photo to him for his inspection. "Same shot, minus the people. Except for the chandelier." His eyebrows drew closer as he glared at the crystal and brass fixture. "How is that possible?"

I took the photo from them and held it out at arm's length. "Gentlemen, we've been had. This isn't the Lincoln bedroom."

Okay, so I was grandstanding. So shoot me.

Unfortunately, neither of them looked very impressed with my proclamation. Michael looked downright dubious. Seybold looked somewhat less doubtful, but he wasn't clear on the concept yet.

"It's simple, really." I pointed to the display screen.

"Chandelier." Then I pointed to the picture. "No chan-delier. Same angle. Same furniture location. The room hasn't been changed in years. They both can't be pic-tures of the same place. Therefore, they're two different places."

"Two different places," Seybold repeated flatly.

I nodded. The thrill of discovery surged through my veins and I savored the feeling for a moment.

"Explain," Seybold said, suddenly getting all Vulcan on me.

"Two places," I repeated. "One real and one a dop-pelgänger, designed to look exactly like the real thing." I waved a hand at the ceiling. "With the exception of the chandelier. And no chandelier probably means no ceiling."

Seybold looked even more confused. "A room that looks just like this but has no ceiling? This is *not* the time for a joke, Miss Cooper."

"It's no joke. It's—"

Michael wrapped his fingers around my arm and squeezed, realization of what he was seeing in those pictures lighting his face.

We blurted out the answer together.

"It's a movie set."

We stood in the curator's office, waiting for Mr. Wallerston to get off the phone.

His office had to be one of my favorite places in the White House because of the organized chaos. Tucked beneath the Grand Staircase, the office itself was asymmetrical, creating an interesting assortment of nooks and crannies, all filled with shelves, and those shelves loaded to the top with books.

The first thing I'd noticed when we moved to the White House was its seeming perfection, despite its age. Every room was cleaned and organized and decorated to the *nth* degree. The staff worked with an oiled efficiency that any five-star hotel would envy. But it took only a few days of living there for me to start longing for a little discord and perhaps a spot of chaos.

Of course, it wasn't like I needed any additional disorganization in my life, but I was simply more comfortable when surrounded by a bit less perfection.

So the first time I stepped into the curator's office, it was like leaving a museum's main-floor exhibit and stepping back into its cluttered storeroom.

I felt at home.

But evidently Michael didn't share my love for the imperfect. He looked around at the piles and piles of books and papers and tried to hide a strong shudder.

A neat freak.

I should have known.

When Mr. Wallerston got off the phone, he apologized profusely, which I supposed was yet another lingering Willa McClaren legacy. Everyone apologizes to me over the most mundane things. I guess they learned the hard way that if they got in the first strike, things went a bit smoother when it came to Willa's histrionic fits.

Michael and I decided not to tip our hand at first, keeping our questions limited, initially, to the amount of access the public had to records pertaining to White House furnishings.

Wallerston slid his chair over to one wall of shelves and indicated the entire case with a wave of his hand. "These are just some of the public reference materials available. We try to cooperate whenever possible with publishers in terms of providing pictures and written descriptions of and histories behind the articles in our rather extensive collection." He pointed to another shelf. "And that's not counting all the books that the

White House Historical Association has published itself over the years."

Michael whistled. "Extensive is the right word. I've never seen so many antiques outside of a museum."

Wallerston laughed politely. "At any one time, the White House holds only a small percentage of the available pieces in our collection. We have almost thirty thousand more pieces in storage at our warehouse in Beltsville and we rotate the stock, so to speak, when needed." He turned to me and smiled. "Or to meet the decorating tastes of a new administration."

Dad, Patsy, Drew, and I had made a visit to that cavernous warehouse to pick out furniture for our private quarters. They'd found what they wanted there and I'd opted to use my own stuff since I was letting go of my Denver apartment for the duration. But while I strolled through the warehouse, watching Patsy *ooh* and *aah* over various pieces of furniture, I found a brass bed that I admitted I wouldn't have minded using for the next four years. Mr. Wallerston had it delivered and assembled in less than three hours.

Michael indicated what appeared to be a history text on Wallerston's overflowing desk. "So you spend a lot of time answering questions about the history of the White House and its furnishings?"

The man nodded. "And the history of the artisans who created them."

"What about nonacademic requests?" I asked. "Do you get many of those?"

Wallerston smiled. "We field calls every day from antique collectors who want advice, information, or a special tour. However, we're limited as to how much we can interface directly with the public. That's why we try to offer as many official publications as we do, so even those who can't take a tour can see what the White House looks like."

I asked my next question in the same mildly inquisitive tone of voice, hoping I wasn't tipping my hand. "How about movie production companies? Do any of them contact you for permission to film here?"

He shuffled through some papers on his desk, as if looking for an answer.

Didn't the man keep computerized records of that sort of thing, like everybody else at the White House?

He turned over one stack, examining, then discarding it in favor of another stack. "More often than you might expect. But we turn down a great deal of the requests. In some rare instances—depending on the content and quality of the production—we might offer a company more detailed photographs or even grant limited access to the house. But mostly, we refer them to the volumes of material already available to them in their local bookstore or through our historical society."

Michael took the next step. "Have you had any recent inquiries from film production companies that are doing White House scenes?"

Wallerston idly restacked the pile of papers on his desk. "Documentary or feature?"

Michael seemed caught off-guard by the question so I stepped in.

"Definitely not documentary. So feature. Or maybe a television production. Somebody who might want to re-create parts of the White House for a fictional story line."

"Nothing too recent, I believe." Wallerston opened up his desk's file drawer, which was packed almost to the point of exploding. "I believe the last time I had a request was six months ago. The inquiries do tend to go in cycles. You know, feast or famine, depending on America's interest in politics," he said, adding a laugh. He thumbed through his files—paper, all of them paper—made an "Aha" sort of noise, then leaned back in his chair, clutching one particular piece of paper.

I craned to see the letterhead. "Who contacted you?"

Wallerston held up a finger as a gesture for us to wait, then turned to his computer. That was promising. I was starting to worry that all of the invaluable knowledge he carried in his head was consigned to the paper chaos that reigned in the room. He pulled up several screens, then finally found what he was looking for. "A Richard Pierce from Paradox Films spoke with me at length in June about a movie he wanted to produce, one that took place partially at the White House. I referred him to some books that have detailed descriptions of the rooms he mentioned and sent him some of our stock photographs."

I dutifully wrote down the information, then gave Michael a quick glance. "Which rooms did he mention he was interested in?"

Wallerston checked his monitor. "Let's see. His main questions were about the Oval Office, the Grand Staircase, and the Lincoln bedroom."

Michael leaned closer to me and whispered, "The Oval Office, too?" He made a face.

I knew what he was thinking. Should we be on the

lookout for yet another roll of film with the same couple doing it in Dad's office?

A series of lurid headlines from previous administrations came to mind. My stomach lurched.

Wallerston continued, thankfully oblivious to the mental images I was trying to erase. "I've not heard back from Mr. Pierce, so I don't know if the movie went into production or not. More often than not, when these so-called producers—if that's who they really are—realize we're not going to let them stage or film their productions here and that proper re-creation is both meticulous and expensive, the projects are abandoned."

"Do you have a phone number for him?"

Wallerston read it off for me and I copied it down. I started to thank him, but he cut me off.

"All right, I've patiently answered your questions," he said, tapping his fingers on the desk.

I realized he wasn't being rude, but it was quite evident that we'd reached a point of saturation; we'd been asking a bunch of questions and not providing much reason why, other than the concept that the current First Daughter seemed terribly nosy about things that were, for the most part, none of her business.

"Now, it's your turn to provide some answers for me," he continued in his same even tone. "Do your questions have something to do with the rather unsavory story on the front page of a very recent newspaper?"

It was no time for hedging. I nodded. "Yes, sir."

"And you're working on the assumption that the pictures weren't taken here but on a set that was built to look like the Lincoln bedroom?"

That one took me by surprise.

It wasn't that I'd underestimated the man, but that I thought he was more concerned with the White House and its antiques than other, more modern conveniences like a fully computerized office. I swallowed my assumptions. "Yes, sir. That's our theory in a nutshell."

After an uncomfortable moment of silence, he gave us a tight-lipped smile. "Then it's a good theory." His smiled broadened to sympathetic. "If there is anything I can do to help, let me know. Perhaps I might be able to authenticate the furnishings in the photograph and prove that they are not those in our Lincoln bedroom."

It was definitely worth a chance. "I'll mention that to Mr. Seybold. But perhaps you ought to call him yourself."

He nodded with enthusiasm. "Indeed, I shall. If there's nothing else . . ." He dismissed us with a nod and reached for his phone.

After we stepped out of his office, Michael and I picked up my Dawg detail, dodged a tour group, and trooped upstairs. By the time we hit the second-floor landing, Michael was starting to breathe heavily.

There was no way this guy ran six miles a day yet was unable to handle a couple flights of stairs. So what was his problem? He didn't strike me as the type of guy who lied about his physical prowess just to impress a woman.

Especially not me.

He signaled for me to stop, trying to hide his gasps for air. "I know . . . a couple of guys . . . in California

. . . who might be able to . . . get us info on Paradox."
Reaching in his inside jacket pocket, Michael pulled
out one of those asthma inhaler units, took a deep drag
on it, then held his breath for a moment.

"You okay?" We definitely didn't need another person keeling over dead in the White House.

He nodded, waited a moment, then released his
breath in a slight whoosh. "Yeah. I haven't had a real
attack in years, not until I started working here. I'm
allergic to something in the building."

"Mold? Mildew?" I offered.

"Politics?" he added with a strained grin. "Who
knows?" He shrugged. "It only happens when I'm here,
mostly in the staircases, so whatever it is, it's pretty
specific and localized." He tucked the inhaler back into
his jacket pocket. "So, like I said, I have some friends
who might be able to get us some info on Paradox and
this Pierce guy."

"And I have a brother who can definitely get us
everything there is to be known. Probably within
minutes."

Michael shot me a look of utter disbelief. "Drew?"

"Nope, the one you haven't met. Charlie."

Twenty minutes later, we sat at my desk, poring over
the files Charlie had sent us. The great thing about the
Internet was the vast amount of data you could find
online and the speed at which you could find it. Charlie
was the master at Net searches, and he'd come up with
a gutload of information about Paradox's upcoming
motion picture *Armed and Dangerous*.

Reportedly it was some sort of spy movie whose two

leads, a pair of undercover agents, had the code names of Armed and Dangerous.

Sounded pretty chintzy to me.

But Charlie said it was a big-budget production with good buzz that was likely to break even on the domestic market and do big box office overseas.

Did I mention that Charlie is a self-professed expert on everything? Not in a snotty, superior, "I'm better than you" way, but in an "Oh, yeah, I read something about that" broad-spectrum way. He has a mind like a sponge, and according to some of my friends, unfortunately, a somewhat drippy personality to match.

But he's my brother and I love him. Unconditionally. Even though he was sometimes a real pain in the rear when we were growing up. With only a year's difference in our ages, we were always in competition to be the best at something. But we didn't necessarily compete in the same fields—that would have made it far easier to come up with a way to determine who was best. We had to compete in totally different fields and try to find a way to compare apples and oranges—to figure if his prowess at running exceeded my sterling ability to jump. It was a never-ending battle between us, as well as battle to define the ever-changing rules of competition.

Luckily, I stopped being jealous of his brains years ago (out of self-preservation and a desire for family harmony), and now I simply use his sponge-smarts for my benefit and we all get along very well.

Charlie didn't let me down. He forwarded us everything from union contract details to location permits to Usenet discussions by people who were working as extras on the film. We now had an astounding amount of information about the film, including one key item: they were shooting the all-important interiors in New York at a place called Trophy Studios.

I won't go into the boring security stuff, but it took me a couple of hours to arrange for our trip to New York, which would happen the next day. That's one part about the First Daughter stuff that I could do without. If it were up to me, I would have hiked it to the nearest Metro station, Metro Center on the Red Line, headed three stops down to Union Station, jumped on a Metroliner, and been in New York in less than three hours.

No muss, no fuss.

And, more important, no security detail.

But that's not how we do things in the White House. Security details, travel authorization, permission for this, regulations for that . . .

Thanks to all the official stuff, we lost the element of surprise. I wanted simply to show up, flash my First Dimples, and talk my way inside.

But to make up for the lost element of surprise, Paradox Studios agreed to give me a VIP tour of their set, and to let me meet the stars and give them a chance to kiss my butt, if necessary. Evidently, some bright boy in their PR department had realized they had a chance to generate some great publicity for the film from an Official Visit from an Official White House Resident.

I had to walk a thin line, gathering as much information and data as I could without giving them any sort of official sanction. They ended up agreeing that we could bring our own photographer, i.e., Michael, who would take all the publicity shots, and we would select which ones the production company would be allowed to use.

They had to be idiots to agree to it, but they did.

So, the next morning, Michael, Mac McNally, and Diana Gates, substituting for Gary Perkins, and I flew in a small commercial jet to LaGuardia Airport, where we were hustled through the terminal and ushered into a black limousine. From there we drove to a rather unremarkable-looking brick-and-concrete-block building somewhere in an area the driver called Astoria.

Honestly, it looked like it ought to have housed auto parts, instead of being a major movie soundstage. I'd had visions of something similar to what you see in Hollywood at the major studios—row after row of large curved-roof hangar-type buildings. I'd been to Universal Studios as a kid. I knew what these things were supposed to look like.

But this was just one squatty red-brick warehouse in a row of similar warehouses that all boasted signs such as "Harcourt Plumbing and Supplies" and "Mega Tire Warehouse."

In fact, you'd have never known this place was a soundstage if it weren't for the large trailer parked outside that had the logo of a lighting company plastered across it and the words "Mobile Theatrical Lighting."

A black-suited man waited at the door, obviously not part of the studio security, but a Secret Service guy on advanced detail from the New York field office. I recognized that emotionless stare into the distance, assessing all possible hazards, foreign and domestic. As much as I appreciate the security, it's still a bit overwhelming to think that advance troops are sent into an area to case the joint, all for the likes of me. I really don't see myself as being that vulnerable, but I promised Dad that I would always allow the Secret Service to do their job, and so I let them do their James Bond stuff.

The advance agent gave us a discreet nod and the car stopped beside him. We were marched into the building, then led down a hallway and through a door that emptied into a quiet soundstage.

A tall, craggy-looking man stood in the hallway and his otherwise dour face transformed into an enthusiastic smile as soon as he saw us troop in. I suspect he hadn't liked dealing with the Secret Service contingent that had arrived before me to scope the place out.

He stepped forward, hand outstretched. "Miss Cooper, what a delight to meet you. I'm Archie Maxwell, the First AD, and I can't tell you how honored we are to have you on our set."

I accepted his energetic but damp handshake. "I appreciate you accommodating my curiosity at such short notice." We stepped onto the soundstage, filled with sets, lights, and a host of other equipment but no people. I made a show of looking around. "It's a lot bigger and a lot quieter than I expected."

He flushed an unhealthy red, as if I'd said something to spike his blood pressure. "Everyone is on the other soundstage right now. I thought we'd start here with what I believe you will find to be familiar-looking sets and where I can answer any of your questions without interruptions. The cast and crew are all quite eager to meet you."

Michael stepped forward, having been relegated earlier to the back with my rear flank. "How far along are you with the movie?" In response to Maxwell's less-than-receptive squint, Michael took another step forward, broke out in what I can only describe as a "big-ass smile," and stuck out his hand. "I'm Joseph Hardy, the photographer the company hired to take the PR shots."

Joe Hardy? I almost burst out laughing. Who did that make me? Nancy Drew?

And since when did America's favorite teen detectives come complete with Secret Service agents?

Maxwell's handshake with the "hired hand" wasn't nearly as enthusiastic as the one I received. Although Michael was the one to ask the question, Maxwell offered his explanation to me.

"We're just about at the end of the production and several of the minor cast members have already been dismissed. It's been quite a grueling shoot. Our leading lady got very sick and had to be hospitalized. We lost some time because we had to shut down for over a month." He pointed toward a break between the sets. "We'll head this way."

"I hope she's all right now."

All this talk about hospitals suddenly made me remember about Perkins's wife; had she'd been released yet? I had to remember to send a note. . . . I stopped to pick my way across the cables that snaked across the floor.

Maxwell mistook my momentary distraction as confusion and reached for my arm to help me navigate around the thick bundles of wire. "Thankfully, she's fine. But it was touch-and-go for a while as to whether we'd continue the production." He led us out of the cable maze and onto a well-lit set of an office.

"This is where the story starts, at the newspaper office, when our intrepid reporters get a tip on a shooting that happens in downtown Washington, D.C."

He said "intrepid reporters" without even stuttering. I was impressed. An overused cliché like that would have made me gag. I realized that he was still holding on to by arm, rather possessively, and had to suppress a shudder.

He continued. "Then we learn that two assassins have been assigned to deal with one man; one assassin is supposed to protect the man at all costs and the other is supposed to kill him. Thus the title 'Armed and Dangerous.' "

"How clever," I lied. "I understand that you've created parts of the White House as some of your set?"

"We have indeed. Two of the key sequences take place in the White House, a verbal confrontation in the Oval Office and a"—he stumbled over the word—"physical one in the Lincoln bedroom."

I couldn't help it. The words just tumbled out of me. "Assignation and assassination. Kiss 'em and kill 'em. Sounds like the perfect combination to appeal to the American public."

Maxwell raised an eyebrow as if realizing for the first time that maybe I wasn't some star-struck blond ditz using her father's presidential connections for a chance to meet her favorite star. If I wasn't careful, I was going to blow our cover story—which, coincidentally, had been that I was a star-struck ditz, using her father's connections.

I'll be the first to admit I have no qualms about using someone's prejudices against him. So to disarm his suspicions, I added a rather silly giggle.

Thus reassured I was indeed empty-headed, he continued. "We expect to do well at the box office. But I suspect what you'd really like is to see these sets and, of course, meet the cast, correct?"

And in that order, too, I hoped. I offered him my ditziest smile. "That'd be fantastic."

Sure enough, he walked us through a maze of scenery flats and suddenly we were entering the Oval Office. I had to blink because it was such a surprise. The room was an uncanny re-creation of my father's office, right down to the color of the curtains and the titles of the books on the shelves.

"Remarkable," I said in honest praise. "I'd be hard-pressed to tell the difference between this set and the original." And that was no lie. Someone had taken great pains to build a credible re-creation of the real thing.

Michael took a couple of cheesy shots of Maxwell and me admiring the furnishings. Although the Lincoln bedroom set was our real concern, Michael and I had agreed on the flight up that we didn't need to make our interest painfully obvious. It made sense to take a few dummy shots elsewhere on the soundstage so that any shots taken in the Lincoln bedroom would seem just par for the course.

What we hadn't covered in our advance briefing was his little "Hardy Boys" joke. Now, I was going to have to remember to call him Joe rather than Michael. Then, once we left, I'd find some more choice names to use. . . .

We spent several minutes in the faux Oval Office and I couldn't help but laugh when I discovered that someone had taken creative license when it came to the photographs on the President's desk. Instead of my father's face or that of any of the former Presidents, someone had pasted on the head of a vaguely familiar-looking actor so that there were shots of the actor greeting Queen Elizabeth, the same actor laughing along with Gorbachev and in serious discussion with a half dozen other world leaders.

Nice touch.

I noticed that the faux President had a picture of a beautiful spouse—who looked about twenty—and two equally beautiful children, who were far too old to have a twenty-something mother. And then they told me that the woman in the pictures, the one who had apparently given birth while still a toddler, was the President.

Ah, yes, Hollywood . . . It has its own persuasive mythology, even here on the East Coast.

In my search to identify our heretofore-unidentified blonde, I noted that this "President" was a redhead. At least in this picture. In real life, who knew?

Next, Maxwell led us through the door that, in the real White House, should have led to the outer office, but in this magical re-creation, we stepped directly from the Oval Office into the Lincoln bedroom. So much for continuity.

As soon as we walked in, I was hit with an undeniable sense of déjà vu. Just like the room before it, the Lincoln bedroom was indeed a duplicate of the original. Michael took some surreptitious shots of the furniture and I maneuvered myself into the same position where the woman had stood, just like we'd planned on the trip up.

When Maxwell's attention was elsewhere, Michael crouched down and took a shot that should match the photo O'Connor had on him when he died.

The phrase "dead ringer" suddenly echoed through my mind and I shivered.

You okay? Michael mouthed.

I nodded, waving away his concern.

When Maxwell turned around, Michael and I simultaneously turned our attention to the ceiling, or lack thereof.

"I can't believe how much this looks like the original," I gushed. "All it lacks is the crystal chandelier that hangs in the center of the room."

Maxwell nodded. "We debated duplicating the chandelier as well, but it wouldn't have been in many shots. Plus, it would have been hard to shoot around."

I looked up and spotted a lighting catwalk positioned right above the bed, only a few feet from the top of the tall headboard. It was at the perfect height and I could easily imagine someone sitting up there, hiding in the dark, shooting a whole roll of film, perhaps without even being noticed. As Maxwell turned away, I caught Michael's attention and pointed it out to him. He nodded and took a surreptitious shot of the catwalk.

Maxwell clapped Michael on the back, only a split second after the shot.

So much for secrecy.

"Now, now . . . save your film, young man," he said

in a tone of voice that bordered on being just a bit too superior. "I have a strong feeling that Miss Cooper would like to get some shots of herself with our handsome leading man. He's on our second soundstage, where they're filming one of the last scenes of the film." He pointed to a door where a red light flashed rhythmically, then went suddenly dark.

Maxwell shot us a toothy smile. "Good timing. They must be between shots. Let's hurry and go on in there while we have the opportunity."

If it'd been up to me, I would have rather stayed in the faux White House set, but we didn't want to raise any unnecessary suspicions. We dutifully followed him through the door and into what appeared to be a warehouse cleverly disguised as . . . a warehouse.

Whereas the previous soundstage had been quiet and empty, this one teemed with life. People were everywhere, from the technicians, complete with black union T-shirts proudly proclaiming their local numbers, to a knot of men dressed in expensive-looking suits.

"Producers?" I whispered, pointing to the small crowd of men.

Maxwell shook his head and whispered back, "Extras."

Talk about feeling stupid. Thank God it was dark and no one could see me blush.

A voice called out over the din, "Let's set up for the medium shot."

Maxwell stepped into a pool of light and waved toward a camera. "Our guests have arrived."

CHAPTER NINE

The room came to a standstill and then overhead lights flared. It was as if the actors and crew had rehearsed their actions—which I guess isn't so far-fetched, considering their vocation. They formed an informal receiving line with an obvious sense of prescribed hierarchy. I noticed the well-dressed extras were relegated to a corner, not even meriting a place in line.

Maxwell led us to the front of the line where a large, bearded man stood. He had so much hair covering his face, I couldn't read his expression—I honestly didn't know whether he was glad to have a break in the action or resented the heck out of us for interrupting his creative process.

However, when he spoke, it was in a soft, pleasant voice, belying my initial concerns. "I'm Marv Schiel, the director. On behalf of Paradox Studios, let me say it's a delight and an honor to have you visit our set, Ms. Cooper." He stuck out a big paw and gave me a surprisingly gentle handshake.

"I'm very pleased to meet you, Mr. Schiel. And, please, it's Eve. Thanks so much for letting us come. I've never been on a movie set before. It's fascinating."

"I take it you've had a chance to see our White House set. What do you think?"

"Unbelievable," I stated, not exaggerating a bit. "It's uncanny how identical it is to the real thing. I can't imagine how you were able to copy everything in such detail. I can't begin to think how much research it took."

He grinned. Or at least I think he did. I saw teeth and heard no growl.

"The credit belongs to our set decorator, James Thestle." He turned to the thin man standing beside him. "Jim, allow me to introduce Eve Cooper, the First Daughter." He added a laugh. "The real one."

Thestle pumped my hand with a frenetic sense of enthusiasm and spoke in a gravelly voice. "You can't know how delighted I am to have you see my set. Delighted. Just utterly delighted."

"Thank you. You've done a miraculous job re-creating Dad's office." I offered him a smile and tried unsuccessfully to extract my hand from his tight grasp; he seemed determined to hold on. "Except for the pictures on the desk."

Concern mixed with a bit of confusion began to flood his eyes.

I tried to disarm his unnecessary concern with my

best smile. "Funny, but the woman in the photographs doesn't look anything like me or my aunt Patsy."

His relief was palpable and everyone within ear range laughed politely.

I leaned closer, hoping he'd release my hand if he didn't think I was going to run away. "So how much research did you have to do? It's so much like"—I almost stumbled over the word—"home, it's hard to believe I'm not there."

He spoke in a conspiratorial whisper. "I used three full-time research assistants who ferreted out absolutely everything they could about these two rooms. One of my assistants had even worked as a White House aide during McClaren's first administration. He was an invaluable help."

Thestle still held my hand and I was starting to wonder if I'd ever get it back.

"As for me," he continued, "I've never even set foot in the White House. We based our entire reconstruction on pictures—from what your people sent us and from a whole library of books. It took us months to build both sets."

I'd admit it. It *had* been impressive in a "Wow, what dedication, what details" sort of way. Then again, I wondered if the cost of creating an exact duplication was really justified. Who else, outside of the White House staff and the former presidential families, could appreciate his thoroughness and attention to detail?

Or even notice it?

I finally managed to slide my hand out of his. "I've only lived there a month, so I bet you know the place better than I do."

More polite laughter.

Either I'd gotten funnier in my old age, or people were giving me mercy laughter befitting my newfound "position." I guess it was one of the downfalls of public life.

We continued chatting about his painstaking research for far too long and then Marv, the director, took pity on us and extracted me from the set decorator's clutches. Marv continued introducing me to other people down the line, assorted assistant directors, electricians, carpenters, etc.

The actors were at the end, evidently lined up in reverse order with the leads last in line. The big finale, I guess. When we finally reached the end, Marv made a real production of introducing me to their leading man, the star of stage and screen, the man who needed no introduction . . .

The guy was undeniably handsome. No, gorgeous in a sort of matinee-idol, George Clooney way.

Trouble was, I knew George Clooney's name and could recognize him across a crowded room (and would fight my way over to him).

This guy?

I had no clue who he was, other than remembering him vaguely from a soap I used to watch in college.

Luckily, everyone seemed to mistake my lack of recognition for being star-struck. I covered my ignorance and made all the appropriate overtures, being oh-so-excited to see him and such a fan of his work. . . .

Whoever th' heck he was . . .

Whatever th' heck he'd done . . . .

The thing I haven't really mentioned up to now is

exactly how we managed to make this visit happen. Normally, I don't believe in using whatever influence comes with my White House connection for my own amusement or advancement. I'd already seen and experienced the legacy that Willa McClaren had left me, having spent her father's entire time in office using and abusing the contacts, perks, and privileges that came with the position.

I know for a fact from a mutual acquaintance that Willa once wrangled an invitation to George Clooney's house.

The bitch . . .

But this investigation—that was another matter. I wasn't doing it for myself, but for my dad. For truth, justice, and the American way. So I truly had no problem using the connections the White House afforded me—for all the right reasons, of course.

When we learned that this was a closed set and that the plot was a closely guarded secret, it was Aunt Patsy's assistant, Sara Cawley, who knew to play the "But the President's daughter is your leading man's number-one fan!" ploy. It was an effective line of attack, but I'd failed to get a most pertinent piece of data from Sara: the actor's name.

So now I had to play along as if I thought what's-his-name was the greatest actor since the invention of the moving picture.

As I stumbled through, trying to cover my ignorance, Diana Gates, Secret Service Agent Extraordinaire, leaned forward and whispered in my ear, "Tony Jenkins, played Marsh in *As Time Goes On* and was Schwarzenegger's sidekick in his latest movie."

God bless that woman.

I remembered Tony Jenkins now. A lightweight actor who made up for his lack of brains and screen presence with his rugged good looks. I figured he was some sort of prima donna, but to my surprise, he was quite polite and kept our meeting on a nice, low-key level, despite the hype others were trying to generate.

He joked about his role in the movie as a presidential aide, saying he'd hoped when the part was first offered that he'd have a chance to bring some dignity back into the position. Then he'd learned that his character enjoyed several rolls in the hay with the female President.

"So much for dignity," he said with a shrug of his very wide and very handsome shoulders. His grin warmed me to the soles of my feet and reminded me that I hadn't had a date in several months.

I did mention that earlier, didn't I?

He continued. "The height of sophomoric humor around here is calling me 'Mr. Lewinsky.' " He leaned closer. "I heard that in the earlier drafts of the script, my character was actually named Lewis."

I winced in his behalf and he laughed in appreciation.

"Thanks. Although I'll admit I don't deserve much sympathy. I came into the role with my eyes open. If I do good, it'll open some doors for me."

Eyes. His eyes were blue.

Okay, I wasn't exactly smitten, but I was enjoying myself. He was handsome, seemingly intelligent, not too taken with himself.

Did I mention he was handsome?

Suddenly there was a nudge in my ribs. Michael

gave me a smile that bordered on insipid. "Miss Cooper, we'd sure like to get some shots of the two of you on the White House set."

Jerk.

The one time I finally got to talk to someone outside of the Great White Prison and Michael had to interrupt me. The nerve . . .

I shot Diana a glance that said, *Hey, you're supposed to protect me. Protect me from him!*

I turned to Tony. (We were on a first-name basis already.) "He's right, you know. I'd love to get some shots of the two of us." I glanced over Tony's shoulder and gave Michael a sickening smile. "In the Oval Office *and* the Lincoln bedroom."

Tony shot me another "warm you to the cockles of your heart" grin and linked his arm through mine. "Shall we?"

Our entourage made its way through the door to the other soundstage, which was now inexplicably dark. Diana gently pushed me back into the lit area, giving me a "not so fast" look. McNally and several other agents fanned around me.

Evidently, they didn't like darkness.

Tony called over his shoulder, "Hey, guys, can we get some lights in here?"

Someone scurried past us in the dark and into the room, and a few moments later, lights flared along the catwalks. Tony waved to a man standing beside a large control deck.

"Thanks, Carlos."

Tony graced me with another unbelievable smile.

"The production guys around here are really top-notch."

Preceded by my Dawg escort, Tony and I walked toward the Oval Office set while Michael and Maxwell hung back a few steps. I distinctly heard Maxwell whisper, "They make a lovely couple," and then I heard a rude, snorting noise that must have originated from Michael.

Maxwell continued, ignoring Michael's unnecessary and, may I say, inappropriate social commentary: "Make sure you get lots of shots of the two of them. Lots of close-ups."

Michael snapped the man a salute. "Yes, sir." He stepped over toward us. "All righty, you lovebirds." He added an outrageous wink. "Maybe we ought to start in the bedroom first."

Tony, who had been holding my hand, strictly in a sweet sort of way, suddenly tightened his grip on my fingers. "Lay off, man. You're talking to a lady."

I gave Michael a sweet smile. "Yeah, I'm a lady." Then I turned to Tony. "Don't mind him, he's an . . . old family friend. He says stupid stuff like that all the time. He thinks it's humorous. We'll start in the Oval Office."

Tony looked at me and then at Michael, then at me again. "So, like are you together or something?"

"No way." Our two voices blended as one.

Tony lifted one shoulder in an artful shrug. "Just checking."

After that rather awkward moment, we recovered as much and as quickly as possible. Luckily, Michael didn't set up the cheesecake shots Maxwell wanted—

not that I would have posed for them anyway. Tony and I simply started talking and Michael took candids.

But it wasn't easy to talk to Tony since I kept falling into his soulful gaze. But I made a concerted effort to make conversation rather than stare. "So . . . uh . . . tell me about the movie. Is there lots of political intrigue?"

"Can't say." Tony twisted an imaginary key in his "locked" lips. "I signed a confidentiality statement."

"Can't you give me a hint?" I pleaded, putting my hand on his arm.

He blushed, then leaned closer. "Promise not to tell? Anyone? Not even your father?"

I solemnly drew a cross over my heart. "I swear."

He leaned closer until his lips were almost brushing my cheek. "All the plots on the Internet are wrong. Marv leaked them to throw the hounds off the trail."

"Smart man." I backed up slightly. I wasn't ready for quite that much closeness. Sure he was a gorgeous man, but I simply was not that fast of a worker. "Then tell me—what's the movie really about?"

He grinned. "Two reporters learn that there's a connection between what appears to be a random shooting in downtown D.C. and an attempt to blackmail the first female President of the United States. I play one of the reporters who goes to work undercover in the White House as a presidential aide. But . . ." He took a dramatic pause. "Little do I know that I'll soon be involved in the blackmail attempt. Madame President tries to seduce me and someone takes incriminating photos of the both of us. But when she's assassinated in the Oval Office, all fingers point to me and I go on the run, trying to prove my innocence."

"It sounds intriguing," I said a bit breathlessly. On purpose, mind you.

He pulled back. "Definitely. It's a real showcase for me. There's romance, action, adventure." He puffed up a bit. "I even do my own stunts."

Michael's camera jiggled a bit and I think I heard that same irreverent snort he'd released earlier.

"We're using the same stunt director that handled my last picture—with Ahr-nold. The man's a genius!"

Tony continued, extolling the virtues of various people whose sole purpose seemed to be making Tony Jenkins look good. Suddenly, Tony Jenkins wasn't looking quite so good to me.

I bet George Clooney wouldn't brag like that.

I listened politely, but suddenly, the momentary thrill of meeting Tony had worn off completely. It didn't matter that he was handsome; he was caught up playing his easiest and favorite role to date: the self-absorbed actor.

I heard every excruciating detail about his past roles, which actors he'd enjoyed playing against, which ones he hated, and the exact details of why. After fifteen solid minutes of listening to his self-aggrandizing soliloquy, I wanted out.

Badly.

And Michael was no help. If anything, I think he was getting a perverse sense of pleasure out of watching as my smile became more brittle and my eyes glazed over.

"Smile, Eve," he prompted.

I couldn't manage more than a grimace.

Tony shifted so that he gave the camera his chiseled profile. "Try this. It's my best side."

No, I'd already learned his best side was his butt, as in watching him walk away. Far away. Out of conversational range. This was one case where I had to agree with the great author who once said, "Pretty men should be seen and not heard."

But, oblivious to my pain, Tony continued regaling me with his acting exploits. I got up and wandered toward the Lincoln bedroom, not because I wanted a change of venue, but because I was contemplating grabbing a pillow from the bed and either covering my ears with it or perhaps using it to smother him.

Michael trailed along, shutter clicking. But I knew he wasn't taking pictures. Earlier, I'd watched him switch to a dummy camera, one with no film. At least there would be no lasting photographic mementos of this torture.

There might be a God, but evidently he didn't mind listening to Tony blather.

As we passed into the next room, Tony continued his monologue. ". . . and then I was invited to the Alabama Shakespeare Festival, where I played Patroclus in *Troilus and Cressida*, Duke Orsino in *Twelfth Night*, Lysander in *Midsummer Night's Dream* . . ."

He droned on, but I wasn't listening.

Something was wrong about the room. Something had been moved, but I wasn't sure what. I stopped in my tracks and Tony bumped into me, then steadied me so I wouldn't fall.

"What's wrong?"

I continued to study the set.

Michael pushed between us and touched my shoulder. "Eve? You okay?"

"No." I shook my head and pointed to the walls. "Something's . . . off."

I almost expected Michael to give me a look that suggested *I* was the one who was off, but to his credit, he wore a look of honest concern.

"Off?"

I nodded. "Wrong. Out of kilter." Why was it so hard to explain this? "Something looks different, but I can't quite tell what it is."

Michael neatly maneuvered Tony out of the way, pushing him back into the Oval Office and then shifting up to join me, shoulder to shoulder, in the doorway. Together, we scanned the room, neither of us stepping beyond the faked threshold as we searched for the inconsistency I could sense more than see.

Tony peered over our shoulders. "What? Where? Is it another fan? You know, we've had problems with some of my more rabid fans trying to break in and meet me. They'll try to steal—"

"Shut up!" Michael and I spoke simultaneously.

I'll say one thing for Tony, he takes direction well. He did indeed shut up.

After a long moment of blessed silence, Michael pointed to the table on the far side of the bed. "There's a lamp missing over there. I think it was there when we left."

Tony pushed between us and walked into the room. "Don't worry. A fan wouldn't try to steal something like that. The guys are probably starting to dismantle the room. They only kept it intact when we got through yesterday with the pickup shots because we knew you were coming today."

He made a great show of looking around the set. "That, or maybe one of the crew has decided to take home a White House souvenir." He laughed at his own joke, making an audience of one.

Then, Tony crossed to the far side of the bed and stopped suddenly, going all pasty beneath his pancaked tan. His "macho-man" squeal was high enough and loud enough to shatter glass. Pointing with a shaky hand toward something out of our sight, he made another sound and then landed on the floor in a dead faint.

Diana and Mac had swung into action before Tony's scream had even formed an echo. I saw Tony fall only because I could see beneath Mac's arm as he pushed me down into a corner and shielded me with his own body.

If this was nothing more than a gag by a two-bit actor with a million-dollar face, he was going to have to deal with several angry Secret Service agents, not to mention one highly incensed First Daughter.

The agents had rules they had to follow, but me, I could fight dirty if I had to.

Michael was the one who stalked over to Tony and poked him with the toe of one shoe. "If this is your idea of being funny . . ."

His voice trailed off as he glanced toward the bed. "Oh, crap . . . It's another one."

"Another one . . . what?" I managed to yell around Mac's protective bulk.

Michael released a shaky sigh. "Another body."

CHAPTER TEN

The agents hustled me out of the room and into the limo. We would have driven off immediately if I'd allowed them to do so. But I managed to convince them that they could maintain my safety there in the vehicle while we waited for news. That, and I figured that the NYPD might not appreciate us pulling a vanishing act.

And sure enough, only a few minutes after we got settled, squad cars arrived, as well as an ambulance. I could see them pointing at the limo and could imagine their conversation:

Who's in there?

The President's daughter.

What President? You mean the President *President?*

Yep.

I dug into my purse and pulled out my cell phone.

"I have to talk to Dad before this filters back to him," I explained to Diana. "God knows what it'll sound like once it gets back to him."

When I got through to his secretary, Jeanne, she explained it was one of those times that he simply couldn't be disturbed. Murphy's Law, I guess. At least I knew she was telling the truth. But she did promise she'd get the message to him just as soon as possible, before he had a chance to hear any half-truths or rumors from any other source.

Her voice grew soft and maternal. "Are you sure you're all right, Eve?"

"Absolutely. We're waiting in the limo and there's plenty of security."

"I'll make sure to have your father call you when he gets free. He's going to want to hear your voice when he finds out."

Relieved, I settled back into the seat and watched the turmoil outside through the smoked glass. Mac stood at the front of the car, playing both bodyguard and lookout. He'd pulled members of the advance team to points around the other three sides of the car so that agents formed a four-sided protective ring around us. A cordon seemed a little excessive in my mind, but I wasn't going to argue with them.

Not today . . .

Michael became my eyes and ears, hanging around the set and reporting back to the car with updates until the police finally threw him out for good. But before he was ejected, he learned some basic details.

The body was that of one of the set's security guards, Oscar Rolanski. The crew and the police theorized that he'd climbed up to a catwalk as a part of his security sweep and he'd simply fallen.

No intrigue.

No assassination attempt.

Just poor timing and an unfortunate loss of balance.

A simple case of "ooops."

As Michael described it, if the poor bastard had fallen one foot over to the right, he would have landed on the bed. As it was, he missed the bed completely and landed on the bedside table, breaking it and his neck at the same time.

I'd like to think it was my incredible sensitivity that made me realize something was hinky in the room when I first walked in, but really . . . I figure it was nothing more than the missing lamp and picture that caught my attention, and that only subliminally at first. The picture in question was that of a young girl which had hung to the right of the bed. Evidently, the guard had knocked it off the wall as he fell. Michael said they had found the mangled picture under him.

Michael hadn't said much since he'd been ejected from the crime scene. He merely sat on the seat beside me, his hands betraying him by shaking. I charitably chalked it up to the sinking temperatures and the snow that had just started to fall.

He spoke in a low voice. "They're not going to let me go back in. I'm lucky they didn't confiscate the film." He patted the camera bag at his feet. He leaned forward and spoke to the driver. "The doors are locked, right?"

The driver nodded. "Yes, sir."

His unusual concern probably shook me more than

anything else. I crossed my arms, trying to ward off the sudden chill that threatened me. "What do you mean, 'Are the doors locked'? Are you saying that you think there's any danger?"

"No, no," he said quickly. Too quickly.

"Michael . . ."

He drew in a long breath. "It's just all too coincidental. Two bodies . . ." His voice faded for a moment, then he seemed to regain some momentum and conviction. "Eve, how many dead people have you ever run across in your personal life—outside of your career?"

I thought about the handful of crime scenes I'd covered during my wire service work in Denver. Most of the time, the bodies had been removed before I came on scene. So essentially, I'd seen only two bodies while working. And of course, none in my everyday life. "None, really," I whispered. "You?"

"Same here—before this, zero. But now we've run into two of them, both connected somehow with this blackmail situation. It can't simply be a coincidence."

It was easier to try to dispute his claim than force myself to believe it. "But don't the police believe he fell on his own? I mean, it's not like he was shot or stabbed or . . ." I couldn't go on, listing all the grisly ways a person could die.

Michael said nothing as he stared out the window beyond me toward the soundstage.

My mind started churning.

Two bodies.

Maybe with no connection at all.

Then again . . .

I shivered.

Michael patted me on the shoulder. "Sorry. Now I've got you worried, too."

I released a sigh that sounded entirely too shaky for my taste. "Two deaths." I watched a single snowflake melt into nothingness against the car window. My mind wandered back to the faux Lincoln bedroom and I reconstructed the scene in my head.

The guard lost his balance on the catwalk and fell over the protective railing, plunging headfirst into the room, knocking the picture off the wall, then hitting the bedside table, where he broke his neck.

I closed my eyes and tried to picture the sight, half hoping I couldn't conjure up something so devastating in my mind. But I've mentioned my highly developed imagination before, right? To my disgust, I had no problem picturing the fall.

Maybe I'd look into some serious therapy later on. . . .

But for now, I had a mental film going forward, then reverse, with freeze frames in all the wrong places.

I opened my eyes to see Michael staring at me.

He covered my hand with his. "You sure you're okay?"

"Fine . . . considering. I'm just trying to picture the fall in my head." I pulled my hand free so I could gesture with it. It became the guard and the other hand, held out horizontally, the railing. "So he slips and falls over the railing, right? That explains why he went headfirst." I demonstrated by doing the universal sign for plunging over a rail.

"Or he slipped and fell under the rail," Michael added.

I repositioned my hands and demonstrated that as well. "Then he would have fallen feet first."

"Unless he got a foot tangled in the walkway and it only released once it supported a substantial amount of his weight as he dangled from it."

"Then he'd probably have a broken foot, too."

"Possibly. At least he'd have marks on his shoes. But when they examined him back there, they said the only things he seemed to have broken were his neck and one shoulder blade, all consistent with a headfirst fall from the catwalk." He paused to scratch his head. "That's enough to kill you, of course. But come to think of it, I don't know if they looked at his feet or not. I guess that's something they'd notice in an autopsy."

My mental movie advanced a few frames. "So he hits the painting on his way down and it falls. Then he lands on the bedside table, headfirst, breaks the table, breaks his neck, and lands on top of the broken piece of furniture."

Even I had to admit it was pretty weird, maybe even sick, how I could talk so calmly, so matter-of-factly about a man's fall to his death. That therapist idea was gaining more strength as we went along.

I rewound my mental movie. "His hand or some other body part hit the frame as he fell. It falls, too, maybe a split second behind him. If so, then how did the picture frame get under him?"

Interest flared in Michael's eyes. "Good point. But if he was flailing around, hanging by one ankle, he could have knocked if off the wall with one of his hands before he fell himself. That's how it would have fallen first. Or maybe he hit it hard while grabbing for something to break his fall, and gave it enough of a push for it to land before he did. It's possible."

Diana piped in for the first time. "But if the picture had simply been knocked off the wall, it should have slid straight down the wall and landed between the wall and the bedside table. It wouldn't have landed under him and been broken."

We all shared a look of discovery and confusion.

"So we're saying we don't think he simply fell?" I said, finding it suddenly hard to catch my breath. "That somehow, something's fishy? That this is maybe a murder set up to look like an accident?"

Michael nodded. "Maybe someone even killed him elsewhere and made it look as if he'd fallen."

"But why?" I asked the question, but I already knew the answer and proceeded to say it aloud. "Because he knew something about how the bedroom set was used to make the blackmail shots."

Diana and Michael spoke at the same time. "Exactly."

We sat there in silence, savoring the not-too-sweet flavor of our epiphany. Then Diana spoke in a soft but firm voice. "But how do you prove it?"

How, indeed? It was a job for Nancy Drew or Joe Hardy or some other fictional sleuth. But was it a job for me?

I closed my eyes. "I don't know. But that won't keep me from reporting our theories to Dad or Mr. Seybold or anybody else with authority."

Michael nodded toward the window. "You may have your chance. Someone's coming."

Archie Maxwell approached the car, accompanied by one of New York's finest. They paused to speak to Guard Dawg Mac and then were waved through the protective grid toward us. Maxwell stooped and knocked on the car window.

Diana lowered the glass a bit and I leaned forward past her. "Any news?"

Maxwell's face was a distinct shade of gray. "The police aren't convinced that the watchman simply fell. They'd like to speak with you."

I was about to respond, but Diana pushed between us. "Tell the lead investigator that Miss Cooper will speak to him just as soon as her counsel—"

"No." I put my hand on Diana's arm. "I don't need a lawyer. I think it's safe to assume that since I was the center of attention while I was in there, every minute of my time can be accounted for by a dozen witnesses. I haven't been out of the Secret Service's sight since I left D.C. I'm definitely no suspect, so I really don't need someone to represent me." I turned to Maxwell. "Can you provide us a quiet and"—I added for Diana's benefit—"secure place where we can talk privately with the police?"

"Absolutely. You can use my office."

Diana rolled down her window all the way, called Mac over, and explained what was happening. Two of the agents went with Maxwell, and Mac, Diana, Michael, and the driver stayed behind with me.

A few moments later, we got the high sign and we left the warm limo, braved the increasing snow, and dashed into the building, where we were escorted to Maxwell's office.

Talk about sterile.

I've seen more personality in a post office cubicle. Maxwell had no personal pictures, nothing to earmark this as his space. Not even a single toy! Even my dad has a Scooby-Doo figurine on his desk in the Oval Office, not to mention a couple of Happy Meal toys hiding in his right-hand drawer in case he has younger visitors.

The only out-of-the-ordinary decoration in the room was the woman, standing by the end of the empty desk. She made her severe black suit look like something off the latest fashion runway in Paris. I didn't have to look at Michael to know he was gaping at her.

Blond, stacked, and with the sort of aloof expression that drove men wild, the woman made Seven of Nine look like a two and a half.

But to my surprise, she ignored Michael and approached me, holding out her hand. "Miss Cooper, I'm Lieutenant Lange," she said in a voice that was just this side of a purr. "I appreciate you delaying your trip back to Washington to speak with us."

As if I'd waited just for her . . .

But this was no time to be snippy. I accepted her handshake. "You're welcome. It didn't feel right, leaving."

We made nice and sat down at the two chairs on one side of the desk. She pulled out a small leather notebook and pen.

"First, I want to assure you that we believe you have nothing to do with"—she consulted her notebook— "Mr. Oscar Rolanski's death. All I want to do is ask you a few questions about your presence here."

"Certainly. Go right ahead."

"How did you learn about the movie set? From what I've been told, this project has been kept under wraps and the set was closed to the public."

Okay, so far, so good. I could answer that one without having to hide anything. "I was talking to the White House curator and he mentioned that a movie production company had approached him about getting information about the house, specifically the Lincoln bedroom and the Oval Office. I wondered how exact a replica could be made based on research books and pictures."

"So it was idle curiosity that made you come here?"

I tried not to squirm. "Curiosity, yes. Idle, not necessarily."

She consulted her notebook. "Would that curiosity have anything to do with the current news story about the pictures taken in the Lincoln bedroom?"

God, I hate it when people pin me to the wall. I tried to match her aloofness with some of my own. "It might." In retrospect, I think I sounded more like a three-year-old who'd gotten caught with her hand in the cookie jar.

Michael decided to insert himself into the conversation. He stepped forward. "Can you blame us for being curious, Lieutenant? Or concerned, even? The newspaper splashed that picture across the front page and there have been rather unsavory implications. And then suddenly we learn that there's a duplicate of the room somewhere else. We had to come see for ourselves how close a duplication it really is."

Lieutenant Two and a Half stood to face him. She

was almost as tall as he was in her own leggy Scandinavian way. "And what did you learn"—she consulted her notebook—"Mr. Hardy, is it?" The merest hint of sarcasm in her voice suggested that she was up to date on her juvenile literature.

"My name's not Hardy," he corrected, not missing a beat. "It's Cauffman, Michael Cauffman."

She raised one perfectly arched eyebrow at him. "Indeed? And here I was so anxious to meet your brother, Frank."

I stood, as well, not wanting anyone to think the conversation was going over my head, literally or figuratively. "Ignore him. He's the White House photographer, has a warped sense of humor, and evidently hasn't read a book since he was a kid. You asked about the room. It's a perfect copy of the original. Right down to the pattern in the rug." I stepped closer. "Those blackmail pictures might well have been taken here instead of at the White House."

She turned that raised eyebrow in my direction. "Then I gather there's more than the one picture I've seen splashed all over the media?"

Okay, it was a slip on my part. But I had a distinct feeling that I was merely confirming what she'd already figured out. We locked stares for a moment.

She might become an ally in our mission. Then again . . .

I broke away, glancing at Michael. I wanted to get a reading from him before I volunteered any information. He gave me a noncommittal shrug.

Fat lot of help he was.

I drew a deep breath and went with my basic instincts. "Confidentially and off the record." It wasn't a question but a demand.

She nodded. "I agree to both."

"Yes, there were multiple pictures. We believe there were at least two rolls taken, each roll from a different angle." I drew myself to my full height, several inches shorter than her. "And in analyzing samples we had from both sets, Mr. Cauffman and I determined that at least several of the pictures were impossible with respect to the physical constraints of the real Lincoln bedroom. Some of the pictures were taken from a position near or above the ceiling, and the room's chandelier would have partially blocked the shot if they'd actually been taken in the real Lincoln bedroom. And we just can't figure out a way to get a camera in position for those shots without pasting ourselves to the ceiling."

Lieutenant Lange (I really wanted to call her Lieutenant Lungs) glanced toward the door and presumably toward the soundstage beyond. "But you think it's possible to manage that camera position from a lighting catwalk or camera boom?"

I hadn't thought about a camera boom, but it made sense. "Exactly."

She contemplated the news for a moment, then raised one perfectly manicured finger. "Wait one moment, please." She moved gracefully toward the door on a pair of heels that had to have cost a couple hundred dollars.

Each.

I was starting to wonder if she was a really cop or a leftover from the *Law and Order* set.

She whispered instructions to an underling, and a

minute later said underling returned with someone in tow.

The young man who stepped into the office looked surly but scared. But he also had a gleam of appreciation in his eye for the leggy lieutenant, as if given a different time and a different place, he'd be standing on some construction platform and wolf-whistling at her along with the rest of the hard hat gang.

Once she ushered him into the room and into the chair, she adopted a benign smile. "Mr. Constantine, would you please tell these people what you told me?"

He flushed. "But you said . . ."

"I said that if you made another pass like that at me, I'd show you six uses of a stiletto heel you've never imagined in your worst nightmares. What I want you to tell them is what you said about the movie being shot here."

"Oh . . . that." The young man's flush faded a slight bit until only the tips of his ears remained bright red. "It's about some chick who's the President and who gets caught doing one of her aides in the Lincoln bedroom."

"And how does Madame President get caught?" she prompted.

He lifted one shoulder. "There's supposed to be one of those mini-spy cameras hidden in a picture on the wall."

I glanced at the lieutenant. "The picture that was destroyed?"

She nodded slightly and turned her attention back to the young man. "Mr. Constantine, earlier you mentioned some nighttime shoots. Should I assume that the director was not aware of them?"

Color rocketed through his face again. "I done told you."

Her expression remained pleasant but noncommittal. "Would you mind repeating it for my colleagues?"

My colleagues. I had to say I liked the sound of it. It sounded much better than "Nancy Drew, First Daughter" and "Joe Hardy, Shutterbug at Large."

After several sputtering starts, the young man's voice dropped to a low whisper. "Forty bucks and you could rent out the set for the night. So's you could say you did your girl in the Lincoln bedroom."

Lieutenant Lange crossed her arms—as best she could. "Who brokered the transaction?"

The young man squinted at her. "Huh?"

She tried it again, this time in simple words. "Who took the money for the honey?"

He muttered something and the lieutenant barked sharply, "Louder!"

"Oscar," he whispered, only slightly louder. "The night watchman."

I swallowed hard. "The dead man?"

Lieutenant Lange nodded. "One and the same."

CHAPTER ELEVEN

All three of us agreed that it was no coincidence that the one person who might be able to shed some light on the blackmail situation was now conveniently dead. Although the lieutenant had nothing to go on other than our unsubstantiated theories, she seemed willing to look for clues that might suggest the late, unfortunate Oscar's demise was more than an accidental death.

I don't know if it was because of my influence (non-existent), my father's influence (as Commander and Chief, he drips with influence), or strictly because she sensed we were actually on to something, but she listened to us. I'd like to think the truth was behind Door Number Three. In any case, we got her assurance that she would look very hard and long at the guard's death and see what she could turn up with respect to his role in the blackmailing conspiracy.

By the time we headed out, the weather had deteriorated into something approaching blizzard conditions. The snow was so bad we couldn't fly, and so we ended up taking the train back to D.C. I don't think the Secret Service agents were too thrilled, securitywise, but at least I had a chance to learn that Diana Gates is a real card shark. I never want to be caught again on the Metroliner with her, a deck of cards, and nothing else to do.

Secret Service agents have perfect poker faces.

Michael didn't contribute much to the conversation. After a half hour of cards, he folded, pleading bankruptcy, and leaned against the window, his eyes closed and an insipid smile plastered on his face.

Dreaming about the beautiful Lieutenant Lange and her stiletto heels, I bet.

When we finally got back home, I had already worked myself into a frenzy, wondering how I'd tell Mr. Seybold about my "confession" to Lieutenant Lange. Although I thought the situation warranted the truth, I wasn't so sure he'd see it that way.

But when I walked into his office to make a clean breast of things, he was on the phone.

"Just a minute, Lieutenant, she just walked in." He covered the mouthpiece of the phone. "It's Lieutenant Lange from the NYPD. She has more information on the Oscar Rolanski case." He turned back to the phone. "Go ahead, Lieutenant."

He listened intently, and every time he said, "Uh-huh," my stomach twisted into a tighter knot. Finally he said, "Good work, Lieutenant. You've got my fax number. Let me know if you find anything else." He paused and shot me a quick look. "And say hello to your father for me, Terry. 'Bye."

He hung up the phone and swiveled in his chair to face me.

"You know her?" I asked, hoping to forestall the inevitable.

"Since she was ten. Her dad and I served together in the Air Force before he became a cop. I always knew she'd follow in her old man's footsteps."

Somehow I figured the unspoken admonishment was "Unlike you, big mouth."

Before I could speak, he stood and stalked over to his fax machine. "I'm the one who suggested she be put on the Rolanski case," he said nonchalantly.

I gaped at him. Who was the man? God? "How did . . . When did . . ."

He waved away my questions. "I wanted to have suitable authority waiting for you as backup if you found anything on the movie set. Then, when we learned a body had been found there, her superiors agreed to let her handle the case even though she works Vice in another precinct."

The Vice Squad?

In those shoes?

He continued. "Lucky for us, she'd worked Homicide in that area before, and the local guys didn't mind her cutting in on their territory."

If my head didn't hurt before this conversation started, it certainly did now. "Then everyone agrees it wasn't an accidental death? We have proof?"

He tapped the fax machine impatiently. "Reasonable proof it wasn't accidental, yes, but nothing so far that points to a particular suspect."

The machine buzzed and then sprang to life, grinding out several pieces of papers. I would have been scanning them hot out of the printer, but Seybold waited until the machine signaled again, and then stacked the papers neatly and returned to his desk.

I stood for a few moments, then my rubbery knees gave out. It had been a long day. Too long. I dropped into the chair at the end of his desk and tried not to fidget too much.

After an agonizing length of time, he finally looked up from the papers. "No fingerprints other than those of the guard and crew members we could reasonably expect to have had business up there were found on the catwalk, but we have smudges that indicate someone was up there wearing gloves—most likely the killer. There are signs of a struggle, one that seems to have been quite vigorous. It looks like the guard didn't go down easy. It appears that one of the klieg lights was broken during the struggle, and there's fresh blood on the catwalk. It's not the same type as the victim's, so it's probably the assailant's."

"That's good," I said. "You can narrow down the suspects. See who's been injured recently. Maybe even track them through recent hospital admissions."

He looked up from the paper. "Hardly. It's only a small amount of blood, so we're probably talking a cut that wouldn't require stitches. On the bright side, the blood type is O-positive, which rules out you and Mr.

Cauffman. Even the media won't be able to pin this on you."

Seybold knew my blood type? I thought for a moment. I knew that wherever Dad would visit, the advance security would arrive there early, making all sorts of contingency plans with respect to hospitals. Part of that was probably to guarantee there were sufficient quantities of plasma compatible with Dad's blood type in case of an emergency. Maybe it wasn't so odd that Seybold knew mine was the same as Dad's.

He probably had earmarked me as a likely donor if, God forbid, anything should happen.

I suppressed a shiver.

But how did he know Michael's blood type? This was getting a little spooky, even for me. I shivered.

"Are you all right, Eve?" Seybold dropped his usual facade and let something akin to real concern shine through. "You look pale."

I hid a yawn. "I'm just tired. It's been a long day. I don't usually stumble into murder scenes more than once a month."

To his credit, he didn't reach over and pat my hand. That would have been a bit too paternal and solicitous for my taste; I have a reputation to maintain as the unruffled First Daughter who can handle anything.

Or any*body* . . .

I swallowed hard. Just not a *dead* body.

He stood and I automatically rose. "We'll talk tomorrow after you've rested."

"Tomorrow," I repeated, appalled at how my voice cracked when I fought against the desire to yawn again.

"But I still need to brief"—I stumbled over the word—"Dad so he knows what's going on."

Seybold glanced at his watch. "He's still in his meeting, and I don't think we should interrupt him or divide his attention at the moment. I'll update him when he gets out. You don't need to wait up for him."

For some reason, I didn't mind that Seybold was literally dismissing me. If anything, it made me feel more like I was part of a real team, that we were all working toward a single goal. Protecting the President included protecting his good name and reputation. Looking at him, I suddenly had faith that he could inform Dad just as well as I could, if not better.

I even managed a half smile. "Yes, sir."

I trudged to the elevator and dumped my Dawg detail at its entrance. Diana and Mac had been relieved from duty the moment they got me into the building, and two fresh but anonymous faces had been assigned to dog me.

I even made it to my bed before collapsing. I'd say I fell dead asleep, but for some reason, after the last couple of weeks, that phrase makes me feel weird.

The next morning, I awoke feeling moderately alert, despite a night's sleep punctuated by a wild assortment of nightmares. The curse of having a good imagination is that it doesn't turn off at night.

But, nightmares aside, what was haunting me now was the fear of opening the paper or turning on the computer to see what new scandals had erupted during the night. I could imagine the headlines, virtual or otherwise: "First Daughter Finds Dead Body in Ersatz Lincoln Bedroom."

Then again, it might have gone far to prove that there were two Lincoln bedrooms in existence at that moment in time.

I almost stumbled into Drew's room, stopping only when I realized it was Saturday morning. The last thing I needed was his rage at being wakened early on a Saturday morning. I wasn't so far out of touch that I'd forgotten how much I had valued my chances to sleep late on weekends when I was a teenager.

I wandered into the dining room and found myself on the receiving end of a bear hug from Aunt Patsy. I didn't realize how much I needed it until I was engulfed in her arms. I just stood there, soaking in her love.

"Mr. Seybold briefed your father last night, telling him all about yesterday's excitement. Are you okay?"

I nodded, my chin bobbing against Patsy's shoulder. "I'm fine. It's not like we saw the man fall. I didn't even see much of the body."

"But another death . . ."

I pulled away so I could see her, face-to-face. "I refuse to believe it was a coincidence. I think he was killed because he knew something important about the set."

"Important—like he knew someone had shot those pictures there instead of here?"

I nodded. "A witness to the truth."

She grew unusually pale. "The dead man wasn't there when you toured the rooms the first time. That means the killer was there in the building at the same time you were."

Suddenly, I had a hard time catching my breath. It wasn't that I hadn't made that same logical leap the night before. I'd been willing and able to accept that the man might have been murdered and that someone there had been the murderer. Maybe my lack of feelings then had been due to a combination of excitement and exhaustion, which allowed me to discuss the situation in dispassionate and even disconnected terms.

But something about admitting in the morning light that it was possible, even probable, that a murderer had been waiting on that movie set, and that my actions had perhaps even goaded him into killing, made me feel very uncomfortable.

I hid my reaction from Aunt Patsy and managed to turn my gasp for air into a strangled gasp of laughter. "You didn't need to worry about me. I had a platoon of Secret Service agents surrounding me." Okay, it was an exaggeration, but I had felt pretty protected. I continued, adopting a smile of assurance that I hoped she didn't see through. "It was a fluke that whoever did this had any opportunity, considering the security measures that were in place. If anything, they tipped their hand. The only people who were cleared to be there were connected with the production company." My own logic started to lift my spirits. "It seems to me this whole thing means we can be pretty sure that the pictures weren't taken here."

My dad's voice echoed across from the doorway. "But believing something and proving it are two different things." He stalked across the room and pulled me into a familiar hug, one that radiated strength and concern and love.

"I should have never let you go there yesterday," he whispered with his cheek pressed against the top of my head.

"You didn't let me go, Dad," I whispered back. "I went on my own. I've been an adult for a while now."

He kissed my cheek and pulled me over to the breakfast table. "I know. But you're my daughter, and I'll never stop being a father. Fathers never stop worrying." He glanced around the room. "We're living a new lifestyle now, and it came with its own baggage. A completely new set of problems and concerns and worries and—"

"—and the highest level of security and protection possible," I supplied. I reached over and poured him a cup of hot cocoa, hoping that I could distract him with routine. "I'm not going to pull a bonehead stunt by deciding I can work better on my own, and dismiss the agents guarding me." I shot him a determined look. "I've never had a problem working within the rules."

His look of concern faded somewhat and he managed a smile. "You're right. You're not my boneheaded child."

We both knew what he was talking about. Charlie won that title, annually. He'd all but turned down Secret Service protection, much to Dad's dismay, but not to his surprise or begrudged agreement. Charlie has lived in his own world all his life, and why would anyone think that would change once his father became the Commander in Chief, the most powerful person in the free world?

Then again, Charlie's life of isolation had some built-in protections, thanks to the intensive security measures his company instituted to protect their technology. Charlie, being the source of much of that technology, was sufficiently protected as well. I couldn't help but think of the poor agents assigned to Charlie, forced to spend their shifts sitting in their cold cars because he refused to allow them onto his company's grounds.

Stubborn cuss.

The offspring Dad ought to worry most about was Drew, who not only had the same boneheaded genes as Charlie, but also the problems compounded by his youthful sense of immortality. Because Drew was a minor, Dad knew his own instructions to the agents about his son's safety would be followed to the precise letter. But I had a sneaking suspicion that it wouldn't be long before Drew grew tired of the novelty of being protected and tried to ditch his protection.

Maybe I could use my most recent experience as an object lesson.

And maybe monkeys would fly out of my . . . never mind, you get the picture.

I didn't want to admit it to either Dad or Aunt Patsy, but I worried that Drew was beginning to see me less as a sibling and more as a third parent.

And, speak of the devil, Drew stumbled into the dining room, dressed in sweatpants and a T-shirt that bordered on the obscene.

Ah, rebellious youth.

See? I'm even starting to sound like a parent.

He rubbed his eyes. "How'd it go yesterday? D'you meet any stars?"

Evidently, Dad had told him where I was going. I shrugged. "One guy who used to play on the soaps."

Drew snorted in derision. I gave Dad and Patsy a little brush-off gesture behind my back. They read my signal and wandered away, realizing I worked better with Drew one-on-one.

"He was ... interesting. Apparently, he played Schwarzenegger's sidekick in his latest movie."

Drew's eyes widened. "Tony Jenkins?"

I nodded, surprised that Drew knew who Tony was.

"You met Tony Jenkins?" he repeated in awe.

"Sure did."

"So is he ... like ... cool?"

I leaned closer, deciding this would be a prime time to play sibling and not parent. "Definitely not cool. He was nice to begin with." I lowered my voice. "And he's totally gorgeous, but it didn't take long for me to see what side of the Force he was on."

"A darksider?"

"Definitely. He's totally self-absorbed. And you know I'm not into the First Daughter center-of-attention stuff, either. After a few niceties, the conversation turned to him. Exclusively. His roles, his connections, his likes, his dislikes, the actors who aren't as good as he is, the ones that aren't as good-looking as he is—the quintessential Hollywood phony."

"You're kidding!" Drew whispered.

"Nope. And it gets better. Something weird happened while we were there. While we were on one set, someone fell off a catwalk in another part of the building. Later on, me and Tony and Michael, while we were taking pictures, walked right up on the body."

Drew's eyes opened wide. "Body? As in dead?"

I nodded. "Absolutely dead. Tony Jenkins took one look at the body, screamed like an opera soprano, and fainted dead away."

"No way!"

I sketched a cross across my heart. "Word of honor. I wouldn't be surprised if he wet himself while he was going down."

Total glee erupted across Drew's face. "Man, wait until I tell Scott. He's Jenkins's biggest fan. It'll slay him." Drew and I shared a laugh that was much too short for my taste. Say what you will about macabre humor, it helps you get through the tough times.

It didn't take long for Drew to grow solemn again. "Then that means you saw a dead body."

I nodded. "Another one."

I have to give my little brother credit; he's not stupid. He raised one eyebrow and nailed me with a knowing glare. "You were there, in New York, because of Mr. O'Connor's brother, right? The first dead guy?"

So what was I supposed to do? Lie? "Yeah."

"And now there's another dead guy." From the look on his face, I knew the gears were turning in his head. It was quite evident he didn't like the answer he was getting.

"You think this second death was connected to the first one?"

Again, I couldn't lie to him. "We think so."

He frowned as he started putting the pieces together. "But you said the guy fell."

Here it came. I swallowed hard. "Fell or was pushed. Evidence is beginning to stack up to make it look more like murder than an accident."

It took only a moment for righteous indignation to rip across his face. "Are you effin' crazy? Isn't it bad enough we had one"—he stopped himself before saying a word that would get him grounded—"freaking stiff in our garden? You had to go look for more?"

Somehow, I had a feeling these were the same sentiments—minus the potential expletives—that both my father and my aunt had wanted to express, but couldn't because of my advanced age and their firm grasp of my legal rights as an adult.

In a way, it was sort of nice, knowing that my little brother, while living in a time when teenagers were supposed to show blanket disdain for everything, actually cared what happened to me. And, judging from his tone of voice, maybe he didn't quite see me as a third parent. He'd never dream of yelling like that at Dad or Patsy.

But then again, unlike them, I could yell back without worrying about upsetting his fragile psyche.

"Of course I didn't go looking for another body, stupid. I was there trying to prove that the pictures in the paper could have been taken there on the set instead of here. They have a complete duplicate of the Lincoln bedroom for the movie. And the guy who died was a night watchman. Whoever killed him must have been worried that he might break down and tell the authorities who took those awful photographs on their set."

Drew didn't back down. "Grammar, sis, grammar. That should be 'whomever killed him,'" he said in a mocking voice. "But you don't *know* who." He started waving his hands around. "It could be anybody. How in the heck are you going to protect yourself from somebody you can't even identify? It could be anybody—a stranger, someone you know. It—"

"Stop." My father inserted himself into our rather heated conversation, using his "He Who Must Be Obeyed" voice. He'd perfected it in Congress. It worked well with battling siblings, too.

He placed a hand on Drew's shoulder. "Son, I appreciate what you're saying and why you're saying it, but you have to put some faith in your sister." He looked at me with a stare that said, *We both know he's right.*

He continued. "She knows what a delicate situation she's in and that the most important thing at stake isn't my career but her safety." He turned to me. "If you can pursue your investigation without placing yourself in harm's way, then continue. But if anything should happen to you . . ." He got somewhat choked up, which in turn made me get all blurry-eyed, too.

I hugged him, then Drew, who was resistant at first and then more accepting. "Listen, you two," I said quietly. "I understand why both of you are concerned, but don't worry. I think I've done all I can. The New York police are investigating the night watchman's death. When they figure out who did it, we'll know who took the pictures, and this whole mess will all be over."

And I sounded so positive, too.

By noon, I'd had no word about the NYPD investigation. I distracted myself by ramping up for the State Dinner we were hosting that night for the new president of some emerging African nation. There's no need to go into a long description of the country's politics and such, because about a month later, that small nation was swallowed up by a larger one.

But, at the moment, I was glad for the distraction as I read over the various reports that protocol had provided concerning the customs of the tiny country and my role at the state dinner as the designated "babysitter" for the foreign president's daughter.

Okay, so she was nineteen and not a baby.

Both Drew and I were being asked to sit with her to provide sparkling, youthful conversation so that the three of us wouldn't get so bored that we'd fall asleep in our soup dishes.

My only problem was that I couldn't figure out how a country so small and so new could have such elaborate rituals already.

I stood staring at my closet, trying to decide what to wear. Aunt Patsy had made several recommendations, including one dress that a designer had sent me in hopes of winning a First Daughter style sanction.

It was hideous, with ruffles in places that God never meant to be ruffled.

I decided to wear a dark green velvet long-sleeved gown with a turtleneck collar. The protocol report had mentioned something about the African country's custom of placing your hand on your exposed neck as an invitation to the opposite sex. It'd be just my luck to wear something low-cut, then forget, scratch my neck, and discover I'd just propositioned every man in the diplomatic party.

The hoopla began at seven with a reception, then the sit-down dinner started at eight. I still had time to kill before the party, and I decided to catch up on my e-mail. In the last few days, I'd been ignoring most of it, only reading whatever bits of information Charlie sent me.

I looked at the "In" box and started sorting the messages into files, deleting the SPAM (yes, the President's daughter gets her unfair share of SPAM, too) and trying to pick out the friends from the merely curious.

I'd just started wading into the good stuff when my phone rang.

"Eve? It's Carl Wallerston. Do you have a minute?" His voice sounded hoarse with some intense emotion.

"Sure."

"Could I trouble you to come down to my office? There are some pictures I want to show you."

I glanced down at my jeans, sweatshirt, and fuzzy bedroom slippers and hesitated for a moment. So far, I hadn't emerged from our private quarters without taking some basic efforts to make my appearance presentable. We're not talking full makeup and the like, but just the standard stuff—clean clothes, hair brushed, etc.

"Sure," I said, forcing myself to sound chipper. "I'll be right down."

You've heard of Presidents' Day? This was going to be Precedence Day. It was high time I proved—more to myself than others—that this wasn't just the White House, but it was my house, my *home*, too.

At least for the next four years.

I did make one concession and gave up my bunny slippers, trading them for a pair of real shoes. But otherwise, when I went downstairs, I went in my grungy jeans, my faded high school sweatshirt (*Go, Rams!*) and with my hair pulled back in a ratty ponytail.

To his credit, my Dawg said nothing about my appearance. (He, with the off-the-rack suit and worn shoes. I wondered what we paid these people. I doubted it was enough.)

Luckily, I ran into no one but house staff on the trip down. Carl's door was open and he was sitting at his desk, which was even more cluttered than usual. Before I could say a word, he jumped up, motioning for me to take his seat. "That was fast."

As soon as I was seated, he shoved a magnifying glass in my hand.

"I've been examining the photos from the paper." He stabbed the top picture with his forefinger. "Look here." He shifted my hand so that the magnifying glass hovered over a small table caught in the background behind the bodies caught in midgyration. It was one of the shots from the role of film we'd found.

"On the table." He pointed to a small plate sitting upright in a stand beside a tall lamp topped with a globe. The picture was clear enough to make out flowers on the plate.

He tapped another picture, this time from one of the ones Michael and I had shot in the real Lincoln bedroom. "And here."

Same location. Same plate.

"And here." It was one of the shots we'd taken on

the movie set before the Grim Reaper so rudely interrupted us. Evidently, Seybold had been feeding him
shots, probably taking the curator up on his offer to try
to authenticate the furnishings. Again, the plate sat in
the same place.

Shivers of excitement began to crawl up my back.
"You mean you've found something?" I began to compare the pictures, looking for discrepancies. "What is
it? Wrong plate? Wrong size?"

"As far as I can tell, they're identical."

Okay, I didn't get it. I told him so. "Are you telling
me that our entire hypothesis was wrong? That the pictures weren't taken on the set?"

He shook his head. "No. I'm telling you that someone took meticulous care in re-creating the Lincoln
bedroom."

Okay, Sherlock, tell me something I don't know.

He turned to his computer and pointed to the screen.
"And, according to my records, that plate was removed
from the Lincoln bedroom from October 16 through
December 30 because it had been chipped and was being repaired." He pushed back from the desk, triumphant. "Any pictures taken in the Lincoln bedroom
during that time frame would not have included this
item. So if the man in these pictures insists that they
were taken in November, then they weren't taken here.
They couldn't have possibly been."

I kissed the man on the top of his balding head.
"You're fantastic, Mr. Wallerston. Absolutely fantastic."

He blushed and brushed down his hair with one
hand. "Thank you, my dear. Hopefully, Mr. Seybold

will share your opinion of my investigative abilities . . .
but I also hope he will demonstrate his appreciation in
a less exuberant manner."

"Have you told him what you've found?" I asked.

"I will do so immediately. I just thought that, since
it was your interview with me that brought me into the
case, so to speak, you deserved to be the first to know."

How can you say thank-you for something like
that—both for the compliment, and for his maybe even
helping to get my Dad off the hook?

I almost skipped into the elevator, optimistic about
the case we were building against media attacks. But
I'm not stupid. So far, most of our proof relied on in-
house records—records that the press would say could
have been changed or altered to support what we called
the facts. *I* knew they hadn't been changed, but in light
of the legal troubles suffered by previous administrations, would the American public believe our claims
this time?

However, if Lieutenant Lange of the NYPD came
up with independent and incontrovertible proof that
provided reasonable motive and opportunity for the
person at the center of this mess, then we might come
out of it not smelling like rose fertilizer.

But could we last that long?

Until then, life and diplomacy went on.

That evening, as we stood waiting for President Ma-
bassah and his entourage to arrive, Michael sidled up
to me, under the guise of taking a picture of me and
Drew. It was an unnecessary subterfuge, but I guess he
was having a hard time getting out of investigative
mode.

He pointed the camera elsewhere. "Got a call right before I left, from Lieutenant Lange," he whispered.

"She had to cancel your date because it was time for her to return to the mother ship?"

Drew shot me a puzzled look. "Wha-huh?"

Michael lowered the camera and grinned at Drew. "She's a heavenly body who is also a lieutenant in the New York PD." He paused, then gave me a quick glance.

I nodded. "He knows everything. Dad insists."

Michael raised his camera and continued talking in a low voice that no one else could hear. "Terry said—"

"You're on a first-name basis already? Whoa . . . Who's the fast worker? You or her?"

He and Drew both shot me the same brotherly scowl. Michael continued. "As I said before I was rudely interrupted, Terry called me and said that so far, they'd found nothing. Glove prints, but not fingerprints. No one was on that set who wasn't supposed to be there— actors, crew, suits."

Drew spoke up first. "Then the killer is part of the production."

I stared at my brother. It wasn't the insight that alarmed me, but his matter-of-fact delivery. It's uncomfortable to hear your fifteen-year-old brother speak about a murderer with so little emotion.

He shrugged as if reading my thoughts. "It's a cold, cruel world out there."

Michael beat me to the punch. "And you live where it's warm, safe, and protected around the clock. Don't start confusing the two."

I wanted to ask him what he meant, but we got the

high sign from a staffer that the hoopla was about to begin. For the next hour, I smiled, nodded, and moved on cue, making nice with the visitors, and not even grimacing when the president's daughter, Anglika, was foisted on us.

We really didn't get a chance to talk until we sat down to dinner. The boy-girl-boy seating protocol had been changed because of uneven numbers. I sat on one side of Anglika with Drew on the other.

Although she appeared to be a painfully shy girl, she wore a colorfully loud dashiki that was hard to miss from across the dining room. Her matching headdress seemed about five pounds too heavy for her head. Compared with her, I felt positively colorless in my dark green dress.

We were starting the soup course when Anglika reached up and grabbed her headdress, which had started to list toward me. She finally said something besides a platitude: "Darn it, I hate wearing this thing, don'tcha know."

She might have been an African princess, dressed to the nines in her native costume, but she spoke with a dead-on North Dakotan accent.

I practically spewed soup across the table. "What?" I managed to say after I finished choking. I could just imagine the story of how she'd learned English by watching American movies.

Specifically, *Fargo.*

"This head wrap," she complained. "It's a real pain." She eyed Drew's suit, which luckily still fit, even though the inauguration had been four long weeks ago.

What can I say? The kid's growing.

Anglika sighed. "You're lucky your father doesn't make you dress up in some sort of ridiculous costume for dinner." She'd overcompensated and now the head-piece tilted dangerously in Drew's direction. "Oh, for sweet . . ." she complained, trying to straighten it.

Drew added to the general misery by sticking a finger in his collar and making a face. "Try wearing a tie."

Okay, maybe the suit didn't fit as well as Patsy and I had thought.

She shot him a warm grin. "Trade you my headdress for your tie."

"Deal." He pretended to start tugging off his tie.

"Drew, stop," I hissed. I turned to Anglika. "It's not that I don't appreciate international trading, but I'm not sure the dinner table is the right place for it."

She released a tinkling laugh that had an infectious quality about it. "Point taken." She turned to Drew. "I guess we all have our own crosses to bear, eh?" Now the accent bordered on Canadian, which, I suppose, was only appropriate, since North Dakota bordered on Canada as well.

Curiosity reared its ugly head and I was powerless to stop myself. "You have an . . . interesting accent. Where did you learn English?"

Her grin amplified. "Prairie Rose Elementary School in Bismarck, North Dakota, then Wachter Middle School, and after that Bismarck High. Now I'm a fresh-man at Minnesota State University–Moorhead. That's right across the Red River from Fargo."

No one has ever said that Drew and I look much alike. Our coloring is different; Drew's dark like Dad, whereas I'm fair, more like my mother. But I knew in my heart, at that moment, we wore identical slack-jawed expressions.

She nodded. "I get that a lot." The head wrap listed forward. *"Uff da,"* she complained while reaching up and steadying it. "This thing is really getting on my nerves."

"You get what a lot?" I managed to say.

"The you've-got-to-be-kidding looks on people's faces." She leaned closer to me. "My dad might be the president of Nimtonzwe, but my mother's a fourth-grade teacher in the Bismarck school district. I grew up there."

We got the entire story, delivered in her dead-on accent, about how her mother had gone to Africa on a Peace Corps mission, fallen in love with a young man, got pregnant with his child, and come back to her hometown of Bismarck to give birth and raise her daughter. It was actually anticlimactic, compared with the "I watched *Fargo* two hundred and forty-eight times" explanation that my overactive imagination had conjured.

Anglika dipped her head as much as her headdress would allow. "I've told you my secret. Now how 'bout you telling me yours?"

I shared a puzzled look with Drew. "What secret?"

She leaned forward, precariously, and lowered her voice to a whisper. "Is it true what they say? That your father is going to step down from office before he's impeached?"

CHAPTER TWELVE

I got angry.

More than angry; I became incensed. I'm lucky I didn't stand up and start yelling. Instead, I forced myself to keep my voice low and my face expressionless, but I couldn't keep the emotion out of my words. "Who is spreading that filth?"

She swallowed hard and pulled back, probably afraid she'd get singed by the fire I was breathing.

"Uh . . . I don't know. I overheard someone talking about it in my political science class."

I tried not to shake my fist at her. It was a struggle. The words "Don't kill the messenger" reverberated in my brain and probably saved us both major embarrassment. Instead, I held my clenched hands in my lap, hiding them beneath the tablecloth. "Well, you tell whoever said that that my father *isn't* going to resign, because he *isn't* going to be impeached, because he *didn't* take any money under the table for his campaign."

She swallowed hard again and scooted her chair away from me as much as she could without landing in Drew's lap.

I've noticed I have that effect on people when I'm really steaming mad. I hadn't felt this incensed since Dad's opponent tried to pull some dirty campaign tricks on us.

Suddenly, I felt someone tap me on my shoulder. I turned to see Michael standing behind my chair. For some reason, his patently blank look irritated me. Hadn't he heard what she said? After all, he lived out there in the "real world." Were these sorts of rumors running rampant? Had he kept them to himself rather than upset his boss or his boss's daughter?

"Uh, Eve, I need you for a picture." He wore a smile that didn't quite reach his eyes. Good thing, too. If I thought he was amused by my anger, he'd have been subject to it as well.

"Not now," I said between clenched teeth. I had a few more dozen things I wanted to say to Anglika.

"Now," he said with more force than I expected. With that, he pulled my chair away from the table with me still in it.

I knew full well that this was neither the time nor the place to raise a stink with him, so I managed to adopt an almost polite smile and excused myself to both Anglika and the poor man sitting on the other side of me, who hadn't said a word to me since we sat down.

With my luck, he'd be a reporter for some big newspaper and my Miss-No-Manners act would land me as the lead story in some politico-gossip column.

Michael gripped my arm none too lightly and made it look as if we were going arm and arm out to the hallway rather than the truth: he was hauling me out there against my will.

"What in th' hell is wrong with you?" he whispered once we were safe in the hall.

I stared at him and suffered my first real moment of White House Elitism Syndrome.

I was the President's daughter and *he* was nothing more than some lowly photographer. How dare *he*—

The realization hit me as effectively as a direct punch to the stomach. It was as if I'd been possessed by Willa McClaren. For one long and upsetting moment, I thought I was going to throw up. I took a quick step to the right, almost as if I thought that would shift me out of Willa's sphere of ghostly influence.

Of course, she wasn't dead, so maybe I was simply learning a terrible secret about myself—that I could be just like her if I allowed myself.

Or maybe it was a lesson about absolute power corrupting absolutely. Either way, I felt sick. I shook my head and felt a sudden chill that made me wrap my arms around myself.

Michael's anger turned into concern. "Eve . . . are you okay?"

It took me a moment to find my voice. "Not really.

You realize what I was doing, don't you? Channeling the Wicked Bitch of the East."

He stared at me, confusion filling his eyes. "The wicked who?"

"Willa McClaren. That was one of her White House nicknames. You know the staff here is discreet by the fact that it never made it into the papers. I was about to lambaste you and the words I wanted to use sounded just like something she'd reportedly say." Another shiver grabbed me. "I don't ever want to sound like her or remind anyone of her. Ever."

Any anger he'd experienced earlier was completely gone now. He even offered a small laugh. "Don't worry. From what I've heard about her, you couldn't sound like her if you tried, much less turn into her, even for a moment."

Little did he know.

He continued. "But I knew I had to get you out of there before you blew a cork. What were you two talking about that got you so upset?"

I drew a deep breath, trying to steady nerves that were still a bit frazzled. "Miss North Dakota and I were discussing the rumors concerning Dad and his impending impeachment."

He gaped at me. "His what?" he sputtered. "What a load of crap. Who in the world is saying junk like that?"

I found his reaction to be encouraging: Anglika's revelation seemed to have caught him by surprise, too. Perhaps he hadn't been trying to shield Dad and me from unsavory gossip and accusations circling the globe. . . . Or perhaps he'd simply not heard this latest one.

Of course, I couldn't use my usual isolation theory as an excuse. How isolated could I be from rumors and innuendos in the White House when I had access to a slew of daily newspapers, a couple hundred satellite channels, not to mention the Internet?

Yet, I did feel isolated.

Alone.

Shoved away into corner and surrounded by Secret Service agents like some stupid porcelain doll. I glanced at the nearest agent, who stood at a discreet distance, close enough to protect, but far enough to pretend he couldn't hear every word I said.

Michael followed my gaze for a brief moment, then turned back to me, new confusion filling his face. "Okay, I understand about the rumor, but what I don't understand is the Miss North Dakota reference. Who are you talking about?"

"Anglika, the African president's daughter." I shrugged in the direction of the State Dining Room. "Engage her in conversation. It's like talking to an extra from the movie *Fargo*." He started to speak, but I waved away his remark. "Never mind. It's a long story, I'll tell you later. But what she's saying about rumors circulating about Dad's resignation or impeachment, that's totally off-base, right?"

He nodded with enough conviction to make me feel a bit better. "Totally. The latest scuttlebutt I heard was that President McClaren engineered this entire thing because your dad edged him out of power in the party."

I contemplated the concept, but it just didn't work

for me. "As much as I'd like to believe that—and I really would—it's too far-fetched. Someone's behind this, but I don't know who or why, and I really don't think it's President McClaren."

"Me, either, but, anyway, that's the latest gossip I've heard."

Applause suddenly rippled through the dining room and both of us knew we had to return to the "festivities," me as First Family set decoration and Michael with a real job to perform. But as we entered, Anglika and Drew were exiting. We all paused in the doorway for an uncomfortable moment.

Drew shot me a guarded smile. "Dad said we could leave before the speech if we wanted to. Me and Angie thought we'd head upstairs and play Nintendo for a while." He gave me the evil eye. "You're going to stay here, right?"

I wasn't sure if I was being warned off because of my lack of decorum while at the table or because Drew was developing a sudden crush on an older woman. Somehow, I didn't think the latter was the case.

At least, I hoped not. It was a complication none of us needed at the moment.

"Uh . . . no, thanks." I turned to Anglika and stuttered through an apology for my less-than-hospitable reaction. She accepted it with surprising grace and offered what seemed like a truly honest request to "forget about it."

In punishment, I returned to the dinner table to endure the after-dinner speeches. Mind you, I think my dad's a good speaker, but even he can't make some subjects too terribly interesting. As he spoke on "Economic Trends in the Twenty-First Century," I battled to stay awake. Every once in a while, I'd catch sight of Michael, who floated around soundlessly, snapping pictures of the guests, of Dad, and, on occasion, of me. Of course, when it came to taking pictures of me, he'd hold the camera at an awkward angle, just to get me tickled.

I didn't have a chance to tell him how I appreciated his efforts to keep me awake until the next day when he showed up just before lunch.

His timing was, of course, impeccable. Aunt Patsy, playing First Hostess with the Mostest, felt compelled to invite him to join us for Sunday dinner.

"There's always enough food," she said with a smile as one of the butlers bustled up with another place setting.

As First Lady, Aunt Patsy had had the responsibility to choose which china service out of the house's immense collection best represented the Cooper administration for family meals, but it'd been no hard choice. She'd fallen to love with the FDR china the first time she saw a place setting in the Smithsonian. It was perhaps the plainest of the twentieth-century pieces in the collection. The presidential seal had been placed along the top edge of the plate and a simple navy blue and gold band circled the plate edges.

Initially, I considered it almost an act of historical desecration to pile our food on such obvious museum pieces, but Patsy stoutly believed it was no more sacrilegious than using Great-Grandma Cooper's china.

Our very first official White House meal had been served on the Reagan china. I remembered the hoopla from when when Mrs. Reagan ordered the china. She'd been quickly vindicated when America realized there weren't enough settings in any one presidential china set to seat a decent-sized state dinner. Dad jokingly complained that he felt like a little kid, being told to eat his entire meal so he could see the pretty pattern on the bottom of the plate.

Me, I didn't like the sight of my mashed potatoes and gravy smeared across the Great Seal of the United States.

So we all sat down, Michael included, to Sunday dinner, eating from the FDR china and chatting about any and every subject except the one that was on all of our minds—those stupid pictures and their growing list of repercussions.

Drew was the most successful in distracting us. He blathered nonstop about Anglika and her RPG-playing prowess. From what he said, apparently, she was taking "Role-Playing Games as a Communication Tool 101" in college.

I remarked that it sounded like the twenty-first-century techno version of "Underwater Basket-Weaving for Varsity Athletes." I'd figured she was pulling Drew's leg. However, Drew staunchly believed exactly what she'd described, as if college were some magical place where your homework could consist of playing video games and your grades were based on your ability to save the virtual universe.

He crossed his arms in defiance. "Angie's doing a term paper on the transmutation of the game with re-spect to processor speed," he said with his sincerest look.

"How interesting," I said, deadpan. "What's next? 'The Financial Effects of Monopoly on Real Estate Prices in Atlantic City'?"

Drew glared at me with a sort of "I know you've just insulted me, but I don't quite understand it" look.

Michael took up for Drew, very much like Charlie would have, had he been there. "Hey, think about it, Drew. The faster the processor and the bigger the memory, the better-looking Lara Croft becomes. I'm just waiting until she gets completely lifelike." He adopted a theatrically dreamy look.

" 'Lifelike' and Lara Croft are not compatible terms," I complained.

Drew turned pointedly away from me and toward Michael. "Yeah, think about her." His voice deepened. "In three-D." His vacant stare was far from theatrical.

I had the urge to kick him under the table.

And then kick Michael for egging him on.

Dad leaned forward with a puzzled smile. "Who is this Lara Croft?" His smile deepened, losing its sense of puzzlement. "And exactly *how* lifelike is she?"

Patsy and I spoke in one unified voice: "Never mind!"

We all managed to distract one another through the rest of the meal and the postdinner visit in the den. Dad was being nice to sit there when what I know he wanted to do was to find some sports show on TV to keep him occupied now that football was over.

He's a Green Bay fan.

Go figure.

Finally, we'd reached the point where Dad had fulfilled his host duties, Drew was wandering back to his room for some up-close-and-personal time with the aforementioned Lara Croft, and Michael was giving me a none-too-secret high sign that screamed, *We need to talk.* Privately.

We excused ourselves and went upstairs to the solarium, where Michael accepted a soda and found a comfortable, stretched-out position on my couch.

He heaved a satisfied sigh. "Man, oh, man, but you guys eat good."

I sat in the end chair, since he'd left me no room on the couch. "A traditional Sunday dinner seems to be really important to the staff. They definitely knock themselves out over it. I think it's because they feel we have such plebeian tastes during the week. If he could get away with it, Drew'd eat a burger and fries every night. Dad's not much better."

He patted his stomach. "Well, some traditions deserve to live on forever, plebeian tastes or not."

We sat in silence for a few moments. When I get stuffed at midday, I usually get sleepy, so I had to fight hard not to nod off. I disguised my yawn with a cough. "So did you come here just to sponge a meal off your boss, or do you have some other, ulterior motive?"

He waited a moment before answering. "Both, I guess. Actually, I was wondering how ol' Drew made out last night with the African Queen."

I was about to tear into him, but I saw a telltale twinkle in his eye that said, *Just baiting you, babe.* So instead of getting on my high horse, I maintained a lower mount. "Very funny. Remember, he's fifteen."

"So?"

"And she's in college. Not in his *wildest* dreams."

Michael stared off into the distance, his smile soft-ening a bit. "I remember harboring some really wild dreams at his age." He shook off his brief reverie. "So, what was with the 'Miss North Dakota' jibe last night? I thought she was some princess or something."

"Evidently, Mommy and Daddy met in Africa, made a baby, and Mommy came back to the United States with Baby Angie in tow. Your 'African princess' ac-tually grew up in Nort' Dah-koda," I said in fair ap-proximation of her flat accent, "and is going to school in Min-ne-so-tah to major in computer games."

Michael looked dumbfounded. "Then Drew was tell-ing the truth? She really told him that?"

"Evidently so. She and Drew played video games up here for several hours. Evidently, she must be making an *A* in her gaming course because, although Drew won't admit it, she *royally* stomped his butt." I laughed at my own pun.

Michael rolled his eyes. "An older and wiser woman, eh?"

"Older than him? Yes. Wiser? That's subject to de-bate. At least she has better hand-eye coordination than he does."

Our conversation faded to silence as we repeated our stalling techniques, perfected during our lunch. Finally, he spoke. "What's next?"

I looked up after a careful study of my nails. "Huh?"

Michael sat up and leaned forward. "What are we going to do next?"

For one moment, one very short and very weird mo-ment, I wondered what he meant by "we."

He continued, evidently oblivious to my momentary

confusion. "What is it the cops on television always talk about? Motive and opportunity? We've done a lot of work toward opportunity—establishing the place where the pictures were probably taken—but we've danced around the other half of the equation. Motive. The 'why.'" He laced his fingers and rested his chin on the top of his knuckles. "Why Stansfield? What does he have against your dad?"

I shrugged. "Why does anybody hate a public figure? Maybe Dad represents everything Stansfield hates, politically."

"Possibly . . ."

We both fell silent.

Then after a minute or so, Michael spoke. "*Cherchez la femme.*"

"The woman in the picture?"

"Among others. Actually, I was thinking about Stansfield's soon-to-be-ex-wife. What's her take on this? It seems to me she's an injured party, too. What if she caught on to her husband's infidelity and decided to publicly expose him, so to speak?"

I cringed over his choice of words, but he had found an angle nobody'd considered. At least, *I* hadn't considered it. "You think Mr. Seybold has talked to her?"

"Possibly. But we could, too." He stopped for a moment, then met my gaze directly. "Talk to her, that is."

For one long moment, it sounded like a great plan. Find Mrs. Stansfield and question her. How simple was that?

Then reality hit me like a dope-slap on the forehead. "Okay, which Hardy boy are you going to be this time? Joe or Frank?"

He blushed. "Okay, okay. I've learned my lesson. We should leave the investigation to the professionals. But aren't you curious?"

I could have lied. I could have made him believe that I had overcome my rampant curiosity. But why lie to myself or to him?

I shifted to the edge of the chair. "Curious doesn't begin to describe how I feel. It's as if I have every right in the world to dig out the truth. More important, I feel like if I don't do it, I can't trust anyone else to do it, either."

He shot me a squinty look. "You don't trust Seybold? A professional investigator?"

I waved away Michael's concern. "Of course I do. He's good, and thorough, too. He's got a lot riding on this. But he doesn't have the same emotional investment that I do. Bosses, even presidents, come and go. But when I look at this mess, I'm not simply talking about clearing my boss. I'm talking about my father. . . ." I couldn't help but let the emotion creep into my voice.

A tear slid down my cheek. "*My* dad . . ."

I have to give Michael credit. He didn't try to soothe me with false platitudes, or tell me that everything was going to be okay, or whitewash my concerns, or blame my outburst on rampant emotions, hormones, or whatever.

He sat there quietly, handed me a Kleenex, and allowed me to blubber and get everything out of my system. After a few moments of drippy silence, I gave a final sniff and straightened up.

"Better?" he asked in a quiet voice.

I nodded. "Yeah. Thanks."

"You know what you need?" A small smile tugged at the corners of his mouth.

Should I be afraid of what he was going to say? I swiped at my eyes. "What?" I said bravely.

"Distraction. When's the last time you left this place?"

"And didn't run into a dead body?" I sighed, immediately discounting my jaunt to O'Connor's apartment. "Seems like never."

"Then I know what we need to do . . ."

Two hours later, I sat on a barstool, surrounded by Michael's friends and my Secret Service detail, sipping a microbrew.

"Better?" he said for the second time that night, this time shouting to be heard above the competing bar noise.

"Absolutely," I yelled back. "You think we could set up an in-house brewery in the White House?"

He stroked his chin in mock thought. "Bet it wouldn't be the first time."

That was the extent of our discussion about the White House, Dad's problems, and even politics in general. Considering that political topics form the basis of most conversations in D.C., I figured Michael had told his friends that the subject was verboten for the night. Instead, we discussed all the movies I hadn't seen yet, TV programs that I had, and books that I intended to read.

In the years of precampaigning, hard-core campaigning, the election, the inauguration, and our introduction into presidential life, my social life hadn't been my own. Sure, I went on elaborate trips, to fancy dinners, met famous people, but it was all for Dad, for the campaign. And during those occasions, I wasn't Eve Cooper, independent, autonomous soul, but merely an extension of my father. While I didn't mind pushing back my own individuality to help represent Dad, I was secretly glad I didn't have to for just this one evening. I couldn't remember the last time I'd been out with my own friends, just to hang out. Even worse, most of my friends now lived a thousand miles away. What I needed to do was find friends in town, but I had the same problem that Drew had: Did people like me because I'm Eve Cooper or because I'm the First Daughter? And where would I go to meet people in this town? Something told me that the Secret Service had strong opinions about the places it was proper for me to mingle.

I took a sip of my beer and watched Michael's best buddy, Craig, throw his head back and erupt in laughter. Craig then turned to me. "Did Mike ever tell you about the time he got caught in the tree while photographing a diplomatic motorcade?"

When I glanced at Michael, he was already in full blush. Evidently, it was a good story. "Go on," I prompted.

"Now, who was that guy again, Mike? Some Saudi sheikh and his harem?" He didn't wait for an answer and continued with his story. "Well, anyway, Mike was standing on the corner near the embassy when the gate swung open, knocking him off his feet. The limo barreled down the driveway toward him." He turned to Michael. "C'mon, you tell the story. You do it so well."

Michael shrugged, his face still containing a telltale tinge of red. "After I fell, the gate started swinging over me. The only thing I could do was jump onto the gate and hold on for dear life. But then it started swinging back toward the wall and it was either jump into a nearby tree or get smashed up against the wall. The only problem is that when I jumped into the tree, a branch snagged my pants—"

Craig interrupted. "That wasn't the only thing the branch snagged."

Michael's face turned from a dusty rose to a flaming red. "Remind me to tell Eve someday about your trip to Vegas," he said between gritted teeth.

Craig colored as well, but recovered nicely. "You wouldn't dare." He gave me a grin. "Let's just say that Mikey-boy has an interesting scar on his butt. The funniest part is that it took the paramedics a half hour to figure out how to get him down."

"Funny only to masochistic souls like you," Michael said into his beer mug.

Craig shook his head. "At least you didn't make the eleven o'clock news. It cost me a nice sum to convince the news crew not to let you be that You'll-Never-Believe-This humor story of the night."

The group started telling stories on one another, each successive story wilder and more unbelievable. The silliness of the banter was exactly what I needed to divert my thoughts. And I welcomed the distraction.

And the beer.

And the sense that I was just the new kid on the

block rather than a new resident of 1600 Pennsylvania Avenue.

We drank, told more impossible stories, and made merry until the wee hours, until the manager tiptoed over to inform us it was closing time. He braced himself as if ready to get an argument from us.

It took me a moment to realize that we must have chosen a place where Willa McClaren had hung out. God, but would I ever escape that girl's shadow?

I was steadier than I expected, making it to my feet without swaying or lurching. I gave him a smile, which seemed to take him by surprise. "Then we had better be on our way. Thank you, sir." I pulled out the wallet I'd stuffed in the back pocket of my jeans and took out my credit card. A moment after I dropped it on the counter, Michael placed his hand over it.

He leaned in closer. "Don't try to pick up the entire bar tab," he whispered. "You're just Eve. You pay your part, kick in on the tip, and just be one of the gang."

"Thanks," I said, and meant it. The last thing I wanted to do was overstep the comfortable position Michael had found for me in his group of friends. I retrieved my Visa card and fished out some bills. I had a five and a couple of ones. I looked up at Michael and grinned at him. "I'm a little short."

Craig leaned over. "Naw, you're just the right size." He snorted in laughter.

Michael rolled his eyes.

I turned to the manager. "Would you take a check?"

The man stuttered, then recovered nicely. "Umm, well . . . sure."

I pulled out my checkbook, snagged a pen from the

bar, and began to write out a check. I hadn't changed my accounts or had new checks printed since we moved, so this one still had my Denver address. I scratched through it and wrote "1600 Pennsylvania Ave., Washington, D.C." Then my mind went blank. I turned to Michael and whispered, "What's my zip code?"

"Two-zero-five-zero-zero. Forget your phone number, too?"

I stuck my tongue out at him. "I remember the switchboard number. That's what I'm supposed to give out."

I handed the bartender the check and started rifling through my wallet for my driver's license.

"No need." The bartender added a laugh. "I recognize you." He glanced at the check. "And thanks for the tip."

I smiled sweetly at him. "Thanks for taking my check."

Much to the Dawgs' dismay, I insisted on walking home. Blame the booze for making me a little more vocal and demanding, but, I hasten to add, politely so. It was only six blocks to the house, and I hoped the brisk outdoor temperature would help me clear my head.

I'd had a lovely evening off from all the worries and the cares that had been dogging me for the past couple weeks. As soon as I got back home, my self-imposed duties would resume. If nothing else, tomorrow was a school day for Drew and I needed to continue my morning mothering role, even if Patsy didn't have any trips scheduled for a while.

Our walk back to the house was uneventful. No marauding terrorists. No screaming picketers. No encounters with unsavory types other than one homeless man who was sound asleep by a steam vent and didn't stir as our entourage trooped by. Most of Michael's friends separated from the pack when we reached the entrance to the Metro station. Michael remained with us for the walk back to the house, seeing me safely to the guard shack.

We stood inside the gate, the Secret Service and guards ever-attentive but giving us a modicum of privacy.

Michael stooped a little to even out the height difference between us. "Feeling better?"

"I do now. But the jury's out on tomorrow morning. It's bad enough facing Drew any morning, but doing it with a hangover . . . I'm not looking forward to that."

He punched me lightly on the arm, reminding me of a guy named Bobby whom I knew in sixth grade. He was always knocking me on the arm. Until that first time that he kissed me. Then I'd responded by socking him in the chest.

"You won't have a hangover," Michael assured me. "You didn't drink that much."

"Maybe not. I'm probably more buzzed than sloshed."

He leaned over and planted a rather sloppy kiss on my forehead. "Then take your cute little buzzed body inside and upstairs. I'll probably see you tomorrow sometime. I'm not sure when."

He pivoted a bit unsteadily. "Night, Eve."

As he departed, one of the Dawgs signaled to a gate

guard by pointing to Michael. The guard stopped him, putting an arm around his shoulder in the old pal-to-pal way. The man asked Michael something in a low voice and, evidently, Michael's answer was sufficient because the guard released him, clapped him on the back, and returned to his station.

As Michael stumbled away, the guard turned to us. "Don't worry. He's walking home, not driving."

"Thanks for checking," I called out. I turned back to the Dawgs. "I guess this is as much a babysitting job as anything else. . . ."

The taller of the two shrugged. "Sometimes." He opened the door for me and a warm blast of air hit us. A moment later, a sudden wave of fatigue hit me. I placed a hand on the nearest Dawg's arm.

"I don't usually drink much. I only had three beers."

"Four," the shorter Dawg corrected.

I nodded. "That's right. I won the last one playing darts, which is pretty good if you think about it. I had three beers and I still hit the dartboard. Then again, as I recall, Craig missed the target completely." I released a big sigh. "And I guess we should be thankful he missed the other people there, too." I giggled. "I can just see you two giving your report: 'We removed our subject from the premises because a bar fight broke out over an errant missile, which embedded itself in a patron's gluteus maximus.'"

The shorter Dawg failed to hide his grin. "Something like that," he tried to say in deadpan.

I drew a solemn cross over my heart. "I promise you I won't be doing this a lot. Going out and getting tipsy. Buzzed." I sighed. "Let's be truthful. I'm just this side of drunk." I shrugged. "Tomorrow morning, I'm going to wake up feeling lousy and curse myself for drinking that fourth beer, and I'll swear off alcohol for at least two months."

I shot them my prettiest smile. "And next time, I'll stop at three, even if I do have a chance to become the darts champion of the universe."

"Good idea," the taller one said. He grabbed my arm, bracing me as my foot hit the landing a little hard and I stumbled.

I made it the rest of the way through the house without help. When we reached the elevator, the shorter Dawg stopped and turned to me. "Would you like for us to get someone to help you upstairs to your room, Miss Cooper?"

"Thanks, but no thanks. I'll be fine. I'm going to hit the kitchen first. I think some toast might help settle my stomach and soak up some of the remaining alcohol." I flashed them a grin, which, hopefully, wasn't lopsided. "I'm really sorry to have dragged you out to a place where you had to watch everyone else have a good time but you had to be on the clock yourselves."

The shorter one blushed slightly. "That's okay.

"It's our job."

"And you do that job very well. I felt very protected tonight."

"Good night, Ms. Cooper."

"Please, it's Eve," I pressed. "And it'll still be Eve tomorrow and the next day, too."

"Yes, ma'am."

I rode up in silence, wondering why it felt as if the elevator were going sideways. Once the door slid open,

I took a few nonstaggering steps toward the kitchen, then changed my mind and headed for the stairs instead. The flight was longer than I remembered, and by the time I reached the third floor, I was exhausted. I dragged myself into my room and threw myself on my bed. Something crackled beneath my shoulder and I rolled over, pulling free a sheet of paper.

It was a sobering note from Aunt Patsy.

> *Roger Stansfield's wife called—thinks you're in that picture with husband—threatening to name you in divorce proceedings. Wants to talk directly to you first.*

I closed my eyes. *Oh, crap . . .*

CHAPTER **THIRTEEN**

Everyone wanted me to stay out of things, to let the lawyers handle the gory details and negotiations and be the ones who provided proof of my innocence.

But I couldn't do that.

I knew in my heart that if I could simply talk to the woman, this whole situation could be stopped, immediately, before it was dragged into the public arena either through the courts or through the media.

Call it faith. Call it naivete. Call it inexperience.

Or call it instinct.

In whatever case, Dad listened to me, long and hard, and finally agreed to let me handle it my way. However, he did insist that I not make the meeting arrangements personally, so it became a matter of "my people" talking with "her people" until we had all agreed on a meeting in neutral territory.

In this case, neutral territory was a private home in Columbia, Maryland, about halfway between Baltimore and D.C. The folks who owned the house were acquaintances of both Alice Stansfield and my aunt Patsy, and the family were willing for us to descend on their home as neutral ground for our little tête-à-tête.

During the trip there, I rehearsed my speech. Dad's legal counsel had grilled me on various aspects of the law, but I boiled it down to three basic phrases:

> *"I've never met your husband."*
> *"I've never slept with your husband."*
> *"That's not me in the picture."*

When we reached the house, there was the obligatory dark sedan waiting outside. More Secret Service Dawgs prowled around on the grounds, and one agent motioned us through the gated driveway entrance.

We followed the thin, winding ribbon of asphalt leading to the house, which was a two-story, red-brick Georgian with white trim. As we drove up, I could see a large wing jutting out the back of the house, as well as a detached five-car garage. That garage was bigger than the last apartment I lived in. And after remembering my apartment, I couldn't help but think about my own car, a '65 Mustang, fully restored. It had been sitting in storage for two months now. Previous White House kids had advised me it'd take an act of God for me to go out driving any time for the next several years. I know it was an exaggeration, but considering the traffic problems in D.C., I wasn't all that sure I wanted to subject myself to the trouble of facing road rage, finding a parking place, or learning all the one-way streets. After all, it wasn't like I had to commute in from the suburbs for the next four years.

Why only four years? I knew that, unless the free world collapsed about our ears, Dad would probably run for a second term, but I also figured that once Drew went to college, I could hightail it out of D.C. and head back to Denver, where I could hopefully regain some semblance of a normal life.

With my Secret Service Dawgs trailing behind me, of course.

Perchance to drive again . . .

Diana Gates, today's assigned Dawg, gave me an inquisitive look as the car glided to a stop. "Ready?"

I showed her my crossed fingers. "As much as I'll ever be."

We exited the car and before we could even reach the front door, it swung open to reveal Esmerelda Mc-Lean, our hostess.

She and Aunt Patsy had met on the campaign trail and developed a fast, strong friendship. I'd met her once before and understood immediately why Patsy had liked the tall, dark-haired woman; Esmerelda had a no-nonsense, positive attitude, and she told you exactly what she thought. In the Beltway world of being polit-ically correct at all times, Esmerelda McLean was a refreshing exception to the rule.

Today, she gave me a pale imitation of her usually broad smile, but did award me with one of her bone-

cracking hugs. "Good to see you again, Eve. I wish it
was under better circumstances."

"Thanks, Mrs. McLean. Me, too. We really appreciate you letting us meet here."

She nodded. "I'll do anything I can to help your
family. You know that."

We did indeed. And we knew she didn't expect anything in return, politically speaking.

She led me through the hallway, its modern black
and gray decorations in stark contrast to the conven-
tional architecture outside.

She paused by a large doorway and nodded inside.
"Alice's waiting for you."

I closed my eyes for a moment and repeated my
litany of lines once more:

> *"I've never met your husband."*
> *"I've never slept with your husband."*
> *"That's not me in the picture."*

But when I stepped into the black, gray, and now
mauve living room, I couldn't edge out a single word.
Alice Stansfield took one look at me and burst into
tears.

So instead of exonerating myself, I spent the first
five, almost ten minutes comforting her. I edged her
over to the couch, where we sat down together. I
couldn't quite say all the usual platitudes like "It'll be
okay . . . everything will be all right . . . it's not as bad
as you think" because, as far as I knew, none of them
was correct.

Instead, I stuck with "You'll get through this . . . we can work together . . ."

The last one got her attention. She sniffed, brushed her hand across her eyes, and leveled me with a stare that looked suspiciously dry-eyed. "What do you mean, 'work together'?"

I reached down and stuffed my hand into the briefcase I'd brought with me. "First, I'm not the woman in the pictures." I shuffled through its contents for my first show-and-tell.

Seybold had provided me a stack of prints from the roll we'd found. I had a variety of shots, presorted in order from tame to squeamishly erotic. I went for the shock value and spread the worst of them faceup across the coffee table.

Call me cruel. But I had to know exactly what role she was playing in this debacle: innocent bystander or compatriot in crime.

She betrayed herself by growing pale. If her tears had been an act, as I couldn't help but suspect under the circumstances, I felt I had regained the upper hand with the stark reality of the pictures. She stared at them silently.

I waited a minute for the full impact of the shots to hit her. There were at least two shots that I placed on top, making sure they were—shall we say—well exposed. If they didn't get to her, nothing would.

I spoke softly. "The only things I have in common with the woman in this photo are that we're both women, and we're both blond." I pointed to one picture where the lighting accentuated the mystery woman's breasts, which were quite voluptuous. "She's got a

much better body than I'll ever have without serious
plastic surgery. Especially there." I tapped the offending and protruding features on the glossy photo. "I'm
willing to strip down if you find it necessary for comparison."

She started to speak, then clamped her mouth shut.
I wondered what she had stopped herself from saying.

I continued. "Also, her waist has to be three inches
smaller than mine, and she's at least two inches taller
than me, judging from the furniture. She has a model's
figure. Whether it's for better or worse, I assure you I
don't."

Then I shot my last volley. "But I do have something
that she doesn't." I untucked my blouse from my skirt
waistband and lifted it to show her the mole. I then
turned, reached into my briefcase, and pulled out *The
Washington Post*. "And so you know for sure that identifying mark wasn't airbrushed out of our shots, you
can see the lack of mole in the picture from the *Post*."

Alice studied both the pictures and me for an inor-
dinate length of time. I've never felt so self-conscious
in my life. And that even includes the inglorious moment when I sneezed in the middle of my father's inauguration oath.

After several minutes, she released a sigh. "It's not
you." This time, real tears formed in her eyes and she
began to cry. "It would have been so much easier if
it'd been you."

"For you, maybe. Not for me."

She hiccuped a laugh in the midst of the sobs. "Point
taken." This time when she wiped her eyes, they were

still red-rimmed and moist. "You mentioned working together. How?"

I gathered the pictures and turned them over so we didn't have to witness the frozen expressions of rapture in them for any longer than we had to. "Your husband has implied that he made a hefty donation to my father's campaign. Even worse, he claims the money was given on behalf of the tobacco industry. Our records don't support this, and it's raised serious questions about my father's campaign finances. Did you know about the donation when it was made?"

She shook her head. "Roger never mentioned it to me. After the story broke, I went back and checked our business records. Roger's books indicated that he pulled out money for the donation from the corporate account, and funneled it through a private account before giving it to your father's war chest. Our personal records also show several large cash withdrawals, which he says are the blackmail payments he made." She regained a little steeliness in her eyes. "To whom, I still don't know. If he knows, he's not telling. But I tend to believe he doesn't. All I'm sure of is that it was a lot of money. Practically every penny we had, all to protect his 'good name.'"

She made a face and tightened her hands into fists. "And what's so *good* about his name? He's the laughingstock of the business now. Everyone knows who he is—the poor schmuck on the front page who got caught with his pants down. 'Poor' is now the operative word in more ways than one—he's taken every cent we have for this little indiscretion."

She had a real head of steam going now and I wasn't

going to interrupt her. It's times like these that you learn more about a person than she expects to reveal. Alice stood up and began to pace around the room.

"I had it all planned," she continued, plunging full speed ahead. "The divorce, I mean. His cheating"—she waved her hand dismissively—"that's not new. He'd done it before, and I knew that if we stayed together, I'd have to expect it again. But he'd started being less discreet. I got tired of him coming in at all hours, smelling of another woman's perfume, of her body." She paused beside the fireplace mantel to examine a framed picture. It was a buddy shot of Esmerelda Mc-Lean, Alice, and another woman, the three of them standing with arms linked, their smiles proclaiming, *Buddies forever. . . .*

"I got tired of watching him appraising other women." She stared a bit too hard at the smiling faces in the picture. "When he walked into a room, you could just see the look of unveiled anticipation in his eyes. He'd pick out his most likely conquest and you could just hear him asking himself, 'When I get her in the sack, will she be a real hellion?' "

Alice paused. *"When,* not *if . . ."* She released a ragged sigh and nodded at the third woman in the framed picture she now held. "Beverly told me he was always propositioning her. At first, she thought he was kidding around. After a while, she realized it was no joke. But I didn't believe her when she told me. I knew he went after women, but figured he'd never make a play for one of my friends."

Alice replaced the picture on the mantle facedown, and I had a feeling that Beverly had finally given in to

Roger Stansfield's insistence, given him the answer he'd been looking for.

"A wife can only take so much, you know," Alice said. Her anger completely drained away, leaving her pale and looking ten years older. "So I told Roger I wanted a divorce. He seemed to take it in stride. We even had some relatively decent conversations about how to break up the household and business finances. I thought it was going to be civil." She spread her hands out, a look of heartfelt despair further aging her face. "But now . . . there's nothing left to split. He mortgaged our house, cashed in our IRA, our investments . . . he used every penny we had to pay off that damned blackmailer."

A moment of heavy silence hung between us. I felt compelled to fill it with the inadequate words, "That's awful!"

"Oh, it gets worse." An even uglier look crossed her features. "The company is going down the tubes, too. Once the story hit the papers, we've been losing clients left and right. They don't want to be associated with us, and I can't really blame them. Even Balfour Industries, the company who started the whole problem in the first place because they wanted to secure a little political largesse with your father, even those rats are leaving our sinking ship." She stared at me. "Of course, they've now realized that their campaign donation bought them nothing in the way of political favor. Roger neglected to credit them as the real source of the money."

I filed this away in my Mental Revelation file. If it

came to it, would she be willing to state that on a witness stand?

She continued. "Together, we have nothing, thanks to him. And half of nothing is still nothing." She buried her face in her hands.

I didn't know what to say. How did you comfort someone in a situation like this? What did you say? *You're not so old. You can start over,* maybe? That would be cold comfort. I said nothing, opting instead to stay quiet.

After a few moments, she gathered up her emotions and turned to me, her control reestablished. "I feel bad, having tried to blame this on you."

I shrugged. "I would have been a good scapegoat. Fairly high profile. Scandalous. Identifiable."

She nodded. "I could have fooled myself into believing it was purely accidental. That he hadn't planned on sleeping with you, but that the temptation to boff the President's beautiful young daughter in the Lincoln bedroom had been too great for him to resist." She gave me a once-over that chilled the cockles of my heart. Somewhere buried in the middle of her statement was a compliment, but it wasn't one I was comfortable with.

She continued. "I even thought he was trying to be somewhat noble, trying to protect your identity, what with you being the President's daughter and all that. But now I don't have that illusion to hang on to." A stone-cold glaze dropped over her eyes and she looked downright scary.

"My husband picked up some tramp, took her to the White House, screwed her brains out, took pictures of it for posterity's sake, then someone got the photos and used them to blackmail him. Not only is he a louse, but he's the stupidest man on the face of the earth."

She unclenched one fist to reveal blood welling up in four curved cuts in the palm of her hand. "I've lost my fortune and my dignity. I used to think I had a chance to get out of this marriage with my sanity. I'm not even sure of that anymore."

I studied her face. A good photographer works on instinct, anticipating what a subject will do, how she will move, what thought process is going through the person's mind. I've learned to read nuances of emotion in the smallest changes in expression.

And everything I could read in the raw emotion that blanketed Alice Stansfield's face said that she was telling me the truth as she knew it.

I suppose it was time for me to return the favor.

I reached into my briefcase and pulled out a second set of photos. She flinched until she saw that the primary subject in the pictures was me and that I was fully clothed. I selected three of the original shots of the naked woman and matched them with the shots of me in the real Lincoln bedroom. Two stark columns laid out neatly on the table, one with a naked blonde, one with me fully clothed.

"You don't need to do this. I believe you," she said.

I ignored her protest. "Paradox Pictures is one of your clients, correct?" Thanks to Charlie, I had that information.

Her expression hardened slightly. "Last time I checked, but that could change tomorrow."

"Are you familiar with their current project, the one that just finished shooting in New York?"

She shook her head. "I don't handle our media clients. That's Roger's responsibility."

"Then you don't know that they're wrapping up a movie, a political-intrigue thriller that takes place partially in the White House."

She shrugged.

I set up a third column, this time with pictures of me, still clothed, taken on the movie set.

I indicated the second column. "These are pictures of me taken in the real Lincoln bedroom." I pointed to the third column. "And these were taken on a movie set in Queens. A Paradox Pictures movie set."

It took a moment for realization to dawn on her face. She leaned closer to the coffee table and examined the photos, her hands clenched as if she was afraid to touch the glossies.

Finally, she picked out corresponding shots from the second and third column. I can't blame her for not wanting to touch the pictures of her nude husband wrapped around another woman.

She cleared her throat. "They look alike. The rooms, I mean."

"They're supposed to. The set decorator was very proud of the painstaking research it took to re-create the original."

I pulled out another set of pictures, the ones that had evidently been taken from the catwalk. She didn't shy from the shot of her husband this time, and openly compared all three shots.

I offered a running commentary. "You can see that the crystal chandelier spoils the re-creation shot we took in the White House. But there's no ceiling on the movie set and therefore no chandelier."

I didn't have to lay any more photos out for her or even mention Mr. Wallerston's revelation about the plate that wasn't in the bedroom during the time Stansfield supposedly had been there.

Alice drew her own conclusion with blinding speed. She stabbed the photograph with her forefinger. "So this shot of my husband was taken in a room with no chandelier. It was taken on the movie set instead!" Animation flickered in her eyes, then dulled to confusion. "But why?"

Why, indeed? I closed my eyes, trying to sort through the confusing assortment of facts and speculations.

Stansfield must have known the pictures were being taken. He had to have seen the photographer—he would have been looking right up at the catwalk in several of those photos. But why was he posing for them? In hopes of using them to blackmail our administration, perhaps? But, instead, had someone else turned the tables on him? That would be ironic—if he was blackmailed with the very shots he hoped to use to blackmail us.

But who would have done it? Sterling O'Connor, deciding he'd rather make a quick buck blackmailing Roger Stansfield?

I shook my head in confusion. Why did everything here seem to boil down to money? Who profited the most from this misfortune? Evidently not Alice . . .

I decided to follow that vein. "When did you first mention divorce to your husband?"

She stared off into the distance. "Last year. We were having a fight and I said something about getting out while the getting was good." A cold glint replaced her look of vague confusion. "We'd had a very good year, last year. If I'd filed right then and there, I'd be walking out of this marriage with one half of a very prosperous business and a substantial personal fortune. But now it's all gone."

"Gone where?" The words slipped right out of my mouth.

She stared at me as if I had suddenly become brainless. "For blackmail, of course."

"For blackmail pictures he posed for? On a movie set where it's normal to see a variety of cameras?"

She stiffened as she began to digest my words.

I continued, my own heart starting to beat faster. "As I said before, the head of my father's campaign finance committee never registered any large donations from your husband or your business. Small personal ones, yes, but nothing like the sums he claims to have given us. And certainly none from Balfour Industries." I gave her my best deadpan stare, despite my own building excitement. "So, if you don't have the money, and we don't have the money"—I leaned forward—"where did that money go? Where is it now?"

I won't repeat what she said. I don't like to use language like that, but most of it had to do with her husband, scatological references, and the ways she might use various implements of torture for their maximum effectiveness.

After she calmed down, our discussion picked up steam (and I'm not talking about the metaphorical steam that had been coming out of her ears, either).

We came to the conclusion that it was a pretty smart scheme, if you thought long and hard about it. Roger Stansfield sets himself up as a blackmail victim and documents his exorbitant extortion payments in a very public arena. By selecting my dad's campaign and the White House as the contributing factors in the blackmail, he defuses and distracts any serious investigation into his own finances. Given a choice, any reporter worth his salt was going to dig into the President's finances before going after an ad exec. Especially when that ad exec says he's a blackmail victim, and has nude pictures of himself spread across half the news venues in the country to prove it.

And the purpose?

Just like Alice said, half of nothing is nothing. If we'd never met and shared information, she would have accepted her husband's financial woes as the truth, because what man in his right mind would set himself up for such public ridicule?

Evidently, Roger Stansfield would—if the ridicule served to save him a tidy fortune in a divorce court.

As we talked, all the pieces of the puzzle started falling into place. I learned that her husband had taken several trips to Europe in the last few months, so we figured he must have a Swiss bank account or something like that where he was stashing his money. Between Balfour Industries's supposed political contribution, and Stansfield's withdrawals from business and personal accounts to pay his purported blackmailer, he had a nice little nest egg tucked away in a place that community property laws couldn't find—and therefore couldn't be divided and given to his lawful wife.

Whoever said misery loves company was right. By the time we'd finished fitting most of the puzzle pieces together, Alice and I felt like old friends.

"Here." I pushed copies of my notes and the photographs toward her. "Use these. If I were you, I wouldn't grandstand with them. But the sooner you get that man into a divorce court, the better." An absurd idea hit me. "Hey, you know what would serve him right? You ought to go on one of those televised divorce shows."

We started giggling together. Ah, sisterhood . . .

But the subject matter was too serious for sustained laughter. Alice's business and financial stability were at stake—not to mention the small matter of the justice she was owed by an unfaithful spouse. My father had his reputation and possibly his political career held in the balance. Alice pushed the notes back toward me. "Isn't your father going to make some sort of statement exonerating himself and his administration from all this? Your proof looks good to me."

I shook my head. "Maybe to you, but probably not to the rest of the American public. Everyone knows what political spin is. They'd simply believe this is another case where the current administration is trying to rationalize or excuse itself—or, even worse, to manufacture evidence. The American public is a bit jaded these days."

I drew a deep breath, knowing that I was taking a very big chance with my father's political career.

I pointed to her. "However, it seems to me that if

all this proof comes from you, then America will believe you, the wronged woman triumphing over her greedy husband. And if your proof just happens to completely clear the White House of all wrongdoing, then so be it. It doesn't matter how the truth comes out, as long as it does. But I'd appreciate it if you can get the big guns invited to the press conference when you're ready to go after your sorry husband."

We smiled at each other—grins of triumph, like those of hunters stalking prey in a dark jungle, ready to bag a record trophy.

"Happy hunting," I said.

CHAPTER FOURTEEN

Dad didn't blow a cork, but his various advisors looked as if they were about to have a collective coronary. In their eyes, I had simply given away the case to the enemy. But even facing such opposition, my instincts still told me I'd done the right thing.

I told Dad exactly what Alice Stansfield had told me, and then what I said to her. He studied me for a moment, then turned to the group of men and women having fits of very vocal apoplexy around us.

"Eve did the right thing. I would have taken exactly the same steps in her shoes. My daughter understands and appreciates the gravity of this situation as well or better than anyone here, and I think she may have given us our best chance to clear up this mess."

As I stood there, I realized for the first time that I

wasn't asking simply for my father's support in my decision, but asking for the support of the President of the United States. A shiver slithered up my spine at the thought.

He turned from his advisors to me, still wearing his Look of Presidential Authority. It was almost frightening, except I knew that beneath it, he still had the same sense of justice, the same morals as when he was simply my dad. I wanted to kiss him, but thought it might not be appropriate at the moment.

But then Dad shone through the facade, giving me a quick wink. "You going upstairs to talk to Patsy?"

I shook my head. "First things first. I need to talk to Mr. Seybold."

He leaned forward and kissed me on the cheek. "I trust your decision, sweetheart," he whispered.

Dismissed, I almost ran to Seybold's office, knowing he was waiting to debrief me. I just hoped he had as much faith in my instincts as Dad did.

It took me almost ten minutes to retell the tale, adding in all my observations and intentions. When I reached the part about the Stansfields' impending divorce, he stiffened in attention.

"So my basic theory is that Roger Stansfield deliberately posed for those pictures, setting himself up as a very public blackmail victim so he could siphon off almost all of his business and personal funds, protecting them from being split in a divorce settlement."

Stansfield shook his head. "You must agree that's a pretty far-fetched theory."

"But not impossible or even implausible. And when you add in his business assets, his personal fortune, even the funds that Balfour Industries thought were going to Dad's campaign, it adds up to a lot of money. And who's to say that he didn't scam any of his other clients by offering to be a conduit for their illegal campaign contributions?"

Seybold laced his fingers. "Then how did Sterling O'Connor get involved?"

I shrugged. "I'm not sure. Maybe Stansfield needed proof that the movie set was truly identical to the real thing and coerced Sterling into taking pictures of the Lincoln bedroom. He might not even have told him why. Of course, that doesn't explain the pictures we found in Sterling's apartment."

"Maybe he took the ones on the set, too."

I nodded. "That's possible, though his brother said he couldn't shoot a vacation photo without cropping off the head of everyone in it. Maybe the pictures of Stansfield were planted in the apartment."

Seybold leaned forward. "Whatever happened, possible or even plausible explanations aren't going to hold up in a court of law or, more important, in the eyes of the American public. We need more. We need concrete proof. And until we get it, all this conjecture is strictly academic." His face hardened. "I understand your theory about Alice Stansfield being a source of public awareness, but I think you've drastically overestimated her possible effectiveness in swaying the media. She'll be lucky if she makes the local paper with her story, much less the national news. Ugly divorces are a dime a dozen. Without concrete proof, rumor and innuendo will go unchecked and we may not be able to save your father's career. But thank you for your work today." He turned back to the papers on his desk, effectively dismissing me.

After that, I figured I had two options: slink upstairs with my tail between my legs, or go out and find that stinking proof.

I don't slink well.

I marched upstairs, each echoing footfall sounding like the word "proof" in my admittedly overwrought ears. When I reached the private quarters, I turned to my Dawg du jour. "I want Diana Gates up here immediately."

"I don't think she's on duty," he offered, in a rather tentative voice for a Secret Service agent.

"Then call her in on duty."

Okay, I was sounding a bit Willa-like, but I had my reasons.

Once upstairs in my rooms, I called Michael and told him to get his ass to the White House and to bring all the photos he'd taken on the set.

"Also, contact the statuesque Lieutenant Lange of the NYPD and get the list of all the names of people at the studio the day we visited. You can have her fax them to me if necessary."

Either he was too stunned or too hungover to argue. He simply said, "Yes, ma'am," and hung up.

Next, I called Charlie and outlined my needs. Bless his heart, he doesn't know how to say no to me, and even better, he loves a challenge, especially when it comes to finding a virtual backdoor into cyberplaces where he shouldn't go. He promised me material in nanoseconds.

Diana and Michael arrived at the family quarters together, about a half hour later, which meant I had to explain myself only once. I pulled them both upstairs to my sitting room.

Once situated, I outlined the plan. "Here's the new stuff. I talked to Alice Stansfield today. As it turns out, she and her husband had been discussing getting a divorce. I think this whole blackmail situation is nothing more than Roger Stansfield's very public attempt to arrange matters so he can sock away every penny he can control, all so his wife won't get anything in the divorce settlement."

Michael gaped at me. "You think he'd be willing to ruin his name and destroy his business just to keep his wife from getting his money? That's a little extreme, don't you think?"

"Maybe, but not if you also consider how big Balfour's campaign contribution was, and the sums Stansfield claimed he paid the blackmailer. We're talking millions and millions of dollars. Plus, who knows how many other companies funneled donation money through him that never reached us? If he's as thorough at planning a scam as he is an ad campaign, he could have rigged all of this to happen at once. Get a big influx of money that the various companies aren't ready to acknowledge giving publicly because the dollars involved represent campaign irregularities, then he creates a very public scandal involving himself, which makes the companies even less willing to connect themselves to him."

Diana leaned forward in her seat, obviously caught up in my explanation. "Then he skips the country, goes to some place where he can't be extradited, and lives off his stockpiled fortune while his ex-wife starves back here."

I clapped my hands in triumph. "Exactly!"

Michael didn't seem to share our enthusiasm or insight. "So what do we do next?"

"I already did it." I drew a deep breath. "I've given Alice Stansfield copies of all the pictures we have—what we found in Sterling's apartment, what we shot here, and what we shot on the movie set, along with the notes to use those images as weapons."

He glared at me. "But why?"

"I believe that if she breaks the story of her husband's scam, the newspapers will pick it up and the fallout will be good for us. For Dad. The more proof we get, the more we give her. Like I told her, the American public has been burned in the past when the White House tries to explain away a scandal. Even if we have the best proof in the world, how many people will consider our explanations anything more than political spin? But the more we feed her, the stronger her case will be. And when she proves that her husband is a thief and a liar and shows how he stole money from her and Balfour Industries and maybe other businesses, and how he never set foot in the White House, it definitely becomes a win-win situation. She wins and we win."

I nodded at the box Michael had placed by his feet. "I assume you charmed the list from Lieutenant Lange and brought the photos?"

He grinned. "Yes, ma'am."

Two respectful "ma'ams" in one day. I really was on a roll.

"Good," I said, savoring my own personal triumph. "Then let's get to work."

We compared the list with the photos we'd taken that day as well as the Secret Service files, courtesy of Diana, to see if anyone had pulled a vanishing act during my visit to the set. You know—killed the guard and then took off?

Diana and Michael both had good memories for faces and names, and we were able to check off names until we whittled the list down to two names—one male and one female—and only one picture of a man we couldn't readily identify.

By process of elimination, that left one woman who was interviewed by the police, but whom we didn't meet or capture in any of our pictures. I'd bet my last dollar she was blond and well built and didn't want anything to connect her to the White House, real or otherwise.

If she was the woman in the blackmail pictures, then had she pushed the guard over the catwalk railing in fear that he was going to spill her secret?

Diana added a new twist to the concept. "Or had someone been blackmailing her and she figured the guard was the most likely culprit? After all, she wouldn't suspect Roger since he's been open about the threats he received."

Conjecture, sure, but it meant we were looking at all the possibilities, including, we hoped, the truth.

But it was Charlie who came up with the best pieces

of information. I put him on speakerphone so everyone could hear the news.

"First, don't ask me how I got this. Okay?"

Michael and I both looked at Diana, since she was the only person in the room who might question the chain of evidence. She lifted both hands in a "Don't look at me" gesture.

"Go ahead, Charlie."

"Lucky for us, Sterling O'Connor used an Internet mail-order pharmacy company for his prescriptions. I was able to get into his account and track that his last shipment of heart medication"—he spewed out the name of a generic drug—"arrived at his apartment one week ago. He signed for it himself. I was able to cross-reference the shipping information and look at his electronic signature. It was the same signature as the shipments before, so it's safe to say he actually received the stuff."

"Then the vial of medicine he had in his pocket shouldn't have been empty."

"Exactly." There was a small pause. "Unfortunately, I wasn't as successful with the bank account information. Those banking folk have some really tough security that I couldn't violate without implicating myself. But I did get into Stansfield's frequent-flyer account and discovered that he made a trip to the Bahamas in July of last year. Ten to one he has a nice offshore account there that no one in the United States can touch but him."

I leaned slightly toward the speaker. "His wife and I figured Swiss bank account—she says he made several trips to Europe."

"Oh, no, those are totally passé. The Bahamian ones are much more convenient."

"Maybe he has both, huh? I'll remember your advice when I get rich and famous. Anything else?"

"I'm working on getting a complete copy of the script for the film *Armed and Dangerous*. I have a lead in British Columbia that might pan out. They have a pretty high reliability factor when it comes to rumor and innuendo."

"Okay, thanks, Charlie. Call if you find anything else."

"Sure, sis. Will do."

I hung up the phone. "Okay, so O'Connor should have had medicine with him, but he didn't. The bottle was empty. Don't you find that more than just a little suspicious?"

Diana nodded. "What else did he have with him? Besides the picture?"

I tried to remember back to when Seybold was listing the things for Dad. "Uh . . . his wallet, a checkbook, and . . . something else." I drew a blank for a moment, then glanced at the phone in my hand. "His cell phone. He had his cell phone with him."

Michael propped his feet on the coffee table and stretched out, lacing his fingers behind his head. "Okay, say for a moment that I want to kill you." He paused to shoot me a grin. "Not that I haven't entertained that thought once or twice so far."

"Ditto," I said, wearing my own sickeningly sweet smile.

"And let's suppose you have a weak heart and I

know all about that. What's the best way for me to kill you without getting my hands dirty?"

Diana supplied the obvious answer. "Trigger a heart attack and withhold medication."

"Right. But what if someone sees you withholding the medicine? Then the cops have a witness and they catch you, dead to rights. Unless . . ."

It was my turn to supply the answer. "Unless you take away the medicine earlier, maybe when I'm not looking or paying attention. Then you wait until I'm in an awkward place and then you call me on my cell and scare the living bejeesus out of me."

Michael straightened up. "Exactly. You saw that picture O'Connor had on him. What if Stansfield and O'Connor met earlier in the day and Stansfield hid the picture in O'Connor's coat while also discarding all his heart medication. Then they separate, Stansfield waits awhile, then calls O'Connor on his cell and says, 'Look in your pocket. If you don't cough up some money, I'm going to tell everyone that you got me and my date into the White House, took these pictures, and have been blackmailing me.' "

I finished the story. "O'Connor goes to his brother for help, starts to go into cardiac arrest, but realizes too late that he has no meds. A bit later, we find his body in the Rose Garden."

"A stiff stiff."

I picked up a pillow and threw it at Michael. "You could have gone a long time without saying that one."

He tossed the pillow back. "I did go a long time. I thought that as soon as I saw the body."

I made a face at him. "You're sick, you know."

Diana stood up between us, placing her fists on her hips. "Can we get back to the problem at hand?" She continued once she had our attention. "Cell phone records," she stated. "We get O'Connor's cell phone records to see if he received any calls during the last minutes of his life. Seybold will have them, I'm sure."

"And Stansfield's, too," I chimed in, trying to beat Michael to the punch. "I bet Alice would give us a copy of anything she can lay her hands on. After all, I gave her the pictures."

Diana continued standing between us. "Well, what are you waiting for? You"—she pointed to Michael—"go talk to Seybold and ask for O'Connor's cell phone records. And you"—she pivoted to face me—"you contact Mrs. Stansfield and see about getting her husband's business and personal phone records. I bet she's gotten them together for the divorce proceedings."

I shot her a snappy salute. "Yes, ma'am."

We regrouped ten minutes later, Michael with Seybold's promise to have the cell phone company fax us the call log from O'Connor's phone, and me having had a very strange and disjointed conversation with Alice Stansfield. I'd left a message on her voice mail. She'd returned the call almost immediately sounding so odd that I noted the number from the caller I.D.

I stood in the doorway between my bedroom and sitting room. "Something's wrong with Alice. I don't know if she's drunk or taking a trip on the U.S.S. *Valium*, but she's not making sense." My stomach was doing some back flips as I imagined the worst: What if she decided that Alice doesn't live *anywhere* any-more? She didn't strike me as the suicidal type; she'd seemed too bolstered by my promise to help her, and too enthusiastic about taking her husband down hard.

I dialed Esmerelda McLean, but her housekeeper answered. When I explained who I was and why I was calling, she told me that Esmerelda had gone to school to pick up her injured child and take him to the doctor. But I pressed and got Esmerelda's cell number and called her.

If she was already a bit harried, dealing with her sick child, she was even more so when I told her about my conversation with Alice.

"Eve, I can't get away. Sebastian fell on the play-ground and the doctor thinks he may have broken his arm. We're waiting now for the radiologist to read the X rays. This just makes me sick. Alice doesn't need to be alone—not at a time like this."

"Do you know where she is? She called me from her cell phone. She could be anywhere."

"She said she couldn't go back home, not knowing what she knew, but she refused to stay with us. I think she decided to go to their Washington apartment. I suspect she wanted to search through her husband's things in hopes of finding more evidence to use against him in the divorce."

"Where in Washington?"

Esmerelda sighed. "I'm not sure. I think it's actually in Arlington. Possibly in Crystal City. I'm sorry I don't know the exact address. It was more Roger's home-away-from-home than hers, so I've never been there." There was a noise in the background. "Eve, I've got to go," she said in a rushed voice. "Sorry. The doctor's ready. Let me know what happens."

The phone went dead.

I turned to my compatriots. "Alice is holed up in an apartment somewhere in Arlington. Maybe Crystal City. Mrs. McLean's not sure where," I reported.

"Then how do we find her? I'd lay odds that the number is unlisted."

"I'll try calling her again and see if she can give me the address."

"It's even easier than that, children." Diana held out her hand for the cordless phone that Michael still held. "May I?"

Three and one half minutes later, we had the necessary address, thanks to the Secret Service and their insatiable quest for knowledge. When I looked at the address, all sorts of alarms clanged in my head. "I know exactly where this is."

Michael glanced at the address in my hands. "Me, too. Crystal City."

"Not just that. It's the same apartment building where Sterling O'Connor lived."

CHAPTER FIFTEEN

According to Michael, who drove the streets almost every day, traffic was lighter than usual, and we made good time crossing the river and driving to Crystal City. The last time I'd made this run, it had been in the dead of night with Seybold and his men. Mac McNally was the second agent in our detail, and when Diana gave him the quick explanation of what we were doing, he responded with a tiny quirk in his upper lip.

Evidently it was his way of showing displeasure. I filed that away in my mental Filofax.

We parked under the front canopy of the building and trooped in, Diana at point and Mac bringing up the rear, both of them spending considerable mental energy observing the area, evidently cataloging escape routes and categorizing every possible threat.

And, for once, I was seriously glad to have such protection. I didn't even try to engage them in any idle chatter for fear of distracting their attention. We entered the lobby, commandeered the elevator, and rose uninterrupted to the tenth floor. I suffered a weird sense of *déjà vu* as we walked down a long carpeted hall, stopping at the very last door.

Was it merely coincidence that O'Connor's apartment was one floor directly below this one?

Diana stood in front of me and knocked on the apartment door. Good security precautions, I guess.

There was no answer.

I craned around her and called out, "Alice? It's Eve. Let me in."

Still no answer.

Michael reached out and turned the knob. The door swung slowly open. As he took a step toward the door, Mac politely pushed him aside and walked in first, gun drawn. Diana reached into her jacket and pulled out her weapon, too. She nudged me back into the hallway corner, placed Michael in front of me, then positioned herself between us and the door.

"Does she know I'm not bulletproof?" he whispered to me.

"You'd probably stop most bullets before they reached me," I answered.

"That's the plan," Diana said between clenched teeth. "Now, quiet!"

We heard Mac call out, "Mrs. Stansfield? Are you here?"

There was no answer.

He tried again. "Mrs. Stansfield?"

After a long moment of silence, he reappeared in the doorway. "I'm going to search the place. Either she's been tossing the place herself, or this mess could be the sign of a struggle or a fast search."

I looked around. "Mess" was indeed the operative word for the place.

"According to Mrs. McLean," I whispered, "Alice came here to look for evidence to use against her husband. So she might have made some of the mess. If I were in the same sort of situation, I wouldn't have been overly concerned with being too terribly neat."

"Maybe she's already found the phone records and left," Michael offered.

"Maybe," I agreed, not wanting to acknowledge the sinking feeling in the pit of my stomach. Something *was* wrong. I could feel it. The unlocked door bothered me.

A few tense moments later, Mac reappeared, holstering his gun. "The place is clear. No one's in there."

Diana motioned for me to go inside and I scurried from my corner and entered the apartment. I knew instantly that no woman had ever lived here—at least not for long.

The leather furniture in the living room, although expensive, was lined up in an awkward row, facing the large-screen television, which was entirely too big for the area. A steel and glass shelving unit held an elaborate sound system.

Ah . . . boys and their expensive toys.

The kitchen looked as if it'd never been used other than to nuke pizza and chill beer. The dirty dishes piled in the sink looked like garage-sale cast-offs, and the unlined garbage can held one of every kind of take-out food container in the known universe.

But the bedroom.

That's where the testosterone ran rampant.

Shades of Austin Powers. The bed wasn't round, nor did it rotate, but that's all the room lacked in being a quintessential swinging-bachelor make-out place. I'd never seen so many animal prints used in one room—leopard-spotted drapes, zebra-striped sheets, and an honest-to-God bearskin rug on the floor. A deer head had been centered above the headboard, and its antlers had been decorated with several pairs of panties, one bra, and a pair of handcuffs. The man clearly had a taste for trophy hunting. A stack of porno magazines sat in a haphazard pile on a bedside table, and the other table was piled high with the sort of sex toys that were advertised in the back of those magazines.

Or so I've been told . . .

I slid out of the room as soon as possible and was rewarded by a look of similar disgust on Michael's face.

"Not up to your decorating standards?" I asked.

He shook his head. "I thought you only saw stuff like that in bad television shows, in the seventies."

"So where's the disco ball?" I asked, taking one more glance at the room and shuddering.

"Probably hiding in the ceiling and activated with a remote control. The same one that probably makes the bed vibrate." He paused. "You think Alice actually stayed here often?"

I tried to picture her putting one foot into the place and couldn't make myself conjure up the mental image.

"I seriously doubt it. I have a feeling this was his bachelor pad disguised as his apartment in town." I glanced around. "So, the important question becomes—where's Alice?"

"Looks like her purse is still here," Diana's voice echoed from the living room. "Coat and scarf, too." Crowding around her, we watched as she used a pen to unzip the purse and look inside. "Wallet, makeup, checkbook . . . no keys. No phone."

I stood beside her, trying to see into the dark regions of the purse. "I know from our visit to O'Connor's apartment that each unit has a designated storage area downstairs. Maybe she went to the basement to see what he had hidden down there. I don't know if her phone will pick up down there, but . . ." I punched in her number and jumped a foot back when her purse blasted in response.

Diana shifted a few more things around, exposing the phone, which was hidden behind some papers. "Correction. Her phone is here."

Michael rubbed his ear in mock pain. "Now, *that's* what I call loud."

"It's because her purse was open," Diana explained. "You have to turn the ringer up that loud so you can hear it when it's buried in your purse."

Michael sat down on the leather couch and began sorting through some papers on the coffee table. "Hmmm . . . credit card bills, utility bills . . . ah, here we go, the phone bills."

"Michael," I warned. "You shouldn't be doing that."

"Why not? It's not like I'm digging through the drawers. The documents are sitting right here. And look

. . . the wireless phone bill for January is just sitting here on top." He studied it for a moment, then turned to me. "Can I borrow your phone for a sec?"

I gave him my cell and watched him consult the bill, then dial a number. A moment later, we heard a muffled ring coming from the bedroom.

Michael grinned. "Oh, look who forgot to take his cell phone with him today." He handed my phone back toward me. "Let it ring until I can find his."

Although I figured we were probably violating several laws, including unlawful entry, I didn't end the call until Michael trotted toward the sound and, a few rings later, shouted "Found it!" in a triumphant voice.

He came back into the room, cradling the phone in a handkerchief. But his triumph was only momentary; Diana held out her hand and after a moment's hesitation, he surrendered the phone. But instead of chastising him, she sat down beside me, pulled out a pencil, and used the eraser to push buttons on the phone.

"I have one like this," she offered. "It logs all outgoing and incoming calls." She continued to push buttons until she hit the right screen. "O'Connor died on the tenth, right?"

Mac grumbled a "Yes. Around two in the afternoon, according to the examiner."

"Someone write this down," she ordered.

Michael reached into his ever-present camera bag and pulled out a small notepad and a pen. "Shoot."

She squinted at the small screen. "Okay—202-555-6453, February tenth, 2:09 P.M., duration three minutes."

Michael dutifully copied down the information and

flipped back to an earlier page of his notebook. "Bingo! That's Sterling O'Connor's cell phone number."

Our smoking gun, figuratively speaking.

Diana handed the phone back to Michael, still protected by the handkerchief. "Put it back exactly where you found it."

Michael shook his head in protest. "He could clear out the phone's memory." He placed the phone on the table, where it was hidden behind a stack of paper. "And then we'd lose this proof."

"Even if he did clear the phone's memory, it'd be okay," Mac said from his spot near the front door. "He can't change the phone company records, and they'll substantiate the same information as the phone shows now. Anyway, we don't have a warrant. We don't want anyone catching us scouting around here. We could all get in big trouble."

I knew what he was saying: "we" was mainly Diana and him. The Secret Service wouldn't look kindly on their slightly-less-than-legal actions. If discovered, Michael likely wouldn't lose his job as official White House photographer, and, as Dad always puts it, when it comes to being his daughter, I'm irreplaceable.

"Okay," Michael said. "What do we do now? Sit around and twiddle our thumbs, waiting for Mrs. Stansfield to return?"

I fought a shiver. "I'm feeling really uncomfortable about all this. I think we ought to be concerned for Alice's safety. Someone needs to go downstairs and look for her." I glanced around, hoping for volunteers.

Diana shook her head. "We go where you go and you have no business going down there."

I glanced at Mac, but he wore his usual nonexpression.

Michael scanned our collective throng for a moment, then sighed. "Okay, okay, I'll go downstairs to the basement and look for her. The rest of you can stay here."

Diana and Mac shared a silent glance. Mac's face stiffened as he reached into his jacket. For one brief moment, I thought he was going to pull out his gun. But instead, he had a small black radio in his hand. He punched in a few buttons, then handed the unit to Michael.

"It's my backup unit. If something goes wrong, push this button to talk. Diana and I will both get the call."

Michael slipped the radio in his inner jacket pocket. "Thanks." He turned to me. "Be right back."

After he left, Mac locked the door, then turned around, placing his back against it. Diana and I sat quietly for a while, until the silence grew too oppressive for me.

"I'm just thinking aloud," I warned. "But don't you think it's more than a coincidence that O'Connor and Stansfield have apartments in the same building?"

Diana looked around. "It makes the missing medicine idea easier to swallow. Pardon the pun. . . ." She made a face, then continued. "And it also explains how they might know each other and how Roger might have gained access to O'Connor's apartment to steal the medicine."

"And plant that film," I added, realizing pieces were finally starting to fall into place. "When we thought the pictures were taken in the real Lincoln bedroom, we assumed O'Connor had taken them. But now that we know they were taken on the movie set, it could have been anybody. In fact, we don't have any evidence that O'Connor was ever on the set. Maybe all Sterling did was take pictures of the real bedroom, empty. Stansfield might have coerced him into doing it by telling him it was research for the movie's set decorator."

I unstuck myself from the leather couch and stood up, unable to keep still any longer. My body wanted to keep up with my mind, which was racing ahead, spurred by both my adrenaline level and the undeniable itch of a problem that needed solving.

I began to stalk around the living room, palms sweaty and heart thundering. "So, what's a plausible chain of events, huh? Stansfield invites O'Connor up here, empties out his medicine bottle while he's not looking, and sends him on his merry way to the White House?"

Diana was slow to answer. "Possibly."

Couldn't she sound a bit more positive?

I continued with my theorizing. "Then Roger calls Sterling. Maybe he'd given him the picture in an envelope earlier and, while on the phone, instructed him to open the envelope. It'd likely be a big a shock all on its own, but add a couple of not-so-veiled threats from Roger about Sterling's contribution to a crime and suddenly Sterling's reaching for heart medicine that's no longer there." I stopped and glared at Diana. "Well?"

Again, she took her sweet time to answer. "It's all possible, but without proof, it's only conjecture."

I glanced around the room. "Until Alice gets here

and gives us permission to look around, I realize it's the best I can do. But what I really want—"

Mac stiffened, signaling for me to be quiet. He did the classic Secret Service "listening to my hand" move, his face betraying no emotion as he said, "Come again, Mr. Cauffman, I couldn't hear you." His gaze narrowed slightly in concentration. "I copy. One moment." Mac turned to Diana. "He says the storage room door is open and there are definitely signs of a struggle. He hasn't gone inside yet."

The two agents shared a silent glance and I could hear them thinking, *He's on his own. . . .*

"So, what are you waiting for?" I demanded. "Go down and make sure he doesn't walk into a trap or something dangerous."

They both shot me blank looks.

I lowered my voice. "I mean it. One of you needs to go down there."

Mac spoke first. "We don't leave our assignment."

I offered them my most calculating smile as I moved toward the door. "Then your assignment, namely me, will be going down there herself." Okay, I'll admit it wasn't too much of a calculated risk. I made the threat knowing full well what their reaction would be.

Mac shifted in front of the door. "I don't think that would be wise."

I stood beside him, pulling myself to my fullest height, yet I still had to look up at him. I'd never realized what a bruiser he was. "And I don't think it's wise to leave Michael down there by himself." I balanced my fists on my hips and turned so I could catch them both in a single, sweeping glance. "So, who will it be? All of us or one of us?"

Diana and Mac shared another silent glance, then she sighed. "You two stay here. I'll go reconnoiter the basement, okay?" She gave Mac another, sidelong glance. "We *could* consider it an act necessary to establish building security."

Mac contemplated the idea, then nodded. "Only if we call in a secondary team for backup."

"I've got no problem with that." Diana started for the door. "I'll make the call and then go down there." She paused, reached into her jacket, and pulled out a radio, handing it to me. "Here. I'll feel better if you have this. It's my secondary, too. We might as well all be in contact." She pulled out her other radio and headed for the door. "Gates to Cauffman."

I tried to ignore the little voice in the back of my head that accused me of making a Willa-style power play. But the difference between the two of us was that I wasn't doing this for me; I was doing it for Michael, to assure his safety. And even better, I wasn't risking my safety in the process, either. I felt perfectly safe holed up in a locked apartment with Mac, him armed to the teeth and both of us one speed-dial call away from a security force that could descend on us like a plague of locusts.

I felt secure. Protected. Safe.

Until a few minutes later when we heard someone outside, fitting a key into the lock. I wasn't really scared until Mac reached into his coat and pulled out his gun. When he motioned for me to move into the kitchen, I did so immediately.

From my hiding place, I could hear voices—a conversation, but I couldn't pick out the words. A few moments later, Mac gave me the all clear.

Still feeling a bit cautious, I stood in the doorway of the kitchen and looked into the living room. "Who was it?"

Mac held out his hand, showing me a set of keys. "The super. He found these in the lobby and was trying to identify which apartment door they opened. Strange. I would have thought—"

He glanced up at me, dropped the keys, and aimed his gun at me. Before I could say anything, someone grabbed me from behind.

CHAPTER SIXTEEN

It didn't take a genius to figure out who my attacker was, even though I couldn't exactly see him.

Roger Stansfield dug the barrel of his gun into my temple. "Don't make any sudden moves."

Mac and I complied. His actions were, of course, impressive. His pistol remained aimed, not wavering at all, at a point slightly over my shoulder. "Just take it easy," he said in a quiet, emotionless tone. "You don't need to do this."

Stansfield betrayed no emotion either, nor did his gun move away from my head. It remained there, pressing coldly against my skin, hard enough to leave a bruise later. That's if the man didn't blow a big enough hole in my head to eradicate the area that would bruise. "Unfortunately, I do need to do it. Thanks to your interference, I've been forced to accelerate my getaway plans. Drop your gun or I will without hesitation shoot the First Daughter dead."

Somehow, I found my voice. "Catching a flight to Rio by way of Nassau?" I wasn't sure whether I was being brave or stupid; I'd always heard there's a fine line separating the two, and now I fully believed it.

He gripped my shoulder with his free hand, his fingers digging into my skin. "I'll plead the Fifth, if you don't mind. My plans are none of your business."

"You made it my business when you got my father involved in this." *Shut up, shut up, shut up,* I screamed at myself.

"You," he said to Mac. "Drop the gun and take off your coat. Remove the radio, too."

Mac glared at us and for one uncomfortable moment, I wondered if he was glaring at me, blaming me for splitting the team in half with my unreasonable demands.

I know I was blaming myself at the moment. That, and wondering where Stansfield had come from. We'd checked out the exits, I thought.

Mac made a deliberate show of placing the gun on the coffee table, then backing away, palms held out. Then, he removed his earpiece and slowly stripped off his coat, revealing his shoulder harness, the holster now empty.

"And now your pants," Stansfield ordered.

Oh, God, I thought, *he really* is *a pervert. What's next? My clothes?*

Mac paused, then began to unbuckle his belt. As his pants dropped, I could hear a small thump as something heavier than I'd have expected hit the carpet. There he stood scowling, pants puddled around his ankles, yet managing to maintain his dignity.

"Now slide your second piece over here."

Sure enough, the clunk had been a second gun, this one smaller, clipped to the inside back waistband of his pants. For one absurd moment, I wondered how uncomfortable it had to be, to have a gun stuck down one's pants. Then I realized how uncomfortable it is to have a gun jammed into one's temple.

After complying, the weaponless Mac looked down at his pants and gestured. "May I?"

Stansfield paused, then released a short bark of laughter. "Yeah. Go ahead. We've had enough unclothed bodies for a while, don't you think? And when you're finished, I want you to lie down, hands behind your head."

Mac pulled his pants on and, after fastening them, stood still for a long moment as if calculating his chances of jumping us, wrestling away the gun, and not getting me killed in the process. Evidently, he decided against the action and instead dropped down, assuming the requested position on the floor.

"Where's Alice?" I asked, still treading that fine "bravery/idiocy" line.

"Around." Stansfield released me with a push toward a chair.

I didn't have to look to know the gun was still trained on me. Rather than watch him, I was trying to catch Mac's eye.

What am I supposed to do? Play along? What?

Stansfield continued, giving me another push. "I hear

I have you to thank for enlightening her." He sounded more than mildly irritated.

I looked up, trying to appear nonthreatening. "All I did was expound on a theory." My thoughts raced ahead. Michael and Diana were in the building. They knew we were up here. Even better, Diana had called for backup.

All I had to do was stay low, stay quiet, and stay alive until that backup showed up. Actually, until well after it showed up—preferably until I'd reached a comfortable old age.

"Lady, your theory has caused me a lot of problems." He walked closer to Mac, shifting his aim from me to him. I knew it wasn't an invitation to play Wonder Woman.

"And I don't like problems." Without warning, Stansfield reared his foot back and kicked Mac in the head. I'll never forget the sound—of the blow and Mac's roaring reaction to it. A second well-aimed kick put Mac completely out of commission.

Up to this point, I'd been able to stay relatively calm, but now panic, among other things, was starting to swell in my throat.

"I suppose I could say that I simply attacked an armed gunman who had broken into my apartment." Stansfield turned to me. "But you . . . your body would be a lot harder to explain." He glanced at Mac. "I saw his partner downstairs, rattling around the storage locker. Nosy bastard."

Bastard? Did he mean Michael? Had he done something equally as brutal to Michael? I began to shiver. Then a ray of hope flickered behind my eyes. If he thought Michael was the other agent in my detail, that meant he didn't know about Diana.

Suddenly I straightened in revelation. Diana's radio. I'd forgotten about it. The trouble was, I wasn't sure how to turn it on so that she might hear what was going on. I had to distract him and sneak a look at the radio controls.

Think of something, Eve.

"How'd you get in here without us knowing?"

He laughed. "Back door. Part of the building's fire escape system. It's got a chain, but it's too long for the door. You can reach in and slide it off."

"That's not very safe," I said, stalling for time.

He laughed again. "My safety isn't really an issue right now. Yours is."

I tried to laugh, but it came out as a rather shaky sigh. "Yes, I guess it is."

"Here's what we're going to do." He stalked around the room, gun still pointed in my general direction, but he was also thumbing through various piles of papers and pawing through a couple of desk drawers. He pulled on a pair of leather gloves, changing his gun from hand to hand as he adjusted them. "I have a flight booked out of Reagan in about an hour and a half. We're going to the airport—you and me." He began to pile the papers from the table in a briefcase that had been sitting beside the desk.

I glanced at Mac, who hadn't moved at all. "Can I check him? He doesn't look good."

Stansfield paused and stared at Mac, then stepped between us to retrieve Mac's guns and radio. "Just in case you were contemplating a very foolish idea . . ."

He grinned. "Go ahead. But don't do anything stupid. Remember, you may come in handy as a hostage, but things also might be a lot easier if I didn't have to worry about you."

I gulped back the revulsion that made my stomach churn and dropped on my knees next to Mac. To my relief, his pulse was strong and he was breathing well enough. But he was going to have a goose egg the size of the Rotunda when he woke up.

If Stansfield allowed him to eventually wake up.

It was as if the man had read my mind.

"I'm not actually a violent person. Well, not usually. Up to now, I've not lifted a hand against a single person. Sterling's death was . . . unfortunate."

I couldn't help it. I couldn't let the statement go unchallenged. "But premeditated, nonetheless."

Stansfield shrugged. He went back to stuffing his briefcase full of papers, keeping the gun and part of his attention on me the whole time.

I continued to take Mac's pulse, using my free hand to pull Diana's radio from my pocket. I used his body to shield my actions as I tried to read the small buttons. I finally found the "Push to Talk" button and the second button that locked it on. Hopefully, Diana would hear some or all of this conversation and know what to do.

"Roger . . . what about the man at the production set?"

Stansfield glanced at me, wearing a look of honest confusion. "Who?"

"You know, in New York. The security guard who died at Trophy Studios. He was the one who reportedly controlled the nonsanctioned nighttime events on the White House set."

"Who, Oscar?" He looked honestly shocked. "He's dead?"

For the life of me, Stansfield sounded as if he knew nothing about it. Then again, after seeing him emote during the televised press conference, I knew he was a good actor and a consummate liar.

He looked down at the gun in his hands. "Damn it," he said in a low voice. "He was a good guy. Trustworthy. Hell of a photographer." His face darkened. "It must have been . . ." His voice trailed off. "That bitch."

I was starting to really believe the old "no honor among thieves" adage. I figured the bitch in question had to have been his partner in the pictures, the one unaccounted person on the set. When she saw all of us trooping in, she must have gotten scared, and killed the only person there who could link her with the photographs.

As I moved blindly back to my seat on the couch, my foot hit something on the floor. I managed to sneak a look without being caught and discovered Michael's equipment bag by the end of the couch, unzipped. His strobe unit sat within tempting reach.

In the proper hands, it could be a weapon. Not a lethal one, but something I could use to distract the man in front of me, perhaps even temporarily blind him.

I had to get that strobe, but Stansfield would notice if I simply bent down and picked it up. Slipping the radio into my jacket pocket, I discovered I had absentmindedly slipped my own cell phone into my pocket rather than back in my purse. Keeping my hand in my jacket, I coughed to mask the electronic beeps that sounded when I hit the "Redial" and "Send" buttons.

I needed a distraction, and I was about to get one.

Two long seconds later, Stansfield's own cell phone rang loudly on the coffee table.

I jumped at the sound, my hand accidentally hitting a couple of magazines that were on the end table beside me. Porno magazines, of course. I looked shocked as I watched them fall to the floor.

Stansfield wasn't the only actor in the room.

He stared at the phone for a moment, then grimaced, silently warning me with the gun. Reaching over to grab the phone, he fiddled with the buttons and turned it off. Meanwhile, under the guise of retrieving the magazines, I managed to snag the strobe, turn it on, and slide it between the cushions of the couch so he wouldn't hear the high-pitched whine as it charged.

He started to put the phone back on the table but instead contemplated it for a moment, then hurtled it across the room, where it hit a marble table and shattered into sharp-edged little cellular bits.

"I hate that thing. Too loud, always ringing at exactly the wrong time."

He sighed, then reached down, unclipped the cord from the house phone. With a mighty jerk, he pulled the other end out of the wall, then knelt next to Mac's still body and began to hog-tie him with the phone cord.

I hoped Diana could hear well enough to know where I was and what predicament I was in. And even more, I hoped that she had backup coming and a plan that would corral this guy without anybody else getting hurt. I already felt guilty enough about Mac, figuring that if I hadn't demanded that the team split, the two of us wouldn't be in this situation.

I hate hindsight.

"There." Stansfield finished tying up Mac and turned to me. I must have flinched because he laughed. "Don't worry. I don't plan to tie you up just yet. You're coming with me."

"On the flight?" If he thought he could get me on a plane with him without a fight, he had another idea coming. He'd never make it past airport security with the gun, and without a gun, he was powerless to control me.

"No, to the airport. I'm afraid you won't be going with me. You're staying behind in the trunk of my car."

Okay, I'll admit it. I'm claustrophobic. The idea of being shut up in his trunk made me shiver in revulsion.

"What?" he said, reading my expression. "Don't like cars?" He stepped closer. "Or is it simply small, dark places?" He reached down and grabbed my arm, hauling me to my feet. Then he leaned into my face, jabbing the gun into my stomach. "Or is it small, suffocatingly dark places," he whispered, his breath revealing the telltale smell of alcohol. Expensive scotch, by the smell of it. How clichéd. The ad man and his scotch . . . "Where the air becomes hot and stale . . ."

The little mental voyage had given me back my sense of proportion. What was being locked in a trunk compared with being here with this madman and his gun? I met his stare, eye to eye, pushed back my revulsion, and said, "No seat belts," in my calmest, most self-controlled voice.

It took him by surprise. He pulled back. "What?"

"There are no seat belts in the trunk," I explained in my most rational tone. "You hit a bump, I hit the roof. You swerve, I slide around. You get in a wreck and I'm in the most vulnerable place. Of course I don't like it."

He threw back his head in laughter. "Then I'd better not get into any accidents on that oh-so-long one-mile drive to the airport." He pushed me back down onto the couch, then leaned past me and grabbed a scarf, presumably Alice's, that had been left on the end table. While his head was turned, I slipped the strobe unit into my jacket pocket. He jerked me to my feet again.

"Put your hands out."

I complied.

He looped the scarf around my hands, then tightened it. "I'll find something a little more secure in the car," he explained as he fit Alice's coat over my shoulders. The coat enveloped me nearly from head to toe. Stepping back, he admired his handiwork. "Good, no one will suspect."

"Suspect that you're kidnapping me?"

He shrugged. "That's such a harsh word. Let's just say this is a forced accompaniment. It's not like I'm taking you across state lines. Just to the airport, where you'll rest comfortably in the trunk. Once I get out of the country, I'll pay an extravagant fortune to use an in-flight phone and alert the authorities as to your whereabouts."

"What about Alice? Are you going to tell anyone where she is?"

He tsk-tsked. "Alice doesn't warrant an expensive phone call anymore. A letter will do for her discovery."

A cold dread filled me. Alice was dead. He'd really killed her. And all his promises about my safety meant nothing if he decided I knew too much, or might alert the authorities before he had a chance to escape the country. He really had a lot more reasons to want me dead than alive.

"Now we're going to take a walk to the elevator, take it all the way down to the garage, and then we're going to take a little ride to Reagan. I guess you can call it a presidential motorcade."

He pushed me toward the door. As I waited for him to open it, I worked my hands to the side and pulled the flash out, hiding it beneath the scarf's edges. I'm not sure what I thought I could do with it—blind him? Probably not. You don't have to be able to see to fire a gun with the hopes of hitting something or somebody as close as I was to him.

If nothing else, I thought, maybe I could use it to signal for help while in the car to the airport.

He made a great show of shoving the gun into my spine to demonstrate his control over me, then we went out the door.

We had taken only three or so steps toward the elevator when I looked up and saw Diana walking toward us. She wore a pleasant smile and held a paper bag in her arms. Anyone who didn't know her would simply think she was a fellow tenant, carrying her groceries to her apartment.

I knew enough not to openly recognize her. I had a feeling she wanted that element of surprise. As we passed each other in the hallway, I could see the barest sign of recognition behind her perfect poker face, which was fine and dandy where Stansfield was concerned, but I had no idea what the plan was, if there was one.

We'd taken a few more steps when we heard her say, "Oops," and the sound of paper ripping. We both turned out of instinct to the right, toward her.

Instead of finding her picking up spilled groceries, she was in a shooter's crouch, gun pointed at Stansfield. "Freeze!" she commanded.

He pulled me in front of himself as a shield, ripped the gun from my back, and aimed it at her. But I was the one who fired. I pivoted, jammed the strobe in his face, and flashed him.

Stansfield screamed in pain and fired his gun blindly. I wasn't sure where the bullet hit, whether it had found a human target or what, because I was in the process of being buried under two Secret Service agents.

I could hear muffled shouts, sounds of a struggle, but no more gunfire. After what seemed like a long time to me, someone shouted, "Clear!" The weight of the two solid men above me lifted off me slowly. "Sorry, ma'am," one voice echoed in my ear.

I surrendered to giddy temptation. "I've been dying to say this my whole life. Is that a gun in your pocket or are you just glad to see me?"

He didn't dare laugh aloud, but when I turned over, the agent who had flattened me wore a guarded smile.

"Just doing my job, ma'am. Are you hurt?" he asked while untying my hands.

"I'm okay," I said, accepting his helping hand and rising to my feet. The shock was making me have trouble concentrating. "And you? I hope nobody else was hurt." I glanced over at Stansfield, who had been cuffed and was being guarded by a circle of armed agents. "Except him. You can hurt him, and it won't bother me much."

"Everyone is fine," the agent said.

"Not quite." I remembered something important. "Mac McNally needs help as fast as you can get it to him, thanks to that idiot." My anger started bubbling up. "He kicked Mac in the head, twice. And Alice, the wife, is missing. I'm worried that she may be injured or already dead. Maybe downstairs in the storage area."

Diana emerged from Stansfield's apartment. "Mac's conscious and making sense. The medical team is working on him."

I couldn't help myself. I hugged her. "You were great. Thanks."

"You kidding?" She gave me a big smile. "You're the one who thought to use the flash in his face. It probably saved his life. We were ready to take him down."

I glanced back over my shoulder. "Then I'm not so glad I had it. He all but confessed he killed his wife."

A voice waffled down the corridor. "She's not dead. At least not yet."

I turned and saw Michael limping from the elevator toward me. "I'd just found her downstairs in the storage area when *he*"—Michael glared at the prone figure on the floor—"jumped me. If Diana hadn't come down looking for me, we might still be there, and Alice might have died."

He looked like he'd been on the losing side of a nasty war. His jacket was torn, his shirttail was half out, and he had the beginnings of a shiner that would do a nine-year-old boy proud.

"The medics are working on her," he told Diana as if reporting to a superior, "and one told me she has a good chance of pulling through this." He turned to me. "Evidently, Mr. Stansfield here slipped his wife a lethal dose of a prescription painkiller. I'll bet they find her suicide note somewhere—probably conveniently typed rather than handwritten." He squinted at me with his good eye. "You okay?"

I nodded. "I've had better moments, but, yeah, I'm okay." I looked down and realized I still held his flash unit in my hands. It had not come through as well as I had, after being slammed to the floor by two Secret Service agents.

"I'm afraid we've had one casualty, though." I held the unit up for his inspection.

A look of horror crossed his face. "My flash!"

What can I say . . . revenge is *sweet*.

Patsy and I sat together at the head luncheon table at the Willard Hotel. Normally, we wouldn't have been seated next to each other, but after my little adventure, Patsy really didn't want much distance between us. Every once in a while, she'd reach over, grab my hand, and give it a squeeze, and I'd smile and squeeze back.

I didn't mind her need for reassurance. I needed it just as much. But it was the overly solicitous attention of others that was starting to wear my patience thin only two days after my big adventure.

I looked across the room and found Michael's lens pointed at me. What else could I do? I crossed my eyes and turned back to my meal.

Michael had survived his ordeal fairly well, too, despite being attacked, knocked unconscious, and locked in the basement storage area with the almost-late Mrs. Stansfield. We both considered ourselves lucky, having had a too-close encounter with a card-carrying murderer.

And Mac McNally was pretty lucky, too. He'd only suffered a mild concussion. I'd feared he would suffer brain damage, considering how hard Stansfield kicked him. Mac attributed his lack of damage to a thick skull and a bit of luck. He also told me to listen to him the next time he asked me not to break up a team. I promised to do just that. He'd earned it.

According to Diana, when she had heard me suddenly broadcasting over her radio, she'd figured out what had happened. She'd just discovered Michael, locked in the storage area, and her worst suspicions were borne out when she heard her radio crackle and me talking to someone. Although she didn't recognize the man's voice, when she heard me call him Roger, two plus two became a very deadly four in her mind.

Grabbing the backup team who had responded promptly to her earlier call for aid, they'd all scrambled into position, trying to anticipate Stansfield's moves based on the conversation I was broadcasting. Later, she told me she'd insisted on being the one who passed us in the hallway, knowing that I'd recognize her.

"And I knew you were smart enough not to tip our hand," she'd said.

Now, she stood a discreet distance behind the dais, watching me wrestle with a rubber-chicken meal while also scanning the crowd for dissidents, terrorists, or, in this case, exuberant ladies who wanted a chance to say they'd met the First Lady and First Daughter. Dad hadn't wanted me to go to the luncheon, but since it was for Mom's charity, he couldn't really argue too much against it. So here I was.

If anything, Michael should have been the one who was ordered to take it easy. He lowered his camera. I figured he was lucky that Stansfield hadn't decked him in the eye he used for aiming.

Michael could have been the media's darling if he'd wanted to. The press had been interested in the story of Secret Service agents having a chance to use their extensive training to prevent a crime against the Presidential Daughter, but when they realized a civilian had been involved as well . . .

Michael sidestepped the hoopla and was back to work the next day as if nothing had happened.

But something had happened. Despite my naturally sunny disposition, I was having a hard time forgetting it. I was okay during the day, but I hadn't had an hour of uninterrupted sleep since that gun had dug into my temple. I kept thinking about what might have happened, all the people who might have died, just because I wanted to play Nancy Drew. One of them could have been me, of course, but that worried me less than the innocent bystanders I would have taken with me. It was pretty harrowing. I even contemplated moving down to the family floor, just to be closer to the rest of the family. But I decided to tough this one out.

I will admit my little adventure did have one extremely good result.

The Washington Post broke the story, and the morning news shows jumped on it with both feet. The arrest of Roger Stansfield for the attempted murder of his wife, Alice, and his armed assault on me, Mac McNally, and Michael Cauffman was the lead story of the day. The *Post* and CNN had done a particularly fine job of ferreting out the details of Stansfield's subterfuge—the pictures taken in the bogus Lincoln bedroom, the campaign contributions that never were, the blackmailer who never existed, and all the other lies Stansfield had told in his efforts to secure a fortune for himself.

The *Post* never mentioned Sterling O'Connor's role in the debacle, which had turned out to be far smaller than we'd thought. But Burton O'Connor sure seemed to be relieved by the sense of closure he received, having learned that his brother's only crime was that of performing a wee-hours impersonation of Burton and taking some nonsanctioned photos of the unoccupied Lincoln bedroom.

All the darkroom equipment, the stashed roll of film, the porno magazines—those had been planted in Sterling's apartment by Roger Stansfield.

The big unanswered question was the identity of the woman in the pictures, who, according to Stansfield, should have been considered the chief suspect in the murder of Oscar Rolanski, the watchman who had fallen/been pushed at the movie set.

Inconsiderate bastard.

They'd get it out of him, eventually. And I trusted that Lieutenant Lange of the NYPD would get that blonde if Stansfield didn't talk.

But best of all, my dad's administration had been

cleared of all wrongdoing, and the retraction was just as explosive and newsworthy as the accusation.

Those things seldom happen.

Especially in Washington, D.C.

PLEASE WATCH FOR SUSAN FORD'S NEXT
FIRST DAUGHTER MYSTERY:

SHARP FOCUS

COMING IN SPRING 2003 FROM ST. MARTIN'S MINOTAUR/THOMAS DUNNE BOOKS

U.S. AIR FORCE ACADEMY PUBLIC AFFAIRS
USAF ACADEMY, CO 80840

ACADEMY ANNOUNCES GRADUATION GUEST
SPEAKER
U.S. AIR FORCE ACADEMY, COLO.—Elliot J.
Cooper, President of the United States of America, is
scheduled to deliver the commencement address to the
class of 2003 at the 45th U.S. Air Force Academy
graduation beginning at 11 A.M., May 28, in Falcon
Stadium . . .

"Good God, Diana. What are you trying to do? Kill
me?" I whispered to the woman who was strapping me
into the seat.

She tightened the harness. "Not at the moment, but I may change my mind if you don't sit back and let me get on with it," she said.

My favorite Secret Service agent, Diana Gates, was in the process of restraining me in what looked to me like a death trap. It was the Secret Service's job to protect me and my family. But I was having some doubts about their intentions right now.

"Are you absolutely sure this is safe?" I asked.

"Nope," Diana said. "But the Air Force is—and they should know." She gave one last pull on a piece of canvas webbing and stepped back, ready to let the professionals take over.

Several Air Force cadets stepped forward at her signal to check over every detail of the tiny aircraft I was sitting in, as well as the straps holding me in it. If I hadn't been so busy worrying about my future survival, I'd have appreciated the view a lot more.

"BRING ME MEN"—that's what it says in big silver letters on the ramp leading up to the Air Force Academy cadet area. When I saw the words, I'd had to hide a smile. The phrase sounded more like the secret plea of a high school girl than a military slogan. Now I was surrounded by an assortment of those very men—trust me, the Air Force's finest are easy on the eyes—and I was literally all tied up and too apprehensive to enjoy it. That was despite the fact that I knew that the men checking my straps were every bit as concerned about my future survival as I was. My dad was, after all, technically their boss.

My name is Eve, and I'm the First Daughter. My father is President Elliot James Cooper, Commander in

Chief of the Armed Forces and Leader of the Free World. I just call him Dad. And because of Dad, I was about to take part in something that the Air Force considered a high treat.

It's not that I mind flying. I like it—in large jets with even larger wings. With bathrooms. And engines—I like having engines. Lots of them. The more, the merrier.

But I was now immovably attached to a flying machine that looked like a child's toy, not an aircraft. And it was completely engine-free. My confidence in the theory of drag and lift shrank accordingly.

Diana moved closer once the fly guys gave her the high sign. "You ready?" Despite the fact that Diana had her game face on—that Official Secret Service blank stare—I'd gotten to know her well enough to realize she was suppressing a small, unauthorized grin.

But Diana's expression didn't keep my attention for long. No, right now I was far more interested in the yellow glider I was sitting in, attached to its tow plane by a rope.

Not a steel cable, but a rope.

A thin rope.

Somehow, that didn't seem right to me.

Diana's attention was elsewhere, scanning the tarmac, as she remained on the lookout for danger. In this crowd it was unlikely to materialize, but it was her job to watch. The glider I was sitting in was parked on the runway of the U.S. Air Force Academy, just north of Colorado Springs, right on the edge of the Academy's 18,000 acres of beautiful Colorado landscape, and we were waiting for clearance for takeoff.

The local Air Force personnel wanted to make sure the time I spent with them was memorable. As I sat in that glider, my face frozen in what I hoped was a pleasant expression, trying not to hyperventilate, I knew they'd succeeded. I was just scared enough to have this moment indelibly engraved on my brain for the rest of my life.

I was here because Dad was to be the main speaker at this year's Air Force Commencement celebration. It's traditional for the President to make the obligatory "For God and Your Country" speech to one of the three service academies each year—working in due course through the Air Force Academy in Colorado Springs, West Point in New York, and the Naval Academy in Annapolis. It was no secret that Dad was thrilled that the Air Force Academy had been first up in the rotation for him. He'd done a tour in the Air Force as an officer, and had stayed active in the reserves for a long time. He might not be an Academy grad, but lots of his best friends were. And those blue-suiters do tend to stick together.

I'd been thrilled, too. I grew up and went to school in Colorado, and had taken the opportunity to come in early to catch up with some old friends. As a consequence, I beat Dad to the Academy by a good six hours.

Dad was due to arrive in Air Force One later today at nearby Peterson Air Force Base, much too late to do me any good. Right now I was the only Cooper in sight. The glider ride was mine. The things I do for the press and my country . . . it always amazed me.

But I needed to look less scared than I felt because the press was watching. I didn't want to let Dad down.

At the edge of the tarmac, the light of flaring camera flashes threatened to blind me as the media took advantage of the photo op. Diana's vision was, I hoped, in better shape than mine. I wouldn't be able to spot a threat right now unless it was the size of a city bus.

"Do I *have* to do this?" I asked, even though I knew I did.

Diana didn't even look at me. "No. But Captain Perky will be so disappointed if you don't."

"Durkee," I corrected. That was the name of the crackerjack military media liaison who had been my guide for the VIP tour all morning. The captain was probably my age, but the severity of her uniform and her haircut made her look older—or at least much more mature. She also knew her facts and figures cold. She was the reason I knew that the Academy grounds covered 18,000 acres.

"Whatever," Diana replied. "Don't worry. People go up in these things every day."

"It's not the going up that bothers me." I said. "It's the coming down. Straight down."

"We've been told the glider has been thoroughly inspected. That shouldn't be an issue," Diana said. In this context "We" meant Diana and the new agent who'd been assigned to me from the White House detail for this trip, John Kingston. Evidently, the higher-ups in the Secret Service thought it was wise to match Diana with someone who was impressively large. Trust me, Kingston was huge. He looked like an agent, all right— a free agent signed by the Washington Redskins, rather than a Secret Service agent.

Lord knows, the Skins could use someone with his heft and reflexes this year.

I glanced at the pilot who was to be my sole companion in this brief foray into the wild blue yonder. He looked like a typical cadet, with his short, dark hair and his chiseled, freshly scrubbed face. His smile could only be described as "Top Gun" cocky.

A fighter pilot-in-training, I bet. Dad had warned me about guys like that.

I knew enough from the tour so far to realize that the patterns of silver rickrack on his uniform meant that he was a "firstie," which was Academy-speak for a senior. His name badge read "Taylor 'The Jokeman' Dobbs." Fulfilling the promise of his nickname, he immediately stepped off on the wrong foot.

"Hello, pretty lady," he said with a wink to Diana. "With agents like you on duty, the security checks will be a pleasure. Can I volunteer for a strip search?" I *think* it was supposed to be a joke.

Rule #1: Never joke with Secret Service agents while they're on duty. That privilege is reserved for my Dad, and even he doesn't try it too often.

Rule #2: Never put the moves on a female agent while she's on the job.

I half-expected to see "The Jokeman" fly across the tarmac and end up with the dusty imprint of one of Diana's black dress flats centered on his back.

But Diana was too professional to lose it over something so insignificant. She merely gave the cadet a glare that made him shrivel up and shrink down like a salted slug.

All the better to fit into a small glider . . .

Deflated now, he turned his attention to me, trying to resurrect his Tom Cruise smile. "Have you ever ridden in a glider before, Miss Cooper?"

"No." That was the truth. "I'm looking forward to it." That was a whopping lie.

"You couldn't have picked a better day. The weather is perfect for a good soar."

Falling on my months of experience in the public eye as the First Daughter, I conjured up a pleasant expression. "Then, shall we?"

I could hear the engines revving on the tow plane, but we weren't moving yet.

Then I felt a slight lurch as the slack was pulled out of the towrope. The little glider jumped forward. A few seconds later, we were rolling down the field behind the tow plane. At first it was really noisy in the cockpit, then the sound level lessened suddenly. I pressed my face to the clear canopy and looked down, realizing that although the tow plane was still on the ground, we weren't.

I wondered if this was what it felt like to ride a kite.

Then the tow plane lifted off and we started gaining altitude. Despite his nickname, Cadet "The Jokeman" Dobbs got down to some serious business.

"See that small yellow handle in front of you?" As I'd said, we were in tandem seating, with me in front, Dobbs in back.

"Yes."

"Pull it," he ordered.

I reached out automatically, then hesitated. The President of the United States hadn't raised a fool for a

daughter—and this guy's tag *was* "The Jokeman."
"What happens if I pull the handle?

"That's the tow release." He chuckled. "It's time for this baby bird to leave the nest."

Oh, great. I swallowed hard, wrapped my fingers around the handle and paused. "I've never done this before. What if I do something wrong?"

He laughed again. "Don't sweat it. You can't mess this up. And if we don't release right, the tow pilot will simply let go of us from his end. So, don't worry. Just do it."

I closed my eyes and pulled.

There was a small mechanical clunk and I watched the end of the towrope come into sight. Suddenly, we were on our own—high up in the sky without an engine.

I wasn't frightened. Much.

I could feel us banking hard to the right. Common sense suggested that the maneuver made sure we wouldn't run into the tow plane ahead of us. But I wasn't brave enough to open my eyes and look, not quite yet. My camera slipped in my lap and I grabbed it instinctively, still keeping my eyes squeezed shut.

In a matter of seconds, the engine noise of the tow plane faded away, leaving us aloft in a majestic silence broken only by the quiet swoosh of air over the glider's surface. Intrigued, I pried open my eyes. Although we no longer had an umbilical cord tying us to the plane, we seemed to be flying successfully without it.

I tried telling that to my heart, which was wedged in my throat.

But after a few dozen thundering heartbeats, I began

to enjoy the feeling of freedom as we soared through the sky.

"You okay?" Dobbs sounded as if he was fairly certain I wasn't. "You know, the air is a little thin up here. We were at 6500 feet before we even took off."

"I'm fine," I said.

Suddenly, any lingering fears I had of heights or of flying without an engine vanished, and I let myself wallow in the beauty of the scenery below us and the freedom of being up in the glider. I felt better than I had since the day Dad won the primary.

Maybe I needed to take flying lessons.

Now *that* would give the Secret Service fits. They were having a hard enough time with my baby brother Drew learning to drive. I almost started laughing again.

Evidently Dobbs realized that I didn't need him to live up to his "Jokeman" nickname. He began to wax philosophical about the wonders of flying. He pointed out red rock formations in the distance, a herd of grazing deer on an athletic field, and what we both believed might have been a bear running across a clear spot on one of the mountain slopes.

I was indeed having a good time, just as everyone had predicted. But after fifteen minutes or so, I realized we were getting closer to the ground. An unexpected sense of sadness flooded me. I'd enjoyed both the flight and Cadet Dobbs' low-key company.

"Time to land?"

"I'm afraid so. All good things must come to an end."

And so they did.

He steered the glider into a long swooping curve,

lining up on the runway, and we descended slowly as we approached the asphalt.

Finally we touched ground—a perfect landing. Just as we came to a final stop, the Secret Service agents flanked the glider, waiting to reclaim their protective-custodial duties.

I started talking before the canopy was completely open. "You were right," I said to Diana as I got out. "It was fantastic." I turned around and shook Dobbs's hand with honest enthusiasm. "Thanks so much. Not in my *wildest* dreams would I have thought I'd have liked it that much. It was so peaceful, so relaxing, so much fun . . ."

The cocky "Jokeman" grin came back, as if, once his feet touched the ground, Dobbs became a different person.

"So . . . you up for trying some aerobatics next time?"

I thought about the state of my stomach in the presence of loop-de-loops, barrel rolls, and other equally unsettling maneuvers. "Thanks anyway. I'll take a pass on that. But the ride . . . it was fantastic! I really enjoyed myself." I shook his hand with honest enthusiasm.

After that, my entourage and I climbed back into the official cars for our next stop on the Grand "Distinguished Visitor" Academy Tour. The written itinerary sheets I'd seen abbreviated that as "DV." I found it tough to think of myself as *Distinguished.*

Before Captain Durkee could resume her narration about the Academy, Diana leaned over and whispered, "You're still smiling. You must have enjoyed yourself." She gave me a quick glance. "When you get home, are we going to have to figure out how to protect you while you take flying lessons?"

"I'm tempted . . ." I laughed at the look on her face, then I shook my head. "Don't worry. It was fun and I'd love to go again—as a passenger—but, no, I'm not going to sign up at the nearest flying school as soon as we get back to D.C."

She looked visibly relieved.

"Good." That came from Kingston. His concise contribution to the conversation caught both Diana and me off guard.

I studied his face. "Why? You said you flew gliders as a hobby. You must like it."

He spared me a quick glance. "It's not that." He turned back to looking out the window for threats. "I've been riding with Drew since he got his learner's permit. One novice driver in the family is enough."

That explained everything. I'm twenty-five, and all grown up—for the most part. But my brother Drew is only fifteen, deep in the thrall of adolescence, and still quite capable of in-line skating his way into the Oval Office during an important meeting to show Dad his latest trick. He's learning to drive, and I think he takes a secret glee in scaring his Secret Service agents to death as he hones his skills. Just before we left for Colorado, I'd heard tales of Drew taking a wheel-screeching right turn on red that had given more than one agent new gray hairs.

Since my mother died several years ago, I've served as a mom-substitute for Drew. That's why I'm unemployed and living in the White House instead of out on my own, making a living, like my brother Charlie, who's a year younger than I am. Heck, Charlie's not only on his own; he's a dot.com tycoon. My over-achieving brother has a very satisfying life in Vermont, where he runs an Internet software business that he built from scratch. It survived the tech sector meltdown in style, and these days Charlie's raking in the cash. Charlie has always been independent to a fault. I am, too, but Drew and Dad need me. At my father's request, I gave up my job and moved in with Dad when he was elected.

I'm not some kind of substitute First Lady. My Aunt Patsy is Dad's official hostess. I'm Dad's unofficial sounding board and Drew's unofficial mother figure. The last year was hard on Drew and the pain wasn't going to end any time soon. I've been doing my best to make things easier for him, but being a teenager is tough enough under ordinary circumstances. Add in a cross-country move to D.C., plus the transition from normal kid to Presidential offspring, and tough doesn't begin to describe Drew's last few months. Despite everything, I know Drew will weather the storm. Of course, I'm Drew's sister. I love him. The Secret Service is merely stuck with him. That includes hair-raising right turns on red and everything.

I reached over the back of the seat and patted Kingston's massive arm. "You have my sympathies. They don't pay anyone enough to ride along with Drew behind the wheel. One terror source in the family is enough, don't you think?"

Kingston almost smiled.

Captain Durkee took up her monologue on the Academy, interrupted by the glider flight, again. "Our next stop will be the Cadet Chapel. It took five years just to design the Chapel. Construction began in 1959 and the building was completed in the summer of 1963. Within the one structure, we have three religious facilities: a Protestant Chapel that seats twelve hundred, a Catholic Chapel that holds five hundred, and a Jewish Chapel that seats one hundred."

I tuned out her facts and figures, turning my attention instead to the building itself. I'd seen it earlier while we were touring the Cadet area, and, of course, I'd seen pictures of it all my life. But until we stepped out of the car and stood in the circular driveway in front of it, staring up at the gleaming spires pointing into the sky, I hadn't realize how truly beautiful it was.

Before we went inside, Captain Durkee pulled us over to the side of the Chapel, so she could point out some of the building's unusual architectural features. Once again, I put on my official First Daughter smile and listened politely.

"As you can see, the main structure is joined to the foundation using a unique pin-hinge connector. We get such high winds up here that—"

We heard a shout behind us.

Then another voice joined in. "Oh, my God . . . look!"

Diana and Kingston reacted fast. They had me down on the ground sheltered between two of the cars before I could think. But then we realized the person who'd shouted was pointing toward the mountain. My agents got off me and started dragging me toward the nearest door leading into the Chapel, but I dug in my heels. It was evident this wasn't about me. The object of every-one's concern was a glider in the distance, skimming much too close to the craggy mountainside.

The glider wobbled from side to side. One wingtip skimmed perilously near a tall tree on the heavily wooded hillside, much closer than "The Jokeman" had dared to take me on my flight. The tiny flier coasted by the top branches with absolutely no room to spare. Then the glider's flight path straightened out and it appeared as though the pilot had regained control of his craft.

Before we could offer a gasp of collective relief, the glider banked sharply to the left . . .

And crashed into the mountain.